IT'S A
DRAGON-EAT-DRAGON
WORLD

TY BURSON

THE MODERN DRAGON CHRONICLES

Chapter 1

Shou left her Palo Alto condominium well before sunrise, though of course time was irrelevant at her age. Still, she had to leave early, if only to avoid her loving and over-protective niece. After a quick check to see if she had her purse and keys, she dialed her niece's cell and left a message, knowing the girl would still be sleeping and that, by the time her niece got up for work, Shou would be well on her way north.

Her niece would be upset, but that couldn't be helped. This trip was important. Ever since Shou had met that young man in Seattle and had seen his friend's dragon with her own eyes, she knew it was only a matter of time. So, each morning, before the city awoke and kicked up every little stink and smell that had settled through the night, she would step out on her balcony, face northwards, and take a big sniff. Today, her marvelous nose caught something.

In Santa Rosa, she bought a coffee from one of those drive-thru kiosks, a pecan torte. She didn't need the caffeine, and she didn't care much for the way the bitter liquid tasted, but the aroma, oh, she practically bathed her nose in the marvelous smell. She was so lost in the competing spices, in fact, that she started to drift into the other lane. A trucker honked, startling her. Shou waved an apology. Reluctantly, she put the cup in the drink holder and concentrated on controlling the automobile. Darned things had been around for a hundred years and she still couldn't decide how she felt about them.

It was a long drive—almost eight hours north along California's Hwy 101. Several hours in, Shou's coffee had become cold and its aroma stale, so she tossed the lifeless brew out the window. She put the cup in a trash bag on the passenger seat and focused back on the drive; marveling at the view. Her ancient eyes took in the gentle, rolling green hills, with their sturdy oaks, until that view transformed into craggy, rugged mountains peppered with slender pines. She would not even get a glimpse of the mighty Pacific for several hours, and still she felt the sort of satisfaction every living creature feels basking in nature. Of course, she could have taken the stunning coastal highway for part of the trip, but that took longer, and sometimes the ocean interfered with her sense of smell.

Every few miles, Shou would pull over and roll down her window, inhaling deeply, just to make sure she was still on the right trail. Thus far, the dragon's scent had grown steadily stronger the farther north she drove.

At Klamath's Trees of Mystery, Shou made a pit stop to visit some old friends and stretch her legs a bit. She wasn't sure exactly when someone had slapped a sign up and decided to charge admission to view the unusually formed trees, but it had become a popular sightseeing spot in the years that followed. Though it was early, there were already quite a few cars in the parking lot waiting for the souvenir shop to open so they could buy their tickets. Shou entered the park without one; no one seemed to notice the elderly woman as she strolled on by. She hummed to herself, passing by the usual favorites: the Elephant Tree, the Candelabra Tree, the Cathedral Trees, all strangely and wonderfully shaped. The tour guides claimed that the trees were twisted by magic—if they only knew.

Shou walked through one enormous tree, the space between its massive roots large enough to fit a car, and then stepped over the wooden rail that girded the path. With no one around, she moved easily, almost gracefully. Humming to herself, she snaked her way around, over boulders and moss-covered tree husks, venturing ever farther from the developed areas. At last, she stopped before a towering redwood. Its surface was covered with knots, a kind of wooden acne that had enveloped the entire tree. Continuing to warble to herself, Shou stepped up to the tree and slapped its bark several times. "Come on, Little Brother, wakey, wakey, get up!"

Almost immediately, one of those knots fluttered, as if it wanted to open. A moment later it did. It lifted like an eyelid, blinked once at the old woman, then closed again. Shou huffed and tried once more, "Up, up, wake up!" The knot popped open, closed, and then dozens of others did the same. All up and down the tree, eyelids of knotted wood opened and closed. At last, half a dozen near the bottom stayed that way, staring at the old woman.

Meanwhile, Shou was rocking back and forth to a new tune. In response to the sad melody, the bark near the bottom of the tree began to darken, and twist—eventually forming something that resembled a face. The tree spoke, "Elder Sister, is that you? It's so good to see you."

Shou smiled, "Yes, Little Brother, look at you. You've grown so tall and strong. How are your brothers and sisters?"

The tree's bark shifted, and the face appeared to be thinking. "We are all here, for now."

"For now? What has happened?" Shou asked.

"Nothing, Elder Sister. It's just the humans. They seem to be crowding us. I never used to see more than a few of them out here, but now? Almost every day they wander by. Some of us say that once humans arrive, it's only a matter of time before the trees are cut down. But I'm not worried; you planted me way out here."

Shou nodded. "Yes, well—"

"Oh, and the air stinks. The other trees think it's getting worse. I don't think it's awful right now, but generally, it's bad."

Shou unconsciously took a deep breath. "Yes," she began, "you are right. The air is not sweet. But I think it's better than a few years ago; at least the humans are trying."

The tree blinked a couple dozen times. Apparently, the other trees did not have an opinion about that. "Why are you here, Elder Sister?"

"I watched a great dragon, still quite young, leave its nest from the north, not far from here, and I need to know where it is. When it's ready to fight for its egg, I should be there," Shou explained.

"A great dragon? That's wonderful!" the tree replied. "Well," it qualified, "it would be wonderful if it's on our side. You sure it's on our side? It wouldn't do us much good if it wasn't on our side—"

"Little Brother—"

"Oh, I should have sensed it if it was close, but I haven't. Why is that, Elder Sister?"

Shou frowned, "I don't know. I only recently found out about it myself."

"Hmm," the tree considered, "I have not heard any of the trees talk about a great dragon. You have seen it? Is it beautiful?"

Shou stepped forward almost touching the tree, "Yes, beautiful—green and gold and potentially quite powerful—like the one who gave him life. I could tell that even from the brief time I saw it. Maybe that's why you couldn't sense it; maybe it is strong enough to shield itself. Who knows? Anyway, I caught the dragon's scent when it left, so I can tell it's almost time; its potency is growing. However, for some reason I'm finding it hard to pinpoint where it's resting." Shou added confidentially, "There will be others looking, so I need to find it in a hurry."

Understanding, the massive tree shook its uppermost limbs, creating a little wind with its leaves. They wafted up and down, grasping for the leaves of other nearby giants. The breeze magically jumped from tree to tree in all directions. Shou sat down on a rotting chunk of wood that was covered with a bright green moss and tiny spiral mushrooms, content to wait. She pulled a plastic baggie of mostly thawed shrimp from her large Coach bag—the height of fashion according to her niece—and, with two spindly, wrinkled fingers, reached in, plucked the tasty morsel, shell and all, and popped it into her mouth. When she finished her snack, she closed her eyes and relaxed, knowing this might take a while.

The park had been open for several hours, and tourists walked the meandering trail of mystical trees, some freakishly formed by nature, some trimmed over the years by ingenious humans, and a few twisted by magic. These were the brothers and sisters of Shou's redwood, who, in their youth, had not been able to make up their minds if they really wanted to be trees, or something altogether different. Their restless spirits molded the trunks and limbs in unusual ways until they eventually settled in, committing to being permanent citizens of the forest. Once human beings had discovered they could profit by that uniqueness, however, the trees had lost all their anonymity.

Around lunchtime, a visiting family barreled down the trail, within earshot of Shou, who was still lingering on the log. "Darn you, kids, get yourselves back here!" yelled an extremely overweight woman between gulps of her diet soda. Her husband, himself easily pushing 350 pounds, was busy playing a fishing game on his cell phone and not paying attention to anything else. The two toddlers tethered to him with a kid leash pulled every which way, but could not break free of his gravity. Three elementary-aged kids were running in between the rest of the tourists, drawing more than a few scowls and the occasional "watch out".

One of the little rascals, a bony and agile boy of eight, jumped the simple wooden rail fence in order to avoid being tagged by his sister. "Gerald," boomed the woman, "back on the path, right now! You'll catch poison ivy again." The older sisters only hesitated for a fraction of a second before following their brother—sure, they risked getting in trouble, but after being cooped up in the motor home, they had to chance it.

"Oh, those darn kids," their mother mumbled. She stopped at the spot where they broke free and waited. Her husband, oblivious, bumped right into her. "Hey, what?" he exclaimed.

She smacked him on the arm, "Darn it, Jimmie, those kids are off in the woods! Go track 'em down," she commanded.

"Huh? I got these two little ones here. I can't go chasing them all through the woods," he complained before returning to the digital largemouth bass that he had almost reeled in.

The mother looked at the fence, and the rocks and all those downed trees she might have to climb over and made a decision. Rather than step off into the wilderness, she opted to yell at them for the next 15 minutes. "Gerald, Tina, and Laveta, get yourselves back here right now!"

Shou opened one eye and saw the boy. She'd heard him and the girls crashing through the forest; their mother yelling after them would have been hard to miss, besides. She sighed and looked over at her towering friend. Most of its eyes were now closed, but a few were blinking. "Little Brother, company!"

A face briefly reappeared before her, and then all the eyes shut at once. Anyone stumbling upon them would see nothing but a wrinkled old woman reclining next to a towering redwood.

The boy appeared first and abruptly skidded to a halt right in front of her. "Hey, who are you?" he boldly asked.

Shou answered, "Just an old lady enjoying a little peace and quiet, or I was." Before she could say more, two girls came flying around a large tree and crashed into their brother. All three rolled around in a melee of knees and elbows. The largest girl got up first, "Hey, Gerald, you stopped." Then she noticed Shou, "Who's she?"

Not letting him answer, she swatted him hard on the arm, "Got you. You're it!"

"Wait. No fair, I stopped playing," he complained.

Suddenly, a strong wind whipped from the north and the massive tree began to sway. Shou looked up and then at the three children. "Is that your mother yelling for you? She sounds worried. Maybe you should get back to her."

The other sister had broken free of the tangle and was already climbing on the downed tree trunk next to Shou. "Naw, if we go back right now, we'll just get in trouble." She stood up on the log, "Gerald, you're it."

"I am not! You..."

He was interrupted by the mass of eyelids that snapped open all at once. "Elder Sister," the tree said, "I know where it is." The girl fell off her log and the other one gasped aloud. She ran over and grabbed her sister close. Gerald snatched up a stick and was going for one of the wooden eyes when Granny swatted it out of his hand.

"Thank you," Shou replied and then she turned to the intruders. "Well, Gerald, Tina, and Laveta," Shou huffed, "I think it's time you got back to your parents."

"No way, hey, how'd you know our names?" Tina asked.

"Yeah, we don't know you," Laveta said. "And what is that?" she said, pointing at the tree.

"Oh, I know a lot of things," Shou said pointing at Gerald. "I know you took your sister's bag of river rocks."

"Huh? I did not!" Gerald lied.

"So, you did do it! You turd!" Laveta yelled, "I knew you did. You lied to Daddy about it."

"Oh, now hold on, Laveta," Shou interrupted. "Didn't you use all of Tina's lip gloss to finish that picture you were drawing yesterday?"

Tina stomped over and grabbed her sister's arm, "You did, didn't you? You little brat!" She gave her a tug, "I'm going to tell Momma on you."

"Absolutely, dear," Shou prompted, "you should go tell your mother right away. You too, Gerald, go tell your father how Laveta broke that necklace back at the souvenir shop and threw it back in the box." Gerald nodded enthusiastically.

The three kids pushed and yelled and hit each other all the way back to their parents, who were waiting for them on a bench. Their dad had given up his fishing game for a hunting game, and their mom was fussing at the toddlers when the trio emerged from the forest. "Hey," their mother yelled, "Over here, right now. You're in big trouble!"

Even though she was a long way off, Shou could hear the mother dressing down the little hooligans. When Shou was certain that the trio had forgotten all about blinking trees, she turned her attention to her wooden friend. "Okay, Little Brother," she said, placing her cheek against the furry bark, "show me."

Chapter 2

Justin's house was situated on the edge of South Pebble Beach Drive, which meant that it was perched directly above the Pacific Ocean. It seemed appropriate, what with Justin's parents being marine biologists and all. It was also convenient considering they did much of their research right in their own backyard. It wasn't a particularly impressive house, but it did have a particularly impressive view. Across the street, past a few Douglas firs and a beautiful Monterey cypress, the land dropped off. Beyond the cliffs, the steel-grey Pacific pushed and pulled against the rocky shore far below. Several stubborn rocks poked out of the water like bad teeth and, on the rare days when fog did not squat on the town, the curve of the coast could be seen far in the distance.

Justin had his own room on the other side of the house with a view of the cul-de-sac, which was fine with him. He was more concerned with what was in his room than what was outside his window. It was a large bedroom made small because of all his neatly organized obsessions: insects according to their order— bees, wasps, and ants to the left; beetles on the right; moths and butterflies in the middle. He had an extensive seashell collection, rock collection, and several jars of buttons. Currently, however, his passion, his obsession, was dragons.

A couple of years ago, Justin and his best friends, Steve and Joy, helped a dragon defeat a demon named Mammon. Since then, Justin had spent hours on end pulling up everything he could on the internet. For a long time, Steve and Joy had shared his enthusiasm for dragons, including all the new facts and theories about modern and ancient dragon lore. Lately, it seemed to Justin that his friends were losing interest. Perhaps, Justin surmised, it was because none of them had seen Dragau for nearly two years, and Steve had not commanded a single bug, much less the variety of animals he had when fighting the demon. Then there was Joy, who, gifted athlete though she was, had not once done anything superhuman. Even Steve's dad, Dragau's caretaker, had not heard from the dragon. Not even once! No one even knew where he was.

At first, everyone involved had been worried. Steve's grandmother, however, seemed to think that given everything that had transpired, coupled with the enormous amount of magic the dragon had used, maybe it had gone into a sort of hibernation. That did not add up for Justin, especially because the dragon slept all the time anyway. Apparently, this was different.

Still, Justin thought, *just because Steve hadn't had any contact with his dragon was no reason for him to forget about it.* Recently, whenever Justin started to bring up the subject, especially at school, Steve was hesitant to talk about it; sometimes he even shushed Justin when they were around other kids. Because of this, Justin was forced to go to the only place where nothing was off limits: the internet. Justin made a couple profiles on fantasy sites where he could openly discuss his latest fascination, even if it also got him lots of junk from Dungeon and Dragons players. Justin wasn't interested in eighteen-sided dice and ninth-level magic users, though; he was interested in real live dragons.

His favorite site was a chatroom hosted by several individuals who scoured the world looking for evidence of the unusual: Bigfoot, the Loch Ness Monster, alien abduction, etc. Ordinarily, Justin wouldn't be interested, but there was a subset of that group who was intensely interested in dragons—specifically his, or rather Steve's, dragon.

➢ Day 702 without a dragon interaction. (DragonKeeper)
➢ Nothing? Your friend still hasn't had any contact? (Dragongirl 1)
➢ No, how about you? Have you found any reliable evidence? (DragonKeeper)

> Not right now. We're on vacation, but when we get home there's supposed to be a town not too far away where they say a dragon appears during certain lunar events. (Dragongirl 1)

> Lunar events? (DragonKeeper)

> Yeah, you know like eclipses and stuff like that. Anyway, tell me again what happened right after Dragau killed the demon. And don't leave anything out. I want to know everything! (Dragongirl 1)

Justin's fingers flew over his keyboard as he explained the extraordinary events of two years ago: how Steve's family took care of the dragon, how two bad guys who worked with a demon wanted to kill the dragon, even how he was brainwashed and ended up in Seattle. It wasn't the first time he had explained it to Dragongirl 1, but this time he typed everything he could remember—and Justin had an excellent memory. When he finished, Dragongirl 1 seemed genuinely impressed.

> Wow, that must have been incredible. Tell me about your friends. Where do you all live? What are they like? How is your school? (Dragongirl 1)

Justin cheerfully complied, though he had been warned more than once to be wary of sickos trolling the internet for innocent victims. Dragongirl 1 could not have been one of those, though—no way. So, Justin described, in great detail, his friends: what they liked to do, where they hung out, along with the town they lived in and the name of the school they went to.

This was the most Justin had ever spoken to a girl, except for maybe Joy, but she didn't count. It wasn't that he had a problem talking to girls, it was more like they had a problem listening to what he had to say. They generally did not seem interested in anything he was interested in, not even beetles, butterflies, or buttons. And if he started in about dragons, they looked at him like he was the bug.

"Justin," a voice from within his house interrupted his virtual conversation, "come on, your dentist appointment is in 45 minutes, and we have to drive all the way to Brookings."

"My teeth are fine, Mom. Why do I have to go? It's a Saturday."

His mother yelled again from down the hall, "Because you need a cleaning, if nothing else. Now get moving or I'm going to throw your computer in the trash can!"

➢ Have to go. Maybe I can log back in later today. (DragonKeeper)

➢ OK, no problem. Have fun. (Dragongirl 1)

Justin logged out and closed his computer. He walked into the kitchen where his mom was fishing in her purse for her keys. Justin scanned the three places she always put them and found them next to a potted plant on an end table by the front door. "They're here, Mom."

"Oh, thanks, Hon. Are you…" She stopped in midsentence. "Justin, why are you wearing that ratty tee shirt? I thought I told you to throw it away. And are those the jeans you wore all week to school?"

Clueless as to why any of those questions mattered, Justin answered, "Yeah." He looked down and noticed the chocolate milk stains from Tuesday. "They're okay; it's only the dentist."

"What about that shirt? It's full of holes and you can't even read what it says anymore. Go take it off and throw it away; get a clean one. And put those jeans in the laundry, too. I bought you five new pairs before school started and I don't think you've worn a single pair."

Justin turned around without arguing and returned to his room to retrieve a clean t-shirt. His trash can was in the corner, but he couldn't throw the shirt away, so he folded it up and put it in the back of his shirt drawer. He went ahead and put his comfortable jeans in the wash since they were in no danger of being destroyed. He opened the chest of drawers full of new pants and stared, unable to commit to the strange clothing. His foot started tapping in agitation until he closed it and went to the next drawer for some clothes he was more familiar with. He pulled out two pairs of pants, but both had holes, which he knew meant they would be instantly rejected by his mother. Instead, he found a pair of camouflage shorts that were almost entirely intact.

"Did you brush your teeth?" Justin's mother called out, from the living room this time, judging by the pitch of her voice.

Justin ran his tongue over his teeth, feeling for any large remaining particles. He hadn't, not this morning. Did he last night? Nope, probably not. He breathed into his hand and didn't smell anything. "I'm ready to go, Mom!" Justin yelled, instead.

Geez, he thought, *that'd be like washing your car before you took it to the car wash. Silly.*

Chapter 3

Three people stepped off the plane. They headed immediately for the baggage section and retrieved several bags. Despite leaving 12 hours ago—traveling from Reykjavik, Iceland to Seattle, and then finally to San Francisco—they looked no worse for the wear. The first of the three, a tall, blond man, lifted the suitcases with ease and loaded them on a wheeled trolley. His companion, a tall, blond woman, walked up to the rental car express lane and entered her info into a self-serve computer. The last, a tall, blond, teenaged girl, bought three coffees before joining the other two on the way to the rental parking lot. They didn't speak.

Once in the car, the girl pulled out the latest iPhone and snapped her fingers. The woman up front passed back a laptop. Using her phone, the girl connected the computer to the Internet. While she waited for everything to come up, she inclined her head toward the man behind the wheel, her gaze expectant.

"Hmm, oh, right," he said before leaving the airport and following signs for HWY 101.

"What are you doing?" the woman up front asked, craning her head to look back. "I thought we knew where we were headed."

The girl ignored her. When she was finished typing, she looked up. "Yes, of course we do. I wanted the program to scan for any more unusual hits before we traveled too far north, in case we need to investigate along the way. I also let them know back home that we landed and gave them our itinerary."

"Were they curious why we are driving instead of flying in the rest of the way?" the woman asked, flatly.

"No, they weren't," the girl replied in the same tone. "By the time the next plane departed, we would almost be there. I explained that to you. We don't lose more than a few hours by driving, and we get a chance to survey the area on the way in."

"I don't understand why it is necessary for all three of us to be here. Surely, one of us would suffice," the woman stated.

"Not your concern," the girl replied. "Here is where we were told to go, so here we are. The truth is that there has been a lot going on in California the last couple of years. It may very well be that we have to split up."

The driver looked sideways at the woman next to him and back in the mirror as if waiting for the next exchange. When neither spoke, he cleared his throat.

"What, Halldor?" the woman next to him asked.

Haldor glanced in the mirror again. "I wasn't told much before joining you in Reykjavik. Berit, why this little town in Northern California? Are we certain it is a breeder?"

"Yes," the little girl, Berit, answered. "My source suggests it resides somewhere in Northern California."

"Humph," the woman up front snorted. "Source. Why don't you tell him what source you're referring to?"

"Brita, you can soften your foolish tone," Berit replied. "There are some things you are not privy to. Perhaps," she added, "when you are elevated to a higher position..." She let the insult hang in the air. "But yes, Halldor, there are good reasons to believe there is a young breeder there. We lost an egg to the Americas centuries ago—"

"We?" the woman interrupted.

"And," Berit continued, "there have been a number of internet queries in that area, especially from one source. He's the one we will speak with first. But if you doubt me Brita, roll down your window. Can't you smell it?" An odd expression lit up the young girl's face, her smile fierce and hungry all at once. "Oh, it's here, and its time is coming!"

Chapter 4

Steve shot out ahead as his goalie booted the ball down to the other side of the field. It hit once, bounced high, and then Steve had it. He never slowed, never hesitated. At a full sprint no one could catch him; controlling the soccer ball didn't seem to slow him down at all. The other team's goalie must have panicked, because he had come so far out of his goal box that he might as well have been a midfielder. In desperation, the goalie threw his body right in front of Steve. Steve stopped the ball, backed it up, and—using both feet—flipped it over their heads to land past the confused goalie. It was kind of a show-off move considering Steve could have just zigged around the poor kid, and the delay did allow two defenders to converge on him, forcing Steve to do some fancy stutter steps to move the ball around them. But, as a third player approached, Steve neatly passed the ball to his cousin Joey, who took an easy shot into the empty net.

His teammates cheered and several ran over to congratulate Joey, but the play, the one that made the shot possible, was all Steve's. Joey gave a grudging nod toward his cousin. After years of feuding, they had finally reached an armistice: they both had ended up on the same team. The nod was not much, but it beat getting insulted. *Besides,* Steve thought as he returned to his starting position, *I already have two today. If I score another, coach will probably move me to goalie so we can't run the score up on the other team.* Steve took his spot as center forward and waited for the ref to place the ball for the other team to kick off.

"Woo-hoo, way to go Steve!" someone yelled from the sidelines. Steve turned and saw Joy and Justin on their bikes on the other side of the fence. Joy waved and yelled again, "Great job!" Then she turned and shoved Justin to make him wave. Steve started to wave back, but hardly managed to raise his hand before his coach told him to get his head back in the game.

As the ref placed the ball, an opposing forward, a kid named Nicholas, tapped it back to one of his teammates. Steve knew Nicholas, as well as the kid who he passed it to. In fact, he knew every other player on the opposing team; there simply weren't that many people in Del Norte County, maybe 30,000, and that was counting the inmates out at Pelican Bay Prison. Besides, there were only three middle schools, and two of them were K-8 schools. It limited the competition. They could travel to Brookings, Oregon, but it was even smaller than Crescent City. Forget about traveling down the coast; that was way too far to go to play other teams. So, Steve and the other players had to settle for playing each other—kind of like taking your cousin to prom. On the plus side, Steve was king on the soccer field. And the other team knew it, too. Rather than risk an embarrassing take-away, they booted the ball down the field whenever he got close. This strategy only delayed the inevitable; before long, one of Steve's defenders got the ball to him. After that, it was all over —thump, goal.

Steve's mom, Jeanie —a tall, pretty woman with flaming red hair— gave him a little wave after he scored. She was sipping her breakfast along with a bunch of other coffee-worshipping parents near the bleachers. Despite the ever-present cold mist on this late October morning, most parents had left the comfort of their cars, though they were only half-heartedly watching the game. Between sips from their paper cups and thermoses, they talked about whatever parents talked about.

As Steve made his way back to the center of the field he noticed Dani, his sister, directing a complicated game of Red Light, Green Light with some of the younger soccer siblings near the playground equipment. She always came to Steve's games, although Steve was pretty sure she had never bothered to watch him play.

Absent was Steve's dad, Roger, who was at home studying for a test on Monday. Roger was enrolled in his final semester of the Emergency Medical Technician course at the junior college. Once he graduated, there was a good shot he would get the EMT job at the hospital. This would help the family's finances, and, perhaps, free him up from his other occupation—renting fishing equipment to tourists from the family business, The Worm Hole, at the marina.

The other side had the ball first, but Steve quickly intercepted a pass and was off again. He did a nice little move to throw off one defender, but quickly found he had nowhere to go. With no one to advance the ball to, he tried to stall with some fancy dribbling until some of his teammates could catch up. Suddenly, he tripped on his own two feet and fell, allowing the other team to take the ball away and kick it down the field. Somewhat bewildered, Steve sat for a second before jumping up and racing after the play.

Both teams had clustered midfield. As a forward, Steve wasn't supposed to drop all the way back on defense, so he went as far as he dared. The ball did get close enough for Steve to make a play, but because everyone was bunched up, he thought he'd kick it back to his goalie for him to boot it across the field. Steve quickly looked to see that the defender was in the right spot and rolled the ball backwards toward the goal box. As soon as he'd done it, he realized he'd made a mistake. Someone yelled and Steve turned all the way around and discovered that his goalie was completely out of position. He was way up front and to the right of the goalie box. Steve's pass happily bounced along with no one to prevent it from scoring a goal for the other team.

The ref blew the whistle and some parent from the other team bellowed into one of those long plastic horns that sounded like a bull elephant on steroids. The other team jumped up and down. Steve stood awkwardly, looking utterly confused. *How did I mess that up? I swore he was near the goal,* he thought to himself. One of his teammates trotted over and patted him on the back. "Don't sweat it. We'll get it back," he consoled.

Steve's coach called for substitutions before they set up to restart and called Steve in. "Shake it off and grab a drink, Steve," the coach said. He wasn't even mad. One of the benefits of being the best player on the team, Steve realized, was that it created a buffer zone of goodwill. Thankfully, that meant the guys on the bench were not overly upset with him either.

Joy waited until everyone cleared away from her best friend before dropping her bike to talk to him. She stooped down behind the bench he was sitting on. "Didn't you look before you passed it back?"

Joy never sugar-coated anything.

Steve took a swig of his Gatorade before answering. "Yeah, I did. I swear I thought Chris was back at the goal."

"Oh well, you guys are still up by three. Maybe with you out, someone else can get a chance to kick the ball," Joy teased.

Steve glowered at her, "Whatever, Miss Ball Hog..."

Justin had come over as well. "Hey guys. Look over at the parking lot," he instructed. Justin was indicating some strangers, a family judging by their similar appearance.

"Aren't they a Nordic-looking bunch," Joy commented.

"What? Oh, you mean because they're all blond," Justin said. "The thing is, there are blond people in several countries and not all are of Nordic—"

"Forget I said anything," Joy said.

"Yeah, either way it's weird," Justin continued as if Joy hadn't said anything. "They're not from here, so why are they watching a soccer game?"

Steve shrugged, "Maybe they're someone's relatives."

"Or," Joy smirked, "maybe they heard that the great Steve was going to suck today and wanted to be here for it."

Steve splashed back some Gatorade at her, but she was too quick and most of it landed on Justin. "Hey," he started to protest, but Steve's coach interrupted them. "You two, quit bothering my players. Get away from the bench."

"Okay, Mr. Evans," they both chimed in. He was a good guy; he fixed their cable TV.

The game continued until halftime with neither side scoring another goal. Without Steve on the field, however, the opponents managed to keep the ball hovering around his side's goal and had taken two unsuccessful shots, which was probably why Steve's coach started him in the second half. Steve immediately went on the attack, anxious to redeem his earlier screw-up. With a nifty little bit of finesse, Steve stole the ball from a kid he knew from Boy Scouts. Without even thinking, Steve broke for the goal. He slipped the ball right between another defender's legs, navigated the ball into position for a perfect shot into the corner of the goal box, but, as he cocked back his leg for the kick, something went horribly, terribly, awfully wrong. His lead leg slipped on something and extended forward, forward in a way that the ligaments of the knee were not meant to go.

Chapter 5

"Why did you do that?" Brita asked. "And why are we here?"

Without taking her eyes off the field, Berit pointed, "See those two children on their bikes? The boy with the curly blond hair is the one I've been chatting with. He's going to help us find the dragon."

"But how did you know he would be here?" Halldor asked.

"I've been watching everything he's typed into his silly little computer for weeks now," Berit said smugly. "I knew this is where he'd be. Now be silent, I want to hear."

Berit closed her dazzling blue eyes and tilted her head to listen to the hectic scene that was erupting around the injured player. Though she was a long way off, she could clearly hear through the pandemonium of the parents and players; she even listened to the mother's fussing. Before she started toward the field, she turned to her companions, "That boy on the internet, Justin—the girl he is with and that boy on the ground are his friends. That boy is the one who is connected to the dragon, and I just gave the dragon a reason to wake up. Now stay here," she instructed.

"What do you mean stay here?" Brita questioned, but Berit didn't bother answering; she walked quickly from the far end of the parking lot and across an empty baseball field. Steve's coach and a couple of players got him to the bench. Silent tears streamed down his face. His mom totally ignored the rules about driving on the field and parked their truck just a few feet away. As gently as they could, a group of adults helped load Steve into the front seat. Fortunately, the hospital was close by—one of the benefits of a small town. Jeanie spotted Justin and Joy as she put the truck in gear. "Hey, you guys! Stay right here and watch Dani, would you? I'll get hold of Roger to come get her."

"Sure Mrs. Batista," Joy replied. "You'll be all right Steve, hang in there!" Joy yelled as the truck started to leave.

With everyone's attention directed at the departing injured player, Berit walked right into the midst of the gathering without drawing attention. "Is he all right?" she asked Joy.

Joy turned around, "What?"

"I asked if he was going to be all right. I'm Berit, my family and I were watching the game from over there," she pointed to the far end of the parking lot.

Joy turned to Justin, who was staring blankly at the new girl. "I don't know," she answered. "It looked like he hurt his knee pretty badly. Listen, I don't mean to be rude, but we need to go get his sister. Come on, Justin."

Joy turned to leave, but had to pull Justin along when he didn't move. "Hey, what's wrong with you? Come on, igit, we need to find Dani."

Justin was staring at the new girl. "Oh, yeah, okay, I'm coming. Nice to meet you," he offered as he followed Joy.

"You, too," Berit yelled. "I'll see you at school."

Joy pulled up to the playground and hollered for Dani, who was nowhere in sight. "Where could that kid be? You see her anywhere?"

"What?" Justin asked absently. "Hmm, oh, I thought she was here a second ago, playing with those other kids."

"Dani! Dani, where are you?" Joy yelled.

Justin rode his bike around the playground, but he kept glancing back at the girl who had rejoined her family. Joy noticed. "Hey, lover boy, you want to focus here? I'm going to ride over to the school. Why don't you see if she's off playing in the woods? God, that kid is such a pain sometimes."

"Sometimes?"

"Okay, if you find her we meet back here." Joy said.

Justin found the red-headed girl in the woods with half a dozen others acting out something Dani had undoubtedly made up. Other parents who were watching the game were attempting to round up their own kids, so Justin did everyone a favor by getting them all back to the field.

"What do you mean she left?" Dani demanded. "She left me? What am I supposed to do? What if they have to amputate Steve's leg? I could be here forever."

Dani, as usual, flustered Justin, so he didn't bother answering. "Come on, Dani, we need to wait for your mom or dad to come get you," he said, instead.

Joy joined them a couple of minutes later. "Hey, you found her. Good."

Dani was still miffed, "Mom should have taken me with her. Like she always forgets about me."

Fortunately, Joy knew exactly how to communicate with Dani, "Look, brain-dead, Steve probably broke his leg and she had to get him to the hospital. She did think about you, and that's why she told us to watch you."

Dani scowled, "I don't need watching. I should have gone with them! What am I supposed to do? Hey, we should go over to the hospital. I can ride on your bike pegs."

"We could head over to the hospital, Joy," Justin suggested, "It's not too far."

Joy shook her head no, "We better wait for her dad like Mrs. Batista said. As soon as he gets here, we can head over there ourselves."

Dani plopped down on the edge of a slide. After a minute, she asked, "Is Steve hurt really bad?"

Justin answered, "Yeah, his leg was stretched out and then the knee bent forward like this." He flexed his wrist joint so that his forearm and hand formed a "V".

"Justin, shut up!" Joy said.

Dani looked forlorn, suddenly, "He's going to lose his leg. Steve's going to be crippled. I'm going to have a crippled brother."

Joy rolled her eyes and gave Justin a dirty look. "What?" Justin asked.

"Dani," Joy began, "Steve is not going to lose his leg; quit being so melodramatic. He might be in a cast or something, though. Hey, you want me to push you on the swing until your dad gets here?"

"I'm not a baby," Dani replied. "You don't have to put me in my swing to get me to shut up." But after a few minutes, Dani walked over to the swings anyway, and Joy followed. Justin parked his bike, and looked around for the new girl, but she was already gone.

Chapter 6

Steve's mom pulled the old pick-up into the student drop zone and started to get out.

"No, I got this, Mom."

"Steve, you've got your backpack and your lunch. How are you going to carry all that with those crutches?"

"It's fine," Steve said as he maneuvered himself out of the truck and reached behind the seat to retrieve his stuff. "Joy said she'd wait by the entrance and give me a hand. Look, there she is."

Jeanie turned and spotted Steve's tall, pretty friend waving from the steps. "Okay, lean over and give me a kiss," she instructed.

"Really, right now? Come on, Mom," Steve protested.

"Hi, Mrs. Batista," Joy said as she trotted up to the truck.

"Hi, sweetheart. You got here early. Thanks for helping Steve out."

Joy slung the extra backpack over her unoccupied shoulder and grabbed Steve's bagged lunch. "It's no big deal. We better go, though; we have different homerooms. See ya later."

"Bye Mom," Steve propped himself on his crutches and waved with a free hand. "Oh, almost forgot. Justin's mom is going to pick us up today, so we don't have to ride the bus home."

"Okay, that's fine," Jeanie answered. "Oh, Steve, do you have all your missed work?"

"Yes, Mom," Steve replied with exasperation.

Steve took each step first with the pair of crutches and then with the good leg while Joy stepped up and waited. "Jeez, this sucks! My armpits are already hurting."

"Get used to it. How long are you on those things?"

"I don't know, a couple of weeks maybe, but I have to wear this brace for a month or so and then I'll get one that moves."

A couple of kids came running over. "Hey Steve, wow, you really did get messed up," one of them stated.

Steve nodded, too busy concentrating on moving up the steps without falling to respond.

"Did you break it?"

Steve waited until he reached the top of the stairs, then faked an easy smile. "Naw, the doctor didn't think I tore anything; probably a bad sprain. She scheduled an MRI just in case, though," he replied.

Steve and Joy were stopped about two dozen more times on the way to class; Steve was forced to tell what happened over and over. Any excitement about being the center of attention was long over by the time they got to his homeroom. "Hey, who's that?" Steve inclined his head toward a clump of kids surrounding a stunningly beautiful girl.

"Huh, oh…That's Berit. She showed up the day you got hurt. She's new, from, I don't know, Europe or someplace where they raise albino, blond people."

Steve looked at Joy and kind of smirked. "Wow, don't like her?"

Joy shook her head, "No, she's fine. I mean she hasn't done anything to me. But, I don't know, there's something…"

"Jealous?"

Joy dangled his backpack out so he had to reach for it. "Please, whatever. I'll see you in the cafeteria. Here, give me your lunch, and I'll bring it with me. Hey, check out Justin."

Steve looked over and saw his friend staring intensely at the new girl. He laughed, "Wow, he's got it bad."

Joy smirked back, "Yup, our boy's in looooove." The warning bell rang, "Oops, hey I gotta go. I need to get to my locker. See ya."

Steve maneuvered the backpack into place and worked his way over to his desk. He was almost in his seat before Justin noticed he was there. "Oh, hey, Steve. When'd you get here?"

"Just now. Joy dropped me off. You okay?"

The teacher entered and yelled for everyone to sit down. A few kids decided that it was the perfect time get up and sharpen pencils, or grab their composition notebooks from the milk crates.

"You need to be in your seats when the tardy bells rings, or I'm counting you tardy. You should have already gotten your things," Mrs. Righter instructed.

"What? Yeah, I'm fine," Justin finally answered once the commotion died down.

The new girl ignored the teacher's warnings and came over. She smiled at Justin before she introduced herself to Steve. "Hi, I'm Berit. You must be the famous Steve."

"Famous? What do you mean?"

"Well, sure. After your accident, you were what everyone was talking about."

The girl had eyes bluer than any Steve had ever seen. Her mouth was large and full and she had a dazzling smile. Then he remembered that she was talking to him. "Oh, y-y-yeah, I'm Steve." The girl giggled.

"Oh, yeah, you already knew that..."

The bell rang. "Sit, everyone. If you are not in your seats before I start taking roll you are late." Berit moved to the front of the class to sit at a trio of desks grouped together and occupied by two other girls. They were waiting for her and the three immediately began to whisper together. One of them looked over at Steve and Justin before laughing. Steve felt his face redden.

"Hey," Steve said to Justin.

"Hey," Justin replied.

"Okay, everyone, the prompt is on the Smartboard," Mrs. Righter announced. "I want five minutes of no talking. I mean it, no talking. Keep those pencils moving! We'll share our writing afterwards. Now, go ahead and start. I said no talking...girls!"

Steve read the prompt, and tried to focus on it, but he couldn't get any traction. He didn't want to get yelled at, so he kept the point of the pencil down like he was scribbling away. As his mind began to drift, he started doodling, an eye, a mouth, bangs. Steve had pictured in his mind's eye the new girl, but what his hand had delivered all on its own was a sinewy lead-grey dragon. He was still thinking of Berit when Justin leaned over to look at what he was doing and frowned. "Hey," he whispered too loudly, "Why are you drawing dragons?" Some of the kids looked up.

Steve was startled, both because Justin didn't know how to whisper and because of what he had drawn. "What the heck? I wasn't drawing a dragon..."

"Steve, Justin," Mrs. Righter, "You can both read what you wrote in front of the class when time's up."

Steve glared at Justin and ripped out the paper from the notebook. He stuffed it into his desk and began writing some incoherent things about why students should be allowed to set the school calendar. *Right, like students would ever be allowed to do that. First, we'd start with vacation, and then every Friday would be a teacher work day. Whatever, what a stupid prompt.*

The rest of the morning was pretty much a repeat of first period: Berit ended up in all of Steve and Justin's classes and neither of them could concentrate. Steve got called out in math during one of those rapid-fire, student-teacher, question-answer exchanges and was completely blindsided. Everyone laughed, and Steve was embarrassed again. Normally, Justin had his back and could rescue him if he was off in la-la land, but Justin seemed as distracted as he was.

The bell for lunch couldn't have rung soon enough. Justin was up and heading for the door right behind Berit before Steve caught him. "Hey, dude, aren't you going to help me get this stuff to my locker?"

It seemed to Steve that Justin had to think about it before he came back, "Oh, sorry. I forgot I told you I'd help."

By the time they got to their lockers and Steve hobbled down to the cafeteria, Joy had already made it through the line and was waiting for them at their usual table. "Here," she said handing Steve his lunch bag. "So, how'd it go? The teachers cut you some slack for being a cripple?"

"Nope, not really. I didn't have all the missing work, but I can turn it in by next week." He reached into his sack for a sandwich. "Still have to do all of it, though. Sucks."

Joy was crunching on a carrot off her hard-plastic tray, "You know, I don't get how teachers think that just because you're home you can do all their stuff. I mean, if you're sick, or hurt, like you, maybe you can't get to it."

Steve nodded in agreement. "Yeah, I wonder if they're grading papers and stuff when they're sick. I doubt it."

"You're quiet, Justin, what's up?" Joy asked.

Justin had his own lunch, a Bento box with nice, neat squares of food: a sandwich with the crust taken off; a green, jiggling block of Jell-O; six neatly-placed baby carrots; and some apple slices with peanut butter. It was pretty much the lunch Justin brought to school his entire student career. Joy reached over to take a carrot and put Justin into a panic attack, but he wasn't even paying attention. She followed his gaze to Berit and then planted the carrot right in the middle of his Jell-O.

"Hey, why'd you do that? I can't eat that!" Justin cried.

Joy turned to Steve for support. "You watching this kid? It's pathetic." But Steve wasn't paying attention either. "God, you, too? You guys act like you've never seen a girl before."

"What, what? I was a, um…."

"Forget it. You two zombies enjoy the view. I'm going to eat with Emily and Rachael." She got up and slipped around Mr. Johnson, the assistant principal who was working the lunchroom to keep kids marginally in line.

Chapter 7

"I mean, look at her," Berit nodded as Joy moved to another table. "She's so...tall. It's almost...freakish." The girl to her right laughed.

David leaned in, "Yeah, that's because her dad is huge. He's a basketball coach."

"But she's a girl," Berit insisted, "she shouldn't be that tall. She's kind of muscular, too." A couple of girls nodded. One added, "She's better at most sports than the boys are."

But Joy was not without her defenders. Tina spoke up, "Well, maybe she is tall. But she's pretty. And she's really nice."

"Oh, of course she is," Berit added quickly. "I didn't say she wasn't pretty. And I'm sure she's great. Still, look at how big her feet are."

A couple of kids did look, but most moved on to another subject. Joy had been popular a long time, and she wasn't going to be overthrown in a single conversation. Berit moved the food around on her melmac tray, intentionally not partaking of the gooey cheese square, and smiled while David told her a story about one of the teachers. During a lull, she reached into her bag and pulled out a crumpled piece of paper. She placed it on the table and smoothed it out with her hands. She didn't say anything.

"Hey," Tina exclaimed, "That looks like one of Steve's drawings! Where'd you get it?"

"It was on the floor in English class. I thought it was a good drawing. Does he draw dragons all the time?"

"No, not anymore," Tina explained. "He used to."

"Yeah," David added, "He used to be all into dragons. I don't think he's talked about them in a long time, though."

Then he laughed, "But Justin, oh, he's still into them. He's such a geek!"

"Really?" Berit asked. She turned to Tina, "But he's so cute. Those blond curls…He can't be a geek."

Lisa interrupted, "Justin? Well, yeah, he is kinda cute," she laughed, "but he's so strange. All you got to do is talk to him. He really is weird. Like last year, I invited everyone to my birthday party. It was a pool party and everyone was swimming and having a good time, and when it was time for everyone to go home, you know where Justin was? He was playing some electronic Lego game with my brother—my brother is ten. Cute, sure, but a total geek."

"Well, I think he's a cutie."

Berit waved to her new friends and crossed the parking lot to where Halldor had parked. She answered a final farewell and quickly climbed into the front seat. "Go, get me out of here before I lose more IQ points dealing with these adolescents."

Halldor started the engine. "Did you have a nice day at school?"

"Don't be smart. Did you or Brita find out anything?" Berit asked.

Halldor waited for a long line of walkers to cross in front of him before turning out onto the road. "I left her at the library. There's a woman there who loves to talk. Brita thought she might learn something about local dragon lore. You want to run over there?"

"Ugh, I don't think I could stomach another minute with a human being. Take me to the house."

Halldor drove a few blocks away to the beachfront rental he and Brita had secured. It was off-season, so the property was reasonably priced and came furnished. They might have found a better one, but they needed a permanent address—a place with a lease so Berit could enroll in school. Fortunately, the owner of the three-bedroom house was fine with a month-to-month agreement. No one seemed to care that they were from out of the country. Eventually, they'd have to deal with questions about employment, but they could draw from numerous lies. Money to live on was not an issue.

Berit was out the door before Halldor had stopped the engine. She bolted up to the front door and turned the knob. "It's locked!"

"Just a moment. I'll be right there," Halldor yelled as he extricated his six-foot-four self from the car.

Berit snapped her fingers and the lock relented. "Never mind. Go after Brita and stop by the marina for some fresh fish. I'm famished."

Berit shut the door behind her without waiting for a reply from Halldor. The house faced the dying sun, but heavy blinds kept most of it out, and the living room was almost completely dark. Without turning on a light, Berit easily maneuvered around the room. She scowled at the cheap décor and ugly furniture: a cheesy picture of a sailboat on the wall, a knock-off Persian rug, a battered couch, a scratched-up coffee table. She sniffed—a dog had lived here once. Before that, a cat. Disgusting.

She opened the door to what was the largest bedroom and found a bed, a simple desk, and a chest of drawers. She opened the heinous mirrored closet to see if Brita and Halldor had put away her new "school" clothes. They were there; one less trivial detail to have to think about. Her laptop was plugged in on the desk. Still in near darkness, she opened the lid. A soft glow permeated the room. She logged into her email and quickly checked to see if she had any new instructions. There were none, although she would have been surprised if there were. She had been at this an exceptionally long time. She typed a short status report and closed the computer.

She started to leave the room to inspect the rest of the house, but paused in front of the mirror. She looked at the perfect beauty who stared back. "Disgusting!" she said aloud before sliding one of the mirrored closet doors over. As always, whenever she wore a human skin, it made her itchy and irritable, and this particular disguise was especially irritating. Still, perhaps more so than any other skin she could have chosen, she knew this one best—its strengths, its weaknesses.

Halldor and Brita wouldn't be back for a while she decided, so she quickly checked the front and back doors before returning to her room. She adjusted the drapes until there was complete darkness, then sat on the floor. She closed her eyes and relaxed. Soon, she was humming. There was a flash of light.

Brita and Halldor returned early. Brita had had enough of the long-winded librarian and had walked over to the marina before calling Halldor. Halldor was therefore able to purchase the requested seafood and pick up his passenger at the same time. He stuffed a five-gallon bucket of fresh crabs into the backseat and they were on their way.

Only a few miles out from the little rental house, they both sensed something was wrong. As soon as they arrived, they bolted out of the car and into the house. There were no lights on except for the glow seeping out from under Berit's door. Brita looked to Halldor, her anger reflected in his face, and yanked open the door.

Berit twisted her serpentine body, covered with what looked like thousands of tiny onyx mirrors. Her fire-red eyes turned on the intruders. Instantly, there was an intensely bright flash as Halldor and Brita switched to their true forms. The magic surrounding the three was blinding, like looking into a welder's flame, but it quickly died, leaving the three dragons facing each other. Halldor's scales were gold and brown, his honey-colored talons slashing at the air. Brita's yellow eyes popped next to her cobalt blue scales. Though none had wings, nor were they as massive as Steve's dragon, each was terrible and beautiful in their own right.

"Enough!" Berit screamed, and the magic flashed again. Her glossy ebony covering was replaced by pale skin and blond hair. Brita growled in frustration as her dragon form was effectively shoved back into her mortal shell. Halldor lay trembling on the floor, the transformation pounding his frail human heart.

Berit climbed to her feet and straightened her dress. As she started to step over the two struggling forms at her threshold, Brita looked up at her, "Why? How could you? You know how dangerous that is for us. What if we were seen?"

Berit stopped, the frown on her face lifting, "Did you bring anything to eat?" She tilted her nose upwards and sniffed, catching the scent from the open car doors. "Oh, good, you did. Don't bother getting up, I'll get it myself."

Chapter 8

A while after the children and their parents had left the woods, Shou thanked her tall friend and set off to find the dragon. The trees claimed it was not far, so she left her car in the parking lot, doubting that she would find any good roads anyway. Of course, trees could be notoriously wrong, especially in their estimation of how long it took to get somewhere. They didn't do a lot of traveling, and their sense of time was for crap—they were trees, after all.

The canopy of leaves overhead snatched away most of the sun's energy and left little for the struggling plants below. This meant Shou encountered a relatively easy walk along the forest floor. Shou followed the whispers above that slipped from tree to tree like a summer breeze. Not every tree could talk, but every tree was alive and capable of bridging the communication between the ones that could—in effect, a sort of forest nervous system. Every once in a while, she stopped and took a deep sniff of air to verify what the trees were saying.

She was only a small distance away from the redwood tourist attraction when a booming voice made her jump, "Well, can you smell him yet?"

Shou twisted her wrinkly old neck this way and that to find the voice.

"Here, here, Elder Sister!" a section of green moss covering a 60-foot pine shimmered before her eyes.

"Oh, it's you! I should have known. You almost made me jump out of my skin."

The moss pinched together as if considering something, and then the tree said, "Wait, that's a joke. Jump out of your skin! I get it! That's a good one."

Shou frowned, "An unintentional pun. You know what I mean. I was so intent on following the dragon's scent that I didn't see you. My, you certainly have grown."

"I'm a tree. What else do I have to do?"

"Ah…true."

The moss on the tree formed a frown, "Maybe if, you know, you came to visit us once in a while, then you'd be able to recognize us from the…" the tree whispered, "…the *stupid* trees."

"If they can't think, why are you whispering?" she asked.

The tree considered, "Ha, ha," it boomed. "You're right!"

Shou smiled, a very human gesture, and mumbled quietly to herself, "Watch who you call stupid." And then she said much louder, "I'm sorry I've neglected you Little Brother—"

"Call me Agaricus Augustas."

"Excuse me?"

"Agaricus Augustas," the tree repeated. "I heard these humans talking, and I thought 'What a great name!' So, can you please call me Agaricus Augustas?"

Shou remained silent while her prodigious brain remembered something. "When you heard them talking, were they by chance picking mushrooms?"

"Huh?"

"Mushrooms, fungus, grows on the ground and on the trees."

"You know what?" Agaricus Augustas said. "I think they were! Why?"

Shou frowned. "No reason. Agaricus Augustas is a great name. Anyway, how long has it been…40 years? I get so wrapped up with my human family sometimes it's hard to get away. But it's impolite to refer to most of these trees as stupid; they're just not much for critical thinking."

Great branches high above shook, sending down clumps of pine needles, "Huh?"

"Oh, never mind. It's been good talking to you, but I need to be moving on."

Shou took a step away, but the tree called her back. "No wait, Elder Sister. Tell me what is happening in the world. You planted me too far away from where the humans visit, so I can almost never hear what they're saying."

"I did that on purpose," Shou mumbled quietly. "Oh, not much. We've been to the moon, and you can microwave your soup in its own can now; we've had a couple hundred wars, some big, some not so big. Television is a lot better because of cable."

The moss surrounding the base of the tree didn't flinch, "Oh."

"Okay, so I gotta go."

"But Elder Sister, I'm, I'm kinda lonely out here. I—the other trees, you know, I listen real hard and sometimes I can catch what they're talking about, but they never include me in their conversations. That means I only have the stupid, um, slow trees to talk to. And they don't talk back to me, so anyway…What was I saying? Oh, oh, I remember, I get bored. Wait a minute, I said bored, and I'm a tree. Get it? Trees make boards. Ha, ha, that was a good one!"

Shou sighed, she didn't have time to provide therapy to the temperamental timber, but he was one of her charges. "Listen to me, Little Brother—"

"Agaricus Augustas, but if that is too hard to remember, how about Agaricus, or Augustas?"

"How about Gus?" Shou asked.

The tree frowned again.

"Never mind, Agaricus Augustas. I will talk to the other trees—"

"When?"

"Don't interrupt," she chastised.

"Sorry."

"I'll tell every sentient, thinking, tree I know that they need to include you in at least some of their conversations. And look," she pointed to where a new path now ran from those within the park. "Now, you'll get some human visitors, too."

The giant tree shook from its roots to the tips of its farthest needles. Unfortunately, a couple of hundred pine cones fell on Shou's unprotected head. "Oh, I'm sorry. I'm so, so happy. Thank you, thank you, Elder Sister!"

"Okay, okay, I've got to go. But remember, don't scare the mortals. You're a tree, so act like one."

"Oh, they can't see us anyway, not the real us," the tree happily answered.

"That's not true." Shou retorted, "Some can. So be on your best behavior."

Shou pressed on, meandering through the majestic redwoods and pines, occasionally encountering some sapling she had planted decades or centuries before. With these, she shared a brief reunion, and fortunately, met no other maladjusted dragon spirits. She was snacking on some dried fish heads and taking her time because she did not want to surprise the great dragon, though he would probably be oblivious. Suddenly, *A-ha*'s "Take On Me" echoed through the forest. It took her a second to realize it was her own phone.

"What now?" Shou muttered as she put the phone to her ear.

"What, Aunt Shou?"

"Oh, nothing, what is it dear?" she asked between crunchy bites.

"Where are you? I stopped by and you were gone."

Shou picked a bone that got stuck between her teeth. "Ouch."

"What?"

"Hmm, oh, nothing, dear, I got a bone, ah...a chip stuck in my teeth. Listen Chen, I got a call from an old friend of mine and drove up the coast to visit her. She's not doing very well so I'll probably be a while."

"Are you sure? Do you need me to send one of the boys to help out?" Chen offered.

"No, she doesn't like people too much. But don't worry, I'll be fine. I'm stretching my legs right now, so why don't I call you when I get in?" Shou suggested.

"Oh, okay, but don't forget, or you'll have me worried sick."

"I won't. Kiss my nephews for me."

Shou hung up and dropped the phone back into her bag. *It's nice they worry about me,* she thought fondly. Reminiscing on the warmth of her adoptive human family, she continued on for several hours, until the fading sun turned down the woodland dimmer switch. Slowly, the sounds of the forest changed. The air thickened with beetles and dragonflies and mosquitoes. Spiders spun to catch their dinners. Bats and owls competed for insects. A pair of deer leaped past Shou. A crafty coyote watched her from under a blackberry bush. A mountain lion picked up her trail, but left her alone.

If the trees were correct, Shou had to be getting close. She could see perfectly well despite the dimness, but it was her nose that she relied on to track down the dragon; its smell was powerful here and getting stronger with each step. She found herself looking down a gully that would soon grow into a ravine. This is what the trees had said to look for, and this is where her sense of smell was taking her. She stepped down carefully and followed the deepening crevice as it zigzagged generally north. When she reached a spot where it widened, she stopped. There, several hundred yards away, she could see a deep indentation in one side of the ravine. She couldn't see what was inside, even with her extraordinary eyesight, but her nose told her what was there.

Shou slowed even more, now. Approaching sleeping dragons was not normally dangerous. After all, it was impossible to sneak up on them because they were still in that semi-conscious state in which they normally operated. But this sleep was different; this was the deep, coma-like rest a great dragon needed to pool all its magic to produce an egg. While in this state, a great dragon could easily thrash around in its sleep and injure a minor dragon like herself.

Shou peered into the cave. It was much larger than it appeared. Shou dug into her bag and checked to see if her phone had a signal. It didn't, which could be a problem. It would mean a hike back out a couple of times a day to make sure she maintained ties to the human world. She did not want her nephews combing all of Northern California looking for her.

She took a deep sniff: a week, maybe two at most. That was her best guess, although probably accurate; Shou had been doing this an awfully long time. She was about to begin her vigil when something caused her to whip around. It was like a crack of psychic thunder. Then another, and once more. Three? Three of them so close? That was no coincidence.

Shou looked into the cave. There was some time yet, but somewhere north, and not too far away, three minor dragons, dragonettes like herself, had shown themselves. That was no coincidence. They would be searching for this very dragon. "No rest for the wicked," she said to herself, then sighed and headed back the way she came. She couldn't smell the intruders yet, not with this dragon's scent so overwhelming, but she'd find them soon enough. She already had a good idea where to look.

Chapter 9

Dani swung the crutch down in a mock attack that Steve parried from the couch. Clap. The sound of aluminum hitting aluminum echoed within the confines of the living room. "Hey, you two, that's not what those are for!" Steve's mother yelled from the kitchen.

"Oh, come on Mom, we're not really hitting. We're just playing," Steve hollered back. "I'm not going to hurt her."

"Heck no, you're not," Dani yelled and then, in her best Puss in Boots imitation, "You're going to die!"

"Dani, go kill your brother on the porch. You'll break something in the house."

"Okay, Mom," Steve replied. "Here, Dani, hand me my crutch so we can go out."

"Let me know when your Dad shows up!" Jeanie yelled on their way out.

"Uh, okay?"

"He's bringing home a surprise," Jeanie said.

"A surprise, what kind of a surprise?" Dani asked. "Come on, tell me!"

"Never mind, go on out and let me know when your dad gets here."

"Come on, Dani," Steve said pointing to the door.

Steve sat on the steps and handed one of the crutches to his sister. They swatted at each other while Dani hurled insults with foreign accents. Steve grew bored quickly, but knew if he didn't keep Dani entertained she would drive their mother nuts. He pulled his crutch back and aimed it like a rifle at his sister. "I've got you sighted; you better run!"

Dani frowned, "That's a sword, not a gun!"

"Rule change; now it's a gun." He cocked the imaginary weapon and Dani ran around the corner of the house. "Pshew, pshew," he fired.

From a semi-prone position around the corner of the house, Dani aimed her crutch and yelled, "Zap, you are fried. I have a laser."

"Yeah, well, I have a cannon and I just blew up the whole corner of the house. So now you're crushed."

"Okay, then I have a missile," Dani countered. "I'm shooting you with a heat-seeking missile. Kapow!"

Steve was about to consider the nuclear option when his dad pulled into the driveway. Sitting next to him in the cab of the truck was his granny. "Hey, Dani, look who's with Dad!"

Dani immediately dropped the crutch and bolted for the passenger side of the truck. "Granny, Granny!"

Steve's grandmother stepped out and wrapped Dani up in a hug. "Lord, child, you're growing like a weed!"

Steve hopped over to where Dani had forgotten the other crutch and propped himself up. "Hey, Granny," he waved.

She walked over and hugged him, the wild mass of grey, wiry hair smothering his face. "How you doing, boy?"

"I'm good. This sucks," pointing to the knee, "but I'm good. You staying for dinner?"

She winked at him and smiled wryly, "Well, if your mom's cooking, then I guess I'm staying."

"Really? Oh, right, gotcha." Granny was being polite; his mom's cooking consisted mostly of vegan meals that imitated other foods, usually without success. "Oops, I forgot! Hey Dani, run and let Mom know they're here," Steve reminded her.

"Mom! Dad's here with Granny!" she screamed as loud as she could.

Their dad came around the truck. With his backpack, faded blue jeans, and hair pulled back into a ponytail, he looked like any average college student from decades past. He smiled ruefully at his daughter, "I think Steve could have done that."

It was a nice night, cool, but not yet cold—the typical Crescent City drizzle absent. Steve's mom suggested they eat on the porch. Steve bit into his fried tofu and vegetables, which were only made tolerable because they were smothered in teriyaki sauce—a concession Jeanie made to get her kids to eat. And yet, his grandmother seemed to be enjoying the meal, and she wasn't known for liking health food.

Steve tried watching Granny without her noticing it. She had changed a lot in the two years since the dragon disappeared. She was moving slower these days and looked thinner. Her dark eyes were still pretty sharp, though, and they caught him staring. "I'm worried," she began. "Roger, why don't you tell everyone what we talked about."

Steve's dad set his plate aside, "Well, after Steve's accident, Granny went through all the family's letters, old diaries—even the one her aunt kept—to see if anything like this has ever happened before."

"You mean like someone breaking their leg?" Dani asked.

"Hush, Dani," her mother scolded, "listen."

"Yeah, but—"

"Dani," her dad added. She folded her arms and huffed.

"No, not the broken leg," Roger continued. "I mean, we don't have many injuries in our family, almost none in fact. But the accident seemed like a good excuse to search for reasons why the dragon has gone."

Before Dani could interrupt again, Jeanie pulled her close. Roger nodded to his mom, and she continued, "I didn't find anything. There's not a single thing written down about a dragon leaving its nest, let alone disappearing. Roger and I haven't had any connection at all. Steve, have you felt anything? Any dreams?"

Steve had already thought about this many times in the last two years. "No," he replied. "But is that so bad?" He added quickly, "I mean, sure I got hurt, but Dad doesn't have to stick around to feed it all the time. And I'm not stuttering, and well, no more demons."

Granny frowned, "It's not just your injury, Steve. There's a complete absence of the dragon's protective magic. Remember, we look after the dragon, but the dragon looks after all of us, including the fishermen. Thank God no one has died, but Roger, what's that boy's name, the one you're friends with?"

"You mean, Anthony? Mom, he's my age."

"Yeah, well, you're all boys to me. Anyway, Anthony," she continued, "he lost a boat a while back, didn't he?"

Roger nodded, "Not him, but his uncle. And Tom Wilkins, on another boat, almost lost his arm last year. There have been a lot of near misses."

"Is the dragon dead?" Dani asked.

Granny hesitated, then shrugged. "I honestly have no idea, child. I'd thought—I'd hoped—one of us would feel something if it did die. But I don't actually know."

"So," Steve said, "what are we supposed to do about it?"

Granny smiled sadly, "I think we have to assume that the dragon may be gone for good."

"It's dead. I bet it's dead," Dani said, mournfully.

"I don't know, honey," Roger soothed. "I don't think so. I think it's gone somewhere. Maybe the fight with the demon really hurt it. Maybe it's healing. We don't know."

"Point is, we need to prepare folks around here for the possibility that we are on our own," Granny explained. "That's mostly folks in the fishing trade, but it's also us."

"What do you mean?" Steve asked.

"I mean, Stevie," Granny said pointing at his leg, "that we have to be more careful. And your dad needs to talk to his fishermen friends and get them to be more careful, too."

Steve kind of drowned out the rest of the conversation. He felt a little guilty. Sure, it had been pretty cool being able to get animals to do what he wanted, but being stalked by a demon hadn't been. Talking to the dragon seemed cool, but it sounded like stuttering to other people, and he hated being teased about that. It did kind of suck that fishermen like Anthony could get hurt, though. *Maybe he was being selfish,* he thought.

"Steve!" his mom got his attention.

"Huh? Oh, sorry, what?"

"Come on in, it's starting to drizzle.

Chapter 10

Shou pulled into the Denny's parking lot well before dawn. It was a frigid morning, made more so by the microscopic ice crystals suspended in the air. Shou got out and looked up at the street lights struggling against the fog. She looked around and saw that she was nearly alone and almost completely hidden by the grey mist. She took a deep breath and stretched her arms overhead. Instantly, a swirling vortex of light erupted all around her, revealing her true form, a vermilion, wingless dragon. Shou spun around like a cat chasing its tail and then stretched up on her powerful hind legs to her full height, almost twice that of a normal man. She dropped back down and her black talons slammed down on something, making a metallic scraping sound. As quickly as she had transformed, she reverted to the elderly, old woman. She blinked at the damage to her car's trunk. "Damn, that's going to be difficult to explain to the insurance people," she said aloud. "Maybe they'll believe a bear did it."

She looked around again. The few customers inside hadn't seen a thing; the policeman parked across the way hadn't either. But somewhere nearby, her little revelation would be like a lighthouse in the storm to any others of her kind. She took a last look at her car and grimaced before she went into the restaurant.

Shou sat with her back to the front doors, but she didn't need to look to know when Berit arrived. No, she would recognize that smell a mile away—more like a hundred miles away. Shou wrapped her aged hands protectively around her steaming mug of coffee and raised it to her nose. She closed her eyes and inhaled the aroma of her black brew, preferring it to that of her old acquaintance.

"I see you're still a coffee addict," Berit announced at her table.

"Who do you think you're fooling?" Shou replied without opening her eyes. "We all have a soft spot for this wonderful concoction." Slowly, she opened her eyes and stifled a slight giggle. "And I see you're a little girl, again. Interesting. I wouldn't have thought you'd pick that disguise again in a million years."

"Ancient history." Berit sat without an invitation, a scowl on her face, "After all, why look like a hundred-year-old bag of skin when you can be bright and new like a pretty penny? No offense."

Shou set the mug back on the tabletop. "None taken. This tired old bag of skin works very well for me."

"That Asian family of yours?" Berit added.

"Exactly. There's never a shortage of elderly aunts and it's easy to show up from time to time with a different branch of the family," Shou explained before she added, "Tell me, are you experiencing all that hormonal nonsense associated with all fourteen-year-old girls?"

Before Berit could answer, the waitress showed up. "Hello, I'm Sarah. What can I get you?"

"Oh, maybe a cup of that delicious-smelling coffee," Berit answered with a dazzling smile.

The teenage waitress nodded and disappeared back to the kitchen. "What were we talking about? Oh, yes, the trials of maidenhood. No, I'm only willing to transform so far. Anyway, it's good to see you again. What's it been 50, 60 years?"

"Hmm, more like 90 I'd say, right at the outbreak of World War I. But you weren't a cute, little, blond girl back then. As I remember, you were a scruffy-looking Russian revolutionary," Shou reminisced.

"Ah, so I was. Those were good, good times," Berit smiled.

Shou raised an eyebrow, "I guess it depends on your perspective."

"So why are you and your friends here?" Shou asked.

Berit smiled brilliantly, "Friends? Oh, my companions. You know, training young ones, teaching them the ropes. You?"

"You know perfectly well why I'm here, you little fraud!" Shou replied with a grim smile. "I won't let you take this one either."

"Either?"

Shou raised an eyebrow. "You haven't guessed?"

Berit smirked, "Oh, I know who this little dragon is."

"No hard feelings?"

"For what? For outsmarting me? For slipping that egg out of the Azores? For getting me stuck on a chunk of rock in the middle of the ocean? No."

"Well, good—"

"That doesn't mean I intend to let you win this time," Berit started as the waitress arrived with the coffee. "Thank you, you can go away now," Berit waved and the young girl whirled around without a word, eyes unfocused as she made her way toward the kitchen.

"Still can't stand them?" Shou asked.

"What? Oh, the waitress. Oh please, I sent her away so we wouldn't be interrupted. Shou, why do you bother? These creatures multiply like ants and destroy everything they touch. Why you continue to support them, I'll never understand. Clearly, you are on the wrong side of this issue."

Shou tilted her aged head as if to consider a new thought and then smiled. "Well, they do make mistakes, I'll give you that. And yet, look at what they have accomplished."

"Pshaw, they poison everything," Berit hissed, slamming down her mug. "They have to be stopped."

"Give me a break," Shou smirked. "You're no environmentalist; you hate humans, pure and simple. Even when they were hardly a threat at all, you and your masters despised them. But they're learning; one day their better instincts will catch up with their technology, and they will be superb." She leaned in and pointed a crooked finger at the dazzling youngster. "This is the same old argument we've had for centuries. You're just mad they haven't destroyed themselves yet."

Berit didn't immediately respond. She was busy creating tiny smoke humans from the steam in her coffee mug. After she had a dozen of them floating in the air, Berit sucked them into her mouth one by one.

Shou sighed, "Lovely, at least you're consistent. So, I don't suppose I could convince you and your friends to stay out of it? Just let the contest be fair?"

"Fair, what's fair?" Berit replied smoothly. "You'll help your little dragon and I'll help mine. What's not fair about that?" Berit leaned in and smiled dangerously, "I do not intend to lose this time."

"The Crusades, the Black Plague, the American Civil War," Shou began, "not exactly losses, by your standards, I would think."

"Diversions, hobbies to pass the time. You and I both know the real game; all the rest means nothing without securing the next great dragon, though it is kind of you to remember."

"So, we're to be adversaries again?" Shou asked.

"Don't take it personally, Shou. Besides, I'm only back-up. You know that little upstart dragon of yours won't defeat mine. But, just to be sure, my friends and I might need to make a little mischief."

Shou didn't say anything and Berit took her silence as permission to continue. "You'll lose again, old friend. When the time comes, my side will have another great dragon and you will have to be content with your silly trees and rodents. You really should forget about these worthless humans and think about what's best for your own kind." She stood up and stretched from toes to fingertips. "And one day, we can leave

these ridiculous forms forever. See you at the party, Shou."
Then she left.

Shou rose as well, reached into her purse, and put a few
bills on the table. She walked to the double set of glass doors at
the front of the restaurant and watched as Berit climbed into the
back seat of a car, her accomplices in the front. Shou cracked
the front set of doors and took in a deep breath, marking the
scent of the other two dragons. She poked back inside the
restaurant for a second, preferring the human smells of coffee
and cinnamon rolls to those of Berit and her friends.

Chapter 11

Half the class was finished with their online math test. Steve wasn't. He had the entire period to finish if he needed it, but he wouldn't. He could sit here for the next two days and still not figure out the three remaining problems. He briefly looked up and saw a couple of kids with their heads down. David had somehow managed to swipe the tape dispenser off the teacher's desk and was making an opaque plastic cube. He smiled at Steve and held it up for him to see.

"You've got 15 minutes left before the end of class," the teacher announced from behind his desk. "Take it if you need it. If you're done, you can lay your head down or read your library books. Log out when you finish and stay off the internet!"

Steve looked around a second time; at least half a dozen kids were looking at tennis shoes or playing BrainPop. He sighed and leaned over to check on Justin. "You done?" he whispered.

Justin smiled and held up his laptop for Steve to see the 100%. Steve groaned. "Hey, you two want a zero? Quit talking!" Mr. Brown gave them his best teacher stare, the blank one with no expression, and then returned to his own computer. Steve wondered if he was playing BrainPop too. Probably not, more likely he was on that real estate site looking for a better house. The same one he was always on when the kids were working on something else.

When Steve looked back at his own screen, however, something was wrong. Instead of a thinly disguised word problem, a YouTube video had appeared. Before Steve could punch the keys to change it, loud music began to blast out of the computer's internal speakers. Suddenly, Justin Bieber was performing his latest hit for the entire class!

"What in God's name is that?!" Mr. Brown yelled as he scurried from behind his desk.

Steve tried hitting the mute button, then closing the screen, and even turning off the computer—to heck with the test—but nothing worked. Kids all around the room were laughing, and Mr. Brown was livid. "It's not funny," he bellowed. He grabbed Steve's computer. "You are in trouble Mister..."

"B-b-but, I d-d-didn't d-d-do anything!" Steve stammered out. More laughter. Some of the kids started mimicking the stutter. It was Steve's worst nightmare; he kept trying to explain and almost every word came out with a few dozen extra syllables. In his head, he screamed, "Stop, stop talking. Shut up, stupid!" But it wasn't what was in his head that the class was hearing. Even in his panic, though, Steve thought to ask himself, *Where is this coming from? Why am I stuttering now?*

B erit was the only one not laughing. "Keep talking, that's it," she whispered. "Make some magic, boy. Let's see that dragon of yours come to your rescue." Then, it happened, Steve's computer made a loud "pop" and smoke puffed out of the keyboard. The laughter changed to screams as each computer in the room did the exact same thing—pop, and then poof. Kids jumped out of their seats. A metallic mist lifted from the dead electronics and clouded the room. Mr. Brown kept yelling for everyone to calm down.

Berit's jaw dropped in surprise. She had expected something, maybe a stray bird hitting the window, or a book to fall from the shelf, something subtle. But this? This was a magical assault! Almost trembling with excitement, she forced her eyes shut and scanned for tell-tale threads of magic that would link the boy to his magical source—his dragon. She could follow that link with magic of her own and then she'd know where it had hidden itself.

There, there it was, a glow surrounding the boy! No, it wasn't possible! It wasn't right, Berit realized. The glow didn't go off into the distance; it led right back to her! Her eyes snapped open. Steve had his head down and he was mumbling to himself. But instead of tapping into his own dragon's magic, he had somehow latched on to her. The boy was leaching the magic from her! It was not possible! She stood up and nearly tumbled over. Someone grabbed her and stopped her from falling. She pushed the well-meaning student away and nearly fell again. On wobbly legs, she headed for the door. Amidst the chaos, no one saw her leave.

Chapter 12

Mr. Brown had no chance of getting the class under control. Besides, when the computers died, their electric souls had ended up fogging up the room with potentially toxic fumes. The best he could do was usher everyone out of the classroom. As the pandemonium poured into the hall, some of the other teachers poked their heads out of their doors to see what the commotion was about. Mr. Brown managed to get one teacher with an aide to go fetch the principal or any other handy administrator.

"Wow, did you see that?" Justin asked. "Every single computer! Oh, man, someone is in serious dog dookie!"

"It was me," Steve said quietly.

Justin peered in the door frame to watch the smoke rise and pool at the ceiling. Mr. Brown shooed him away and pulled the door shut. "Hmm, what was you?" Justin asked Steve.

"Shh, keep it down, Justin," Steve quietly insisted. "It was me. I made the computers blow up. Just, just like I did all that other stuff."

"You were stuttering again?"

Steve nodded. "Yeah, right after that video started."

"You're not stuttering now," Justin observed.

"No, I guess it has stopped. But I was stuttering back there and then everything exploded. It was like before when I'd stutter and unexplainable things happened."

"Like ants biting your cousins, or elk rescuing you, or the bears—"

"Exactly."

"So, you think the computers blew up because of you?" Justin asked with a frown. "That doesn't make any sense. You haven't even heard from your dragon!"

A couple of heads turned their way. "What's that Justin? What are you talking about?" Emily asked. Before he could open his filterless mouth, the principal turned the corner and headed their way. Mrs. Wren, who was the definition of old school, took one look at the situation and immediately started issuing orders, "Now! Line up ladies and gentlemen. Quiet! No talking, and that means you, Mr. Thomas. Okay everyone, to the library. Move!"

Steve started to hop down the hall, which prompted Mrs. Wren to send Justin for a set of crutches from the nurse's office. "Wait here, young man," she instructed. She took a peek into the computer lab and quickly shut the door before the smoke escaped into the hallway.

They heard Justin before they saw him. He rounded the corner in a hurry and got tangled up with the aluminum crutches. Mrs. Wren grabbed the clanking metal from him, giving him a disapproving look. "Thank you, Justin. I'll take it from here."

Steve tried the crutches. They were adjusted too high so he had to set them and kind of take a jump forward; he looked like an uncoordinated insect. *Great,* he thought, *one more way to look ridiculous.* He followed behind Justin and tried to enter the library as inconspicuously as possible. Of course, he forgot to tell Justin that he didn't want to draw attention.

"None of this makes any sense," Justin announced as they passed the checkout desk. "With no dragon, there's no magic. And, even when you did use Dragau's magic, you affected things in the natural world; not computers."

Steve quickly looked around, his face beet red. Thankfully, the library was a zoo. Mr. Brown was doing an admirable job of making sure everyone sat down, but he had given up on trying to keep them quiet. He kept looking apologetically at the librarian, who pursed her lips in frustration. Steve plopped down his crutches and sat as far away from most of the kids as he could. He didn't want to talk, he was almost afraid to, but he had to quiet Justin down.

"Listen," he whispered, "I know I never blew up anything. But like, this time it felt different. I was so mad, like I always used to get, and you know, I started stuttering. But I felt something different. I can't really explain it. It wasn't a good kind of feeling, like when I could link up with my dragon. It was...it felt wrong. I don't know."

Justin considered for a minute. "What was up with the Justin Bieber video? Was that you, too?"

Steve shook his head miserably. "No way, are you insane? Come on. All I was doing was trying to finish that s-s-stupid t-t-test...." He slowed down and took a deep breath, afraid of what might happen if he could not stop stuttering. "No, it wasn't me. Someone, or something, put it on."

Justin slapped the table, "Demons! The demon is back!"

Heads turned their way, and a couple of kids at the next table stopped talking. Steve shook his head violently "N-n-no. Justin, c-c-can you think about maybe whispering?" He took a breath, "Maybe, I don't know, maybe?"

Justin frowned, "Have you seen, you know, any smoky stuff like before, I mean before the computer smoke? Anything like what happened? Hmm, no? Okay, then it must be something else. Plus, you haven't had any contact at all with..." he paused and looked around, but nonetheless said too loudly, "...the dragon." His eyes were alight with excitement.

Steve inwardly groaned. There was no way he could keep talking to Justin about all this here at school. "No, listen, we'll talk to Joy later. Right now's not a good time, okay?"

Berit slipped away from the rest of the class and into one of the girls' bathrooms. She was breathing heavily, her pulse was racing, and her legs felt weak. Twice in her long life, she had been trapped in a mortal form, but even then, she had never felt so weak, so vulnerable. She stopped in front of the mirror above the sink to look at the hated face, certain that she would see a nightmare. Nothing—the human girl staring back looked completely normal. Something impossible had happened. She had never heard of a human doing what the boy had done. It was impossible. She started to use her magic again, but stopped herself. No, what if he did it again? Could she risk it? And besides, she felt a little woozy. No, she needed to get out of here and contact someone. Not those two idiots she brought with her; she'd need some answers from Iceland.

She took a deep breath and checked herself again in the mirror. She straightened a stray strand of hair, and adjusted her stylish skirt. A perfect human doll. "Blah," she said to herself and then stepped back out into the hall. It was empty. She stomped boldly toward the front entrance where a district security officer stood watch. Berit waved her hand confidently to dismiss the annoying little female in her silly, blue uniform.

"Whoa there, girl," the young woman said. "Just where do you think you're off to? Do you have a pass to be out of class?"

Berit stopped. "What? Are you talking to me?"

The guard placed put her hands on her own hips and cocked her head. "Do you see anyone else in this hallway? What is your name, and where are you supposed to be?"

Berit willed the woman to take her annoying self somewhere else. She waited...but nothing happened. Instead, the presumptuous woman approached her. "Well, what's the matter with you? You forget who you are? Come on, let's see where you're supposed to be." She ushered Berit into the office.

"Don't touch me!" Berit demanded.

"No one's touching you, honey. But you can't wander around unsupervised in the halls. Come on, in you go."

"What is happening?" she asked herself. "Where was her magic? Not again!" Becoming desperate, she waved her arm, intending to send the thousand loose papers in the main office flying through the room. Nothing. *If she was trapped in this body, again,* she thought, *she'd jump from the highest building.*

She allowed herself to be sat down outside the assistant principal's door, while the officer asked the secretary about her. "Hey, Mrs. Wallace, can you look up and see where this young lady is supposed to be? She doesn't feel much like talking right now. In fact, she wouldn't even tell me her name."

The heavy-set women smiled, "Berit, why didn't you speak to Officer Washington? Let me take a look here. Oh, here's the problem. She was in Mr. Brown's class, the one that had the incident a bit ago. That's probably why she's so upset. Did you hear about it, Officer Washington? All the computers, all at once exploded! I bet it really upset poor Berit here."

You don't know the half of it, Berit thought to herself.

"Yeah, I heard all the commotion on the radio. Weird," the security guard agreed. "So, what should I do with her?"

"I'm right here; quit talking as if I'm not. You don't have to do anything with me," Berit answered for herself. She pulled out her cell phone and tried her "parents."

"Ah, dear, you can't have that out. It's supposed to be in your locker," Mrs. Wallace explained.

Berit glared at her. The darned thing got no signal in this building anyway. She stuffed it back into her purse. "So, you want me to take her back to Mr. Brown? I think his class is in the library," Officer Washington asked.

"No," Berit replied. "I need to see the nurse. I need to call my...mother. I don't feel well."

Chapter 13

That morning, Shou sat comfortably near the lighthouse, alone on a bench overlooking the crashing breakers, a now cold cup of coffee still tantalizing her with its aroma. It helped overcome the briny ocean smell, which made her hungry. Despite the allure of stinky fish, it was a good centralized spot. From here, she could catch wisps of the young sleeping dragon miles to the south, as well as keep a nose on Berit and her two assistants. And she liked watching the birds; they enjoyed a freedom she sometimes wished for.

Though Shou had possibly the most developed sense of smell in the dragon world, that wasn't what alerted her this morning. Being a creature of magic, Shou, like all dragons, even minor ones, was sensitive to magic. Someone had used magic so powerful that it gave her a bit of vertigo; she set a free hand on the bench and took a deep breath, aware that she might have fallen if she had been upright.

At first, she wondered if Berit and her friends had done something to Justin or one of the other children. After searching through thousands of smells, she caught their scent, relieved to find them smelling like average middle schoolers—not particularly pleasant, but alive and will. But then she detected the boy, Steve, the one who spoke to the dragon. His smell was pungent, like a slap to her face. He was saturated with magic, but Shou knew that was not possible. A few more sniffs confirmed that the boy, in fact, had more magic within him than he could control; it was dangerous. She needed to find him immediately.

Berit had to fake a tremendous migraine for the nurse to let her call her "mother." When Brita arrived, she played it up in front of the nurse. "Oh, how's my poor baby? What happened? Are you okay? Let's get you home and into bed!"

The nurse explained that there had been an incident, and she was sure that Berit was just a little shook up. Berit followed Brita out the front of the school with her head down, but inside, she was livid. If she could have spewed vomit all over Brita, she would have. Instead, she got into the back seat and slammed the car door. "To that wretched little house, now!" She yelled at Halldor, who had been waiting in the car.

Brita had to get one last jab in, "Don't you want to talk about it, darling?"

Berit spoke one ancient word of power, picturing Brita's forehead smashed up against the front windshield, but nothing happened. *Damn, damn, damn, damn, what has that kid done to me?* "Get me to the house. Something horrible has happened."

Brita looked at Halldor who shrugged and started up the car. She started to say something else, but the look on Berit's face made her close her mouth—antagonizing Berit was never a good idea.

Berit bolted out of the car as soon as they arrived and slammed right smack into the front door. It did not open for her as she commanded. She quickly turned back. Neither of her companions had seen. She stood back and closed her eyes. She concentrated with all her being and reached out to the doorknob and gave it a twist. Click, it opened. Relief flooded through her and then Brita yelled, "It's open. We left in such a hurry, we didn't lock it." *Damn, damn, damn.*

Without replying, she went to her room and shut the door. She immediately booted up her computer, quickly scanning through her emails—nothing important. She did not expect there would be; she was usually left free to accomplish whatever her great dragon commanded of her without much interference. She started composing a summary of what had happened, of what was happening. Somewhere in Iceland, a functionary, much like her two assistants, would read the email and relay it to someone higher up—perhaps even the Great One himself, though that was probably unlikely. In any case, it would take a while to get a reply, so there was nothing to do except wait.

Berit had lost her powers before, even been stuck as a human—twice! Though centuries had passed, she still had no idea who had done it, but she sensed this time was different. A human was the culprit, a boy. She had walked among mortals for centuries and had encountered many guardians before, but none had ever displayed this…this ability. They had displayed magic, yes, when connected to the dragons they looked after. But never anything like this.

She considered trying to revert to her true form. What if she couldn't? No, she decided, she would wait for an answer and would continue to try little things, unobserved of course. She didn't know if Brita or Halldor knew. They were smart, especially Brita. If she didn't have it all figured out yet, she would soon. Would she try and take over? No, whatever this was, it was likely only temporary. She would get her powers back; she had to. In the meantime, what to do? Perhaps she could get some answers from that simpleton Justin. She logged onto that ridiculous fantasy website and entered the chat room. She selected Justin's Internet alias and typed:

➤ Hey DragonKeeper, are you there? Haven't talked in a while. (Dragongirl 1)

While she waited for a reply, she took a seat in the chair, her pathetic human legs dangling a foot off the ground. Apparently, the imbecile wasn't hovering over his keyboard right now. Fine, she'd have to wait. Sooner or later, he'd log on, and then maybe she would learn something useful.

Chapter 14

"What are you doing?" Steve asked.

Justin looked up from the little origami dragon he had folded on Steve's desk. "What? Oh, nothing, I made a dragon, see?"

Joy bounced off the bed to take a look at what Justin was doing. "He's the one who should be obsessed with dragons," Joy pointed to Steve, "not you. What is your deal?"

Justin looked at the tiny white dragon he had fashioned. "What do you mean?"

"Dragons, you know, big lizards with wings." Joy snatched the little figurine.

"Hey, give it back," Justin protested.

"Come on guys, stop it," Steve insisted. "Joy, give it back. It doesn't hurt anything, and you know it's his thing right now."

Justin mimicked, "Yeah, it's my thing right now, so give it back."

Joy started to crunch it and throw it back, but stopped. "Fine," she dropped it on the desk. "Here, take it. But maybe you should see your shrink about it."

Justin took the tiny dragon and started flying it around. "Already have. But my mild form of Asperger's not worthy of therapy, thank you very much."

"Okay, fine, but can't they give you some kind of pill or something?" Joy asked. "They've done wonders for my mom, as long as she stays on them."

Steve shook his head, but Justin had already stopped and carefully placed the dragon on the desk and sat back down. He didn't say anything. Finally, Steve spoke up, "Joy, don't you remember back in elementary school, back in second grade. Justin got pulled in and out of school all year long. That's when they first tried to figure out what was wrong with him. Do you remember how he came back sometimes? It was because they had him all dopey on medication."

"Selective serotonin reuptake inhibitors," Justin intoned, "plus, a bunch of socialization therapy. Didn't mind the therapy so much, even though it was boring. But the pills had all kinds of side effects. I didn't like that."

Steve looked pointedly at Joy who shrugged a soundless "Sorry" behind Justin's back. Steve inclined his head toward Justin. Joy sighed and walked over to Justin and wrapped him up in a powerful hug. Justin stiffened up, preferring not to be touched. Sensing his discomfort, Joy released him and apologized for the remark.

"It's okay," Justin replied.

"You're still a geek," Joy replied.

"I know. And you're still a missing link."

Joy smiled, "That's me. Okay, enough of that Kumbaya stuff. So back to what happened at school. How can you be sure, Steve? Isn't it possible, you know, that something normal made the computers blow up?"

Steve gave her the "Are you stupid?" look. "Really, come on, all of them at once?"

"And it happened after he started watching the Justin Bieber video," Justin added.

"I w-w-wasn't watching any videos! That's wha-wha-wha-wha-whaaat I m-m-mean!" Suddenly, the pencil on the desk started to vibrate, and then a cup, and then it seemed as if the entire room was experiencing a minor earthquake. Joy stifled a yelp with a hand to her mouth. Justin tried grabbing things as they fell off the shelves, catching nothing. Suddenly, everything stopped.

Joy recovered first and asked the obvious question, "Steve, was that you?"

Before he could answer, Justin butted in, "Of course it was! It was like the computer lab. It's got to be Justin Bieber! He's the common denominator. Steve is allergic to Justin Bieber."

Steve looked at his friend, but didn't immediately answer; he was afraid to. Slowly he responded, "No, it's not that. I m-m-mean, I'm not allergic to J-J-Justin Bieber. Something m-m-made that video come on during my test and when Mr. Brown yelled at me, I got mad…"

Joy finished the thought, "And that's when everything blew up. Like now when you started to get upset. Steve, since when have you been able to blow stuff up or shake a room?"

Steve plopped down on the bed next to Joy and shook his head. "Today."

"And you're stuttering again," Justin pointed out. He picked up his tiny paper dragon off the floor and pointed at it. "Guys, it has to be connected to the dragon. Steve, you aren't magical all on your own. The dragon is, remember. No offense."

"Jeez, don't you think I know that?" Steve replied with exasperation. "But I haven't heard or seen anything from the dragon in a long time. And there's something else." Steve paused, trying to figure out how to explain it. "I know it wasn't because of the dragon, because whenever I did any magic, I could feel a connection to it. This was different. I didn't feel the same way at all. I kind of felt like I was going to puke. You know, a little sick to my stomach. I still do."

The front door banged open, and Dani came storming into the room. "Steve, hey Steve!"

"Get out, Dani," Steve automatically replied.

Dani automatically ignored him. "Hey guys, what's up?"

"Oh, hi Dani," Joy replied. Justin sort of waved.

Dani dropped on the bed behind her brother and Joy. "What'cha doing? Does Mom know you have people over with no one home? You're supposed to ask first, Steve."

"It's Justin and Joy. Mom's not going to mind. Now get out," Steve said.

"I like it here," as she propped herself up on one elbow, "it's good company. What'cha talking about?"

"N-n-nothing. Now get, I mean it," Steve scolded.

Dani turned to Joy, "He thinks he's my boss, but he's not, especially since he's, you know, temporarily crippled." She pointed to Steve's knee and made like she was snapping a stick in two. "Did I tell you guys what happened today? Okay, so Eloise, Joy you know her sister, she plays on your volleyball team. So, she's like, 'Well, I told you he liked you.' She was talking about Bobby. And I was like, 'No, he doesn't-'"

"Dani, sh-sh-sh-sh-sh-shut up!" Steve yelled.

Dani stopped, her face started to flush bright red. She was about to go all Mount St. Helens when a rap at the door stopped her. Dani huffed and jumped off the bed, "I got it." Joy looked to Steve, who waved it off.

Dani swung open the door and yelled in surprise, "Hey, I know you. Come on in."

"Dani!" Steve yelled. "Joy, g-g-go see who that i-i-idiot let in, please, while I get my crutches."

"Sure." Joy quickly stood up and pointed to the crutches against the closet as she was leaving. "Justin, grab those."

Justin wasn't paying attention, so Joy had to repeat herself, louder this time, "Justin, hand those to Steve."

"What? Oh, yeah. Okay."

As soon as Joy walked into the living room, she stopped. "Shou! Shou! Wow! Hey, guys, it's Shou!" Joy heard Steve hustling in on his crutches, then turned back to Shou. "Sorry, I meant to say hi. What are you doing here?"

Before Shou could answer, Steve and Justin joined them. Dani pulled the old woman to the couch and plopped right down next to her and began asking her questions.

Shou shushed Dani for a minute and smiled at them all. "I'm not going to try and deceive you. I am here for a reason, which I'll get to in a moment. Something happened today, didn't it, something very unusual?"

Justin nodded his head while Joy and Steve stared at Shou. "Yup," Justin started, "Steve was watching Justin Bieber videos in class and—"

"I was n-n-not watching st-st-stupid Justin Bieber videos!" Steve yelled. "I was taking a math test and th-th-th-th-th-the s-s-s-stupid video j-j-just came on."

Suddenly, the coffee table started to levitate off the floor. Everyone watched as it hovered about two feet in the air. Dani looked to her left and then her right, like she was waiting to cross the street, and then she tackled it.

"Whoa, hey, what are you doing?" Joy burst out. Justin sat there stunned. Steve looked sick. Dani had managed to get a good hold and was attempting to subdue the possessed furniture, "Come on, you stupid table." When she had climbed aboard, she pulled in her feet and sat cross-legged like Aladdin. "Hah, look at me, I'm flying!" she yelled.

Imperceptibly, Shou dipped two of her weathered old fingers, motioning the table down. However, instead of planting itself firmly on the floor as Shou commanded, it rose higher and even started to slowly spin. Shou suddenly dropped her hand, her face pale and pained. Meanwhile, the table descended and finally settled back to the floor. Steve bolted for the bathroom as fast as he could hop.

Dani threw her arms wide and began to flap. "Hey, why'd it stop? Make it start again!"

Shou began to rise and had to catch herself on the edge of the couch. Joy immediately went to help her. "Are you all right, Shou? You look terrible."

Shou could barely talk, "Fine. Just a minute."

From the bathroom, they could hear Steve retching. Justin hadn't moved during the whole event. His eyes bored into

Shou's. Finally, he spoke, "Shou, you know about all this, don't you?"

Shou closed her eyes and nodded. She was breathing heavily. Steve returned, his face pale from puking and wet from the water he had thrown on it. Shou spoke first, "Dear, how long has this been happening?"

Steve hesitated before answering, but Shou continued, "Not your connection to the dragon. I mean this, like what just happened."

Steve was very confused. "H-h-how do y-y-you know about D-d-dragau?"

"Dragau?" Shou repeated. "Interesting."

"W-w-why are you here? M-m-maybe I sh-sh-should call my dad."

Shou nodded, "Yes, maybe you should. And your mother, and most assuredly that grandmother of yours as well. This is serious, young man. I don't think you have any idea how serious."

Dani was following the conversation back and forth and repeated Steve's question, "How come you know about the dragon, Shou?" But before she could answer, Dani turned to Justin, "You told her, didn't you? You told her all about Dragau."

"I did not! I haven't said a word about Steve and the dragon to..." Justin hesitated, "...to Shou. Nothing."

Shou interrupted, "No, Dani, no children. Justin did not tell me anything about your dragon. I need to explain some things to you all." She stopped, "But, perhaps, it would be better if your parents were here first. Steve, can you call them?"

Steve nodded and went to the kitchen to use the phone. As he was calling his mom, Justin's own cell phone went off in the other room. He didn't realize it until Dani said his pocket was buzzing. "Huh, oh, hi Mom," he answered. "No, I'm at Steve's...Right now? Come on, Mom. I'm right in the middle of something...But, that's not fair...Fine...Bye."

Steve hobbled in a minute later. "Dad's in class right now, and Mom is finishing up a house," he said. "She should be done in about 30 minutes. Granny didn't answer." He took a look at Justin, "What's going on?"

Justin stood with his arms folded and a scowl on his face. "I gotta go home. Right now."

"Really? Now? Why?" Steve asked.

"Stuff, stupid stuff. Shou, I want to know what's going on too," Justin replied almost in tears. "I'm not leaving."

"You go on, Justin," Shou instructed, "and I'll come by your house later and visit. I probably owe your parents an explanation as well. Okay?"

Justin looked like he was going to explode, but Shou smiled at him and gently said, "Go on now. I'll see you soon." He stood up and walked to the door, not bothering to say goodbye.

"Is he gonna be okay?" Joy asked.

Steve nodded as he settled on the couch, "Yeah, he's fine."

Shou took the interruption to collect her own thoughts. As soon as Justin left, she opened up her senses, careful not to use any magic, just to get a feel for any of it lingering around, like dipping your finger into the tub to test the water. Only she had to yank it back immediately; it was scalding hot. The boy, Steve, was flooded with magic, a black and purple tornado of magic. His aura looked nothing at all like a human's should. In fact, it looked a lot like her own. She had never encountered anything like this in a human. *By the Great Dragon,* she thought, *this is how we look to each other.* She desperately wanted to confirm her suspicions by trying a little magic again. But if it affected the boy like before, then it could be dangerous for him and maybe for her as well. "Steve, how do you feel? Still bilious?"

"What?"

"Nauseous, sick to your stomach?"

"I know w-w-what n-n-nauseous means," he said testily. "And yeah, I am. Hot, too, like I g-g-got the flu."

Dani covered her mouth, "Don't breathe on me!"

Steve gave her a dirty look. "Why do you ask?"

"Because I'm going to Jesse's house this weekend, and I don't want to be sick!"

"Not you, you m-m-moron," he pointed at Shou. "Why do *you* want to know?" he asked again.

Shou considered her words very carefully, "You are flooded with magic right now. And humans aren't meant to house that kind of power—"

Joy interrupted, "What do you mean 'humans'? Aren't you human?"

Shou smiled, "Please dear, let me finish." And then she had a thought, staring at Steve, who cradled his crutches across his lap. "Steve, when did you hurt your leg?"

Chapter 15

Justin stomped home, mumbling angrily to himself. He stopped to kick at every rock, stick, or loose item along the road, and he missed most of them, which only made him angrier. It wasn't far from his house to Steve's, but it took him longer to get there than it should have. He forgot to turn everything off before he left for school—so what? And he forgot to take out the recyclables—big deal! That was no reason to make him come home right now. His mom had no idea what was going on; this was way more important.

It was hard for him to remember to turn off all the lights and lock the place up. Ordinarily, his brother Larry or one of his slum dog friends would be sleeping over so there was no point in turning everything off. But since Larry had gone off to college, there was only Justin and his parents. "College, hah!" Justin said aloud to himself. UC Santa Barbara was close to Ventura and a bunch of other surfing spots, which was the real reason Larry went there. Justin had heard his brother brag about it to his friends dozens of times. Larry wasn't fooling anyone. Justin felt that if his parents wanted to make sure Larry studied, they should have sent him to Arizona or Montana or someplace a long way from the California coast.

When Justin got home, his mother was waiting, "What took you so long? Never mind, I need to go back out, so I left you a list of things to do on the kitchen counter. I also put something in the refrigerator for you to heat up. Your dad and I should be home around six. I moved the recyclable container back into the garage. If you get done early, finish your homework."

"Yeah, but if I hurry up and finish, can I go back over to Steve's?"

"No, Justin, you can't. You've got to learn some responsibility," his mom lectured. "You can't leave everything on in the house. Don't you remember last month when you left the oven on all day? Now, I've got to go."

She moved to give him a kiss on the cheek, but stopped herself; Justin wasn't a touchy-feely kind of kid, especially if he was mad. "All right, get your stuff done."

"I got it, Mom," he grumbled.

"Love you," she said as she slipped out the door.

Justin went into the kitchen and found the 'To-Do' list. At first, he didn't even look at it; instead, he balled it up and chucked it at the sliding glass door. Then he kicked at it and hit a chair instead. It sucked being uncoordinated. He had, however, vented most of his anger and nothing was broken— foot or furniture. He bent and picked up the note. It wasn't too bad: empty the trash, put away dishes, gather up his dirty clothes. He started with the first item, emptying the trash, and then worked his way down the list.

At item number four—gather up dirty laundry and put into laundry room—Justin headed to his bedroom. He was about to empty out his hamper when he noticed his computer screen. He had a message waiting for him from Dragongirl 1. He looked at his list; he was nearly done, so he set it on the desk and logged into the chat room.

➤ Hey, you on? (DragonKeeper)

He waited a minute or so, and got nothing, so he started to log off.

➤ Hey, you're back. Haven't heard from you in a while. What's going on? Any dragon sightings? (Dragongirl 1)

➤ No. But crazy stuff. My best friend blew up a bunch of computers today. (DragonKeeper)

➤ What? (Dragongirl 1)

➤ Yeah really. In math, he got mad and bam! Made everything blow up. (DragonKeeper)

➤ Wow, does he know how? (Dragongirl 1)

> No. That's why Shou turned up to tell him. (DragonKeeper)
> Shou? Shou turned up where? (Dragongirl 1)
> You know who Shou is? (DragonKeeper)
> No, I mean, what's a Shou? (Dragongirl 1)
> She's that old lady I told you about who found me in Seattle. She's here and I think she knows something about why Steve can blow up computers. Oh wait, and he made his sister fly too. (DragonKeeper)
> What? (Dragongirl 1)
> Well, the coffee table actually, but Dani was on it. I'm not kidding. (DragonKeeper)
> Amazing! What's her name, Shou? What was she doing? (Dragongirl 1)
> Huh? I don't know. Why? (DragonKeeper)
> I figured since she might know what was going on, then maybe she was trying to help. (Dragongirl 1)
> No, she kind of looked sick. Then I had to leave. (DragonKeeper)
> So you didn't get to hear what she had to say about everything? (Dragongirl 1)
> No, I forgot to do a bunch of chores before school this morning and had to come home. (DragonKeeper)
> That sucks! So, you think this Shou truly knows what's going on? (Dragongirl 1)
> I don't know. Maybe. She was going to talk to Steve and his family when they got there. (DragonKeeper)
> You think she's still there? (Dragongirl 1)
> Probably. Steve's mom was going to come home in a while and I think Shou wanted to talk to her too. Does it matter? (DragonKeeper)
> No. I guess it really doesn't. I'm just curious how this old woman would know anything, that's all. Hey, oh crap, I

have to get off now. This is so cool. Let me know if you find out more. (Dragongirl 1)

➢ OK, bye. (DragonKeeper)

Justin started to close out of the chat room, but decided to leave it in case she got back on. It was awesome to have someone like Dragongirl to talk to. She seemed genuinely interested in what he had to say. He ran through the conversation in his head, kind of imagining what it would be like to actually meet her in person. He was sure he would be able to talk to her as easily as he did in a virtual world. He tried to picture what she'd look like. At first, he thought she might have looked a certain way, but lately, whenever he thought of her, the new girl Berit was who he saw. "What if she really did look like Berit?" he asked himself. Of course, she wouldn't. She was probably a normal-looking girl. Beautiful girls didn't spend their time online talking about dragons. Still, it was a nice thought. He started to stand, saw his list, and rolled his eyes, remembering that he had a few chores left.

Berit opened up a file and found the address she wanted. Then she slapped the lid down on her laptop and jumped for the bedroom door. "Hey, you two, quickly, get in here," she demanded. Two other bedroom doors opened and Berit's companions joined her in the living room. "Listen, I want you both to go over to this address; 112 Stanton. Wait there for Shou, and when she leaves pick her up and bring her here."

The pair looked at each other, but as usual, it was Brita who spoke up, "I suppose you are going to enlighten us as to why we should go near someone you said was so dangerous. Wasn't it you who said we should stay away from her? I think it was, wasn't it, Halldor?"

Halldor's head swiveled to look at each of them in turn, then put up his hands as if to say, "Not getting into the middle of this."

Berit held her temper out of necessity; she had no power at the moment. "The old woman is vulnerable right now. It's important that I talk to her, so I need you to hurry."

Halldor shrugged and started for the door, but Brita didn't move. She raised an eyebrow at her mentor in a very human gesture. "What aren't you telling us, Berit? What happened at the school today?"

"I said to go, now," Berit said quietly. "We can't risk her getting away."

"Halldor..." Brita instructed, "...stop. Shut the door and wait a minute. No Berit, I don't think I'm going anywhere right now. Not until I get some answers. You know what I think? I think something happened to you today, something with your powers maybe? I think you'd better come clean, or I might have to contact home for some new instructions."

Berit snapped and instinctively reacted. She swung her arm in an exaggerated arc and slapped the upstart dragonette. Besides the loud pop of hand on face, nothing happened. Brita grinned, her smile widening until she broke into laugher. Between guffaws, Brita managed, "So, the almighty Berit has no—"

At that moment, the air seemed to sizzle, like lightning just before it crashes down, and the next sound was Brita's body slamming into the far wall. Berit's magic had returned to her! It was now her turn to laugh. She raised her chin up and Brita was pressed up against the ceiling, her face smooshed into the popcorn ceiling. "Mmmm," she mumbled.

"What? What's that? I can't hear you. Just a minute." Berit smiled and Brita dropped to the floor. She stood over the dazed woman and waited for her to slowly rise to her feet. When Brita finally was able to stand, Berit was in her true form, a glistening black wingless dragon. The jaws, though not massive, were frightening and inches from Brita's face. In a guttural voice not suitable for human ears, Berit spoke, "Never challenge me again. Now, go! I don't know how much time you have."

Halldor was out the door and gunning the engine before Brita could even reach the car. As they backed up, a pretty, blond girl stood on the porch and waved at them.

Chapter 16

Shou got up before anyone else and opened the door to reveal a surprised Jeanie. "Ah, hello, Mrs. Wang," she managed to say as she put her keys back into her purse. Dani jumped up to drag her mother into the living room with everyone else.

Jeanie said, "So, ah, Mrs. Wang, are you going to tell me what this is all about?"

Shou smiled and nodded, "Yes, dear, of course. And I'm sorry for the surprise of it all. Is your husband coming home soon?"

"I'll have to leave to get him in an hour. He's still in class."

"Oh, that's unfortunate," Shou mused. "I wanted to talk to all of you, especially Steve's grandmother—"

"Talk to her about what, Mrs. Wang?" Jeanie interrupted. "What is going on?"

Shou leaned on her cane, actually needing it thanks to Steve "Can we all sit? I have some things to share with you."

The living room was small with only a lumpy couch and an equally lumpy loveseat. Steve had his knee propped up over the arm of the loveseat, his color finally normal. Jeanie motioned for Shou to take a seat next to Steve and stepped into the kitchen to return with a dining room chair She passed it to Joy and pulled Dani to the large couch with her. "Okay," she announced, "we're all comfy now. So, can you please tell me why I had to rush home from work?"

Shou tapped her cane lightly against the floor. "I know about your family, and its connection to the dragon—"

"I knew it!" Dani exclaimed.

"Shut up, Dani," Steve hissed.

"Steve, don't tell your sister to shut up," Jeanie said. "Dani, be quiet."

Shou went on, "Before I continue, Steve, can you explain what happened at school to your mother?"

"How do you know anything about what happened?"

"I'll get to that, I promise, when you've finished."

Steve told the story, leaving out Justin Bieber. Before he could get to the part about this afternoon's weirdness, Dani interrupted again. "And then I flew!"

"Dani, let him tell it!" Joy reprimanded.

"Okay, okay, I mean the coffee table flew, and I caught a ride like this!" Dani started to sit on the table.

"Get off that table! What's wrong with you? What is she talking about?" Jeanie asked.

"Please, please, everyone," Shou soothed. "Mrs. Batista, the young lady is right. The table did fly…because of Steve, or, more correctly, because of me. This is complicated, so I'll ask you all to please just listen," she turned to smile at Dani, who snapped her mouth shut, cutting off whatever it was she'd been about to say.

Shou began, "Your dragon is in a deep sleep. Yes, Dani, I know the dragon is always asleep. Right now, however, is a special time and he requires a special sleep—one in which the great dragon cannot be disturbed. You see, only the great dragons, like yours, can produce an egg—"

"Our dragon's a girl?" Dani asked excitedly.

"You want to go to your room?" Jeanie asked. "Quit interrupting!"

"No, Dani, not really. Your dragon, like all dragons, is neither male nor female."

"So how come you keep calling it a he?" Dani asked.

"More out of habit, really. I tend to refer to dragons the way the humans do."

"So, she could be a girl," Dani insisted.

"It doesn't matter Dani," Steve said.

"Pronoun discussions aside, your dragon will produce an egg, or rather, *could* produce an egg. You see, right now your dragon is hibernating to conserve all his magic. That magic will be the beginnings of another great dragon, or perhaps several lesser beings like myself. No," Shou said, holding up her hand to halt the questions on all of their faces, "this is not my true form. I'll get to that."

"Your dragon is not the only great dragon in the world. In fact, your dragon is a relative baby. Older, powerful beings have been around since well before your kind ever started walking around on two legs. When the time is right, your dragon will fully awake, the magic inside him at its most powerful. When this happens, one of those ancient dragons will come and there will be a terrible battle. If your dragon should win and destroy the other dragon, then it will produce an egg which will hatch when your dragon thinks the time is right."

"If, however, the other dragon should prevail, then it will take the younger dragon's magic and from that magic, a number of lessor creatures will be born—creatures like myself."

"Why not another, what do you call it, great dragon?" Joy asked.

"There won't be enough magic," Steve said.

"That is right," Shou said. "It takes the all the magic of the egg and the dead dragon's magic to create another great dragon. Otherwise, like I said, minor dragons are born."

Dani cocked her head and asked, "So you hatched? Like a bird?"

Shou laughed. "No, we don't come from actual eggs. It's simply easier to think of the magic that way. The magic does condense into a small sphere. And even though we do not become great dragons, some of us are quite strong, able to change forms and do powerful magic in our own right; others are not so powerful, or even particularly intelligent. These simple creatures often take more or less permanent forms like trees or rocks. We live as long as the great dragons, but because we aren't as strong, we can move around the human world without wrecking it."

Shou paused, reading the room. When no one said anything, she continued, "Steve, you and your family are caught in a battle that has gone on for centuries, millennia. There are some great dragons, nearly all actually, that believe that mankind is a cancer. That everything you do harms this world. Your history is one of growth and destruction. Whenever it looks as if you will completely dominate this planet, the great dragons have knocked you back down. The only thing that keeps them from wiping you out completely is that great dragons do not get along. They are territorial and do not cooperate with each other. If they ever coordinate their efforts, humanity will be in big trouble."

Shou nodded, mostly to herself. "I happen to believe the opposite. I believe that you will find a way to become a great species without destroying this world. The ancient dragon that gave me life thousands of years ago believed the same. It is why I have spent my life trying to help the great dragons sympathetic to your kind. Unfortunately, there aren't many left. It is why I am here to help your dragon, and you."

"How?" Steve asked, "How are you supposed to help me? And what does all this have to do with me blowing stuff up?"

Shou considered a moment before answering, "When I met Justin and heard his story, I knew there was dragon magic involved. When I came here, I could tell that your dragon was beginning its time. I knew others would find out as well. There are dragonettes, like myself, who are here to influence the coming conflict. If these creatures can find your dragon, disturb its rest, then they can weaken it. Even if they don't find it, they can hurt it by hurting the things it loves."

"Oh, God," Joy exclaimed. "It's that girl Berit, isn't it? It's her and her parents!"

Shou clapped her hands in amusement, "Yes, yes, my girl. My, you are all so wonderfully perceptive. I can see why your dragon is so close to you."

"It's not my dragon," Joy replied, "It's Steve's and his family's."

"Hmm, is that so?"

Chapter 17

"Berit is a dragon? Really?" Steve looked ill.

"I knew there was something about her, and the way you and... Oh no," Joy said.

"Oh no is right," Steve replied miserably.

"What's the matter children?" Shou asked.

Joy cocked her head at Steve. "Well?"

"Well, what?"

"Well," Joy said, "you and Justin had a thing for her."

"I did not have a thing for her; I t-t-thought she was c-c-cute—"

Danny giggled, but Joy cut her off before she could say anything. "Maybe, that was it for you, but Justin? Justin has it bad for her."

Shou sighed. "Oh, no. That's awful, but he would not be the first Berit fooled. Perhaps I should talk to him?"

Steve and Joy looked at each other. "Or, maybe one of us will," Steve said.

Suddenly, there was a loud bang at the back door. Before anyone could move, a familiar voice yelled from the kitchen, "Hey, where's the party?"

"Dad?" Dani called back.

Steve and everyone else turned to see his father emerge into the living room. He smiled quizzically at everyone and dropped his heavy book bag in the corner.

Jeanie spoke up, "Hey, babe. I didn't think you'd be done for another 30 minutes."

"The professor wasn't feeling well, so he cut us lose early. Kathy gave me a ride home," Roger replied.

Dani ran over to her dad and pointed back at Steve. "It's not fair, Daddy. Steve gets to talk to dragons and blow stuff up."

"What? What is she talking about?" Roger asked.

"Dani, give your dad a minute," Jeanie instructed.

"She's fine," he said. "What's going on?"

Dani huffed and pointed to Mrs. Wang, "She's a dragon. Not like our dragon, though. Our dragon's going to have a baby. Not like a real baby because the dragon's not really a girl, but she's here to protect it. Oh, and apparently some other dragons are here to steal it. But like now Steve gets to steal magic from dragons which is totally unfair!" She stood with her hands on her hips. "Oh, and he blew up a bunch of computers at school," she added.

Roger looked at his wife who shrugged, "Yeah, pretty much."

Suddenly, Shou began to sniff at the air. She got up and approached the front door.

"Mrs. Wang," Joy asked, "are you all right?"

"Hmm, oh, I'm sorry, my friends. I smell something, or someone really. Mr. Batista, was there anyone outside when you came in?"

"There was a car parked a little down the street. It doesn't belong to anyone around here," Roger answered.

"I wonder what they want?" Shou remarked. "Are they here for Steve, or for me?"

"Who, Mrs. Wang? Who are you talking about?" Jeanie asked.

"Those people out there are like me, dragonettes. It's possible they're here for Steve, but that seems unlikely. If Steve can steal their magic, it might be dangerous for them. And they wouldn't dare come for me...Unless, they knew that I'd lost my magic, but no, how could they? Hmm, very strange," Shou mumbled absently.

Roger walked over to the window and pulled the curtain back enough to peer down the street. "Okay, so there are people, no, dragons, out there in a car watching the house. Is that right? Are these, are they dangerous, Mrs. Wang?"

"Oh, completely, and call me Shou, please. Little dragons like them have started wars. But not those two, they're too young. I'm sorry, Steve, but I'm afraid it's this ability to siphon magic away that's drawn them here. Though what they want, I'm not sure."

"What do you mean siphon magic?" Roger asked.

"That's like what I was trying to tell you!" Dani said, pointing at her brother, "Now, he can even suck magic away from dragons. This is totally unfair."

"Dani!"

"Nobody listens to me!" she insisted.

Still confused, Roger asked, "Do I need to grab my shotgun?" Ever since Steve got kidnapped by a demon and its human lackeys, Roger had kept a loaded shotgun under the bed.

"No, no, it wouldn't do you much good. Besides, it's not that dangerous," Shou answered. "They wouldn't dare go directly against me. I don't know what they'd want with Steve. Wait! Yes, yes, I have an idea."

Chapter 18

There was moment of silence as Shou thought about what she was going to do. Dani interpreted that as an invitation to speak up. "This is not fair!"

"Are you c-c-crazy, Dani?" Steve yelled. "Y-y-you want this s-s-stutter? Or, d-d-demons chasing you? And n-n-now, I apparently, suck up magic and b-b-blow things up? Oh my God, are you nuts?"

"Take it easy, son," Roger said.

"Steve, I want to help you," Shou said. "Will you trust me?"

Steve nodded weakly.

Poor, boy, Shou thought. There was more she could tell him and his parents that might help, but that would have to wait. Shou used her superior senses to look around the room. She was a little nervous because she didn't want to trigger any response from Steve, but this wasn't so much using her magic as it was perceiving things differently.

Shou looked from human to human, but saw nothing out of the ordinary, just their softly glowing mortal auras. Joy's flickered a little brighter than average, but nothing to be concerned over. When she got to Steve, however, she saw the swirling colors of dragon magic, though they were a tad dimmer than before. He was still containing an extraordinary amount of magic and he needed to rid himself of it before…Well, she didn't exactly know what, but chances were it would be catastrophic for him.

She spoke to Steve directly, "Steve, you are holding on to magic that your human body was never meant to contain. It could be dangerous. I want to try something to release it, and get my own magic back."

Shou then asked his parents, "I know you don't really know me, but I think I can help him and protect us from those outside. May I try?"

Roger and Jeanie looked at each other and did that psychic thing married couples did when they'd lived together a long time. They answered simultaneously, "Okay."

Shou shed the herky-jerky movements of an old woman and gracefully knelt next to Steve. "Steve, I want you to close your eyes and listen. I'm going to speak with you like your own dragon. Don't be frightened. You'll know what I want you to do."

To everyone else, she said, "I'm going to speak to Steve in my own language. Roger, you might understand some of it because you are a guardian, but please don't interrupt. Now listen, Steve."

Chapter 19

Roger cleared off the couch for Steve to lie down. He had his knee propped up over a couple of pillows. Shou closed her eyes and sat in the chair Roger had brought over to her. While everyone held their breath to see what was going to happen next, Shou began speaking in crumbled consonants, a soft, mildly soothing mantra. Steve sat there, nodding his head occasionally. After a while, Dani asked if she could go to her room because this was booooring. "Shh," her mother admonished, then thought better of it. "Fine."

Steve understood everything Shou was saying. She was telling him to relax and to try to feel the energy cursing around inside himself. As she spoke, Steve began to feel a little separated from his own body, like he was slipping out of himself, like he was a balloon tugging at a string. It was an experience he'd had before when talking to his own dragon. At the same time, he noticed that he could see everyone in the room very clearly even though he had his eyes closed. As his awareness grew, he was able to see the real Shou. She was a magnificent creature! As big as a horse and the color of cooked lobster, she reminded him of those dragons on a Chinese menu—majestic and slithery, all at once.

"Thank you, I think," Shou replied. She turned her large head in his direction and, with a mouth full of dangerous-looking teeth, attempted a ridiculous smile.

"Don't be afraid, Steve. You've seen more impressive dragons than me."

"I," Steve fumbled for words, "well, not quite this close."

Shou winked one of her jet-black eyes. "Well, you have a dragon's eye view right now. What do you see?"

"Obviously, you're right in my face. And you're not Shou anymore," Steve explained. "You're, you look like one of those dragons you see at a Chinese food restaurant, but you knew that, right?"

"What else?"

"Nothing, I see my mom and dad, and Joy—"

"And?" Shou prompted. "Relax and take everything in."

Steve took a breath and attempted to calm all the thoughts running around in his head. He discovered that once he quit trying so hard, his awareness opened up. Suddenly, he was outside their house, looking down. He could see a few neighbors out and about. Ms. Agnes' cat was half in and half out of Big Joe's trashcan. A pair of seagulls were gliding northward along the coast. On a whim, Steve focused on them and expanded his view to include theirs. It was then that he saw the pair of strangers, a man and woman inside a new car. But they weren't a man and a woman; they were dragons, like Shou. He was golden brown and she was a deep, dark blue.

"Shou! There are—"

"I know, you see them exactly as I do," soothed Shou. "If Berit were with them, you would see her true form, as well. But don't worry about them—"

"What do you mean don't worry about them? Didn't you say they were here to hurt Dragau? Or us?"

Shou moved her sinuous neck like a slinky, her snout and maw of teeth came even closer to Steve, now. "Ignore them, Steve. Bring your attention back here. You see the magic that surrounds me? Good. Now look at yourself."

"Wow, I'm like—"

"Me. Exactly. I want you to focus on your knee. I want you to remember how you injured it, the way it felt right at that moment," Shou instructed. "Picture the way the knee felt before the accident, the way it moved. Picture your knee moving that way now, easily with no pain. Can you imagine it?"

"Yes," he replied.

"Good. Now, I want you to gather all that magic inside yourself and I want you to focus only on your knee. Picture the good, healthy knee moving freely without pain. Strong. Do you feel it?"

"Yes."

Shou inched in even closer, "Now, Steve, tell me how strong the knee is, how healthy—"

Steve spoke as if in a trance. "My knee doesn't hurt anymore. It's healthy and I can move it. It's strong."

And suddenly...it was.

Chapter 20

"Nervous?" Halldor asked.

Brita didn't immediately answer. She sat in the passenger seat staring out the window. The sun was below the horizon; only orange and pink and gold remained in the western sky. Porch lights were turning on. Cars were returning to their driveways. Finally, Brita replied, "No, something happened today that Berit isn't telling us. She had no power; I could feel it!"

"Was that before she slammed you into the ceiling?" Halldor asked.

A woman with a baby strapped to her front and a pair of schnauzers walked by where they were parked and gave a little half wave. Brita ignored her and Halldor's question. Halldor waved back at her. "So why are we going after the old dragon now?" he asked.

Brita scowled at her companion. She couldn't understand why he was here; he was as dense as a brick. "Don't you see? Whatever happened to Berit today is happening to Shou. Berit told us to stay away from her initially. The only reason she would send us after the old crone now is because she must have lost her powers as well." Brita mused further before continuing, "And Berit found out. It had to be that kid she talks to online."

Halldor nodded and reached into his shirt pocket for a cigarette. He turned it toward his mouth and a tiny flame teased the end into lighting. He inhaled deeply, burning nearly half of it in one drag.

"Smoke that disgusting thing outside!" Brita snapped.

Halldor cocked his head, "What? Are you joking? We're dragons! You know, we breathe smoke and fire."

"Those disgusting things reek with paint, butane, acetic acid, ethyl alcohol, industrial solvents, along with five or six hundred other vile ingredients," Brita lectured. "That little piece of humanity you stuck in your mouth is what's wrong with the entire human race. It's why these worthless things need to be crushed back to the stone ages."

Halldor climbed out of the car and poked his head back in, "I like blowing smoke rings." He grinned and shut the door before he caught Brita's angry retort, then leaned back against the shiny black car. He drew in a long drag from the sliver of toxicity and held all those nasty chemicals in his lungs. He then leaned across the hood and slowly exhaled. A three-foot long smoky image formed itself into a prancing unicorn right in front of Brita's side of the windshield. Brita said something that Halldor couldn't hear and then produced a very human gesture with her middle finger.

Halldor started to laugh, but stopped when a brilliant light shot out of the house they were watching. Halldor blinked, seeing blue dots before his eyes, like turning on and off a light bulb in the middle of the night. He dropped what was left of his cigarette and jumped back into the car. "You see that?" he asked.

"Of course," Brita snapped.

"What do you think—"

"Listen, don't you hear? It's the old woman, and, something, no, someone else is talking...That's impossib—"

Light exploded out of the house a second time, leaving the pair momentarily blinded.

Chapter 21

Shou slipped out the back door as soon as she could get away from the excited family. Her magic had been restored the moment Steve healed his own leg and, after graciously receiving the Batista's thanks, she'd managed to get away with a promise to come back and tell them more. But first, she had Berit's underlings to deal with.

Shou walked around the detached shed and, just to make sure she wouldn't be seen, she snapped her fingers. A little fog streamed toward her from the direction of the coast. It pooled around her legs and climbed up around her until she was completely covered in a heavy grey mist. Good, either she was far enough away from Steve not to have her powers siphoned off, or, more likely, he was not presently distressed about anything. Eventually, she would have to figure out which was the trigger. If he didn't learn to deal with this newfound ability, then he was a danger to her kind; there were others who would not abide such a talent in a human. Steve could be in real trouble.

Shou released the fog and a billowing wall of it engulfed the two young dragons and their vehicle. Shou followed it in, taking her time, step, step, plant the cane, step, step. When she reached them, they were attempting to start the engine. "Oh, no, kiddies," Shou smirked and climbed into the back seat. Brita spun around, "Who, what are you…How did you sneak up on us?

Ignoring her, Shou reached out her cane and poked Halldor in the shoulder, "So, children, why don't you tell me why you are parked outside of this nice family's house?"

"Listen, you old bat, we don't answer to—"

Suddenly, Brita's head bounced off the dashboard. "Hey, quit it or—"

Boom.

"I said to—"

Boom.

"I'm going to tear your—"

Boom.

"If you don't stop this, I'll—"

Boom.

Halldor threw up his hands in surrender. "Okay, okay, stop, please. We're supposed to bring you to Berit."

"Why?"

Brita shook her head at Halldor to stop him from answering.

Boom.

"Because," he began, "she said you were vulnerable right now."

"And how would she know that?" Shou asked.

At first Halldor refused to answer, but when Shou leaned forward, he continued, "Something happened to her today. She didn't tell us about it, but somehow she lost her powers for a while. She thought you did too."

"Shut up, Halldor," Brita started, "don't say—"

Boom.

Halldor sighed, "It's the kid. Berit talks online to this Justin kid. He's a friend of—"

Shou stopped him, "I know who he is. Tell Berit I'll be visiting her soon." Then she got out of the car. So Berit was not only playing with the boy's emotions, she was also pumping him for information. The thought of this made Shou angry; she had taken a liking to that boy, and to see him duped, or worse? Awful. The more she thought about it, the angrier she got. As the car carrying Berit's apprentices started to pull away, Shou gave them one last look.

Boom.

Chapter 22

"Careful, Steve," Jeanie instructed. "You may not be completely healed."

Steve was jumping from one leg to another, doing deep knee bends, and generally trying everything he could to prove his miraculous recovery was a hoax. But it wasn't. "Does it hurt at all?" Joy asked.

He shook his head, "Nope. I don't feel any pain. Hey Mom, do you think I can start playing soccer again?"

Jeanie looked over at Roger who was looking out the front window. "What? Oh, probably," he said absently. "Hey, that car is gone. Shou must have driven them off." Roger returned to the couch next to his wife. Seated, their height difference wasn't too pronounced. He whispered something into her long red hair. She nodded.

Steve knew a conspiracy when he saw one. "What is it, you guys?"

Roger answered, "I don't think you should go right back to school tomorrow. One, Shou said you were in danger, and two, if you show up with a perfectly healed knee, well, how are you going to explain that?"

Dani's radar had asserted itself and she walked into the room, "What? He doesn't have to go to school? Are you kidding me? He gets all the family magic *and* he gets out of school? Oh, my, gawwd!"

Joy put her hand on Dani's shoulder, "It's not like that, Dani."

Dani shrugged her off and started stomping off to her room again, "This sucks. Steve gets to do everything; Steve gets to skip school, Steve gets to make stuff fly around..." She continued listing her grievances all the way down the hall, until she slammed her door shut.

"Dani—" Roger began, but Jeanie stopped him. "Don't, hon, let her be for now. Joy, do we need to get you home?"

"Oh yeah, home. No, I can walk."

"Yeah," Steve chimed in. "I can walk her. My leg feels fantastic."

"No one is walking anywhere tonight," Roger replied. "Remember those people watching the house a while ago?"

Steve spoke before thinking, "They weren't people; they were dragons. Oh, um, but they're gone, Dad."

Jeanie supported her husband, "Yes, they're gone right now, Steve, but will they be back? We better take Joy home. And then we need to talk."

"Oh, wait a minute," Steve interjected, "you're not thinking of dumping me off at Granny's again, are you? Come on, there's nothing to do out there, and everyone else will be in school, so it'll only be me."

Jeanie grimaced, "We haven't decided what we're going to do tomorrow. We do need to make sure Joy gets home safely tonight, though."

Steve remembered his last long stay at his grandmother's. It hadn't been too bad, especially once Justin and Joy showed up, but that was during the summer and now they'd be in school. And there was that thing that happened when Justin got amnesia and got adopted by an Asian family; and the thing when they were attacked by the demon; and the thing when Steve got kidnapped. Suddenly, Steve had a logical epiphany. "Mom and Dad, listen. Don't you remember that last time you tried to keep me safe at Granny's? And this time it's no demon, so Granny's magic yard elves won't help. If they want something from me, Granny isn't going to be able to stop them, but if I stick around here, Shou might."

"He might be right, Roger," Jeanie agreed.

Roger was up and pacing. "So, we pretend everything is normal? Damn, I wish I'd never heard of dragons."

Inwardly, Steve kind of agreed. If he was honest with himself, part of him liked being able to make strange and wondrous things happen, like the time he made ants attack his cousin, or when he was actually talking to his dragon and got to see the world like he did today with Shou. Of course, having a demon invade your mind was disgusting, and blowing up computers was not cool—not to mention the whole Justin Bieber fiasco. Worst of all, this stuff made him feel like a freak—Steve didn't know what he'd do if it got out at school.

"What are you doing?" Jeanie asked her husband, interrupting Steve's thoughts.

"Well," Roger answered, "first we'll take Joy home, and then I'm going to make a few calls. If we can't hide from this, we're going to need some help."

Chapter 23

The dark thunder cloud had miraculously settled on the ground. It moved from Stanton, south on Del Monte, and then turned back north on Pebble Beach. Every once in a while, a lightning bolt erupted from within. Even though Crescent City was routinely covered in fog, it didn't usually have storm clouds trooping through the streets. The only reason the freaky phenomenon was not drawing more attention was because the rest of the weather was so lousy and many would-be witnesses were already indoors.

Inside the determined cloud stomped Shou. She was livid. Berit was a tyrant—a conniving, maniacal thug bent on throwing mankind back into the stone ages, but the audacity that Berit would send underlings to haul her in? Like some wet-behind-the-ears lizard? It was insulting, and out of character. It was also troubling. Berit was a manipulator, and she was good at it. Let the humans do all the dirty work. If they get hurt, well, they were only humans after all. That was Berit's style. Sending those hatchlings only illustrated how far Berit might be willing to go.

Then there was Justin. That nasty dragon was stringing that poor boy along. The more Shou thought about how broken-hearted that kid was going to be, how foolish he was going to feel when he discovered he was being used…Another lightning bolt erupted within the cloud. A passing car pulled over and began taking pictures before Shou realized she was dragging along her own angry little storm. "Oh, shoot!" she chided herself. A moment later all anyone saw was a drenched old lady shuffling along with the use of her cane.

Why would Berit risk an open confrontation? Was she that desperate? If she was, then Shou was worried. Steve was in greater danger than she had let on. Could he potentially upset the contest between the great dragons? Even if he couldn't, he could certainly create a distraction.

It left Shou in a bit of a quandary. Unlike Berit, who had the support of the great dragons in Iceland, which translated into an extensive network bent on destroying human civilization, Shou had few allies—her human friends and a relatively small number of dragonettes she had rescued over the years. Although Berit preferred to work alone, it was clear her dragon overlords could and would send reinforcements. As powerful as Shou was, she could not be in two places at once.

This was not the first time Shou wished her own great dragon had survived, but she was old enough not to dwell on what could not be helped. She realized that her mental wanderings, along with her spindly old legs, had led her to Justin's house just as a beat-up van turned the corner and parked right in front of her. Its music continued a moment after the motor shut off.

A tall young man, who Shou immediately recognized as Justin's older brother, Larry, jumped out. She watched him try to open the back doors of the vehicle, curse and then crawl back inside from the front and return with a large laundry basket full of crumpled clothes. Shou leaned forward on her cane, wondering if she should tell Justin about Berit and fill in his family about what was going on, when another car pulled in behind the van. Two other boys about the same age as Larry got out and entered the house. Shou suddenly had an idea.

Chapter 24

"Joy," Roger asked as they pulled into her driveway, "do I need to let your mom know why you're so late getting home?"

She shook her head, "Nope, it's all right. Thanks for the ride, Mr. Batista. Bye, Steve."

As soon as she opened the door, Joy knew something was wrong. Every light in the house was on, the television in the living room was blaring, and the vacuum cleaner was running unattended in the den. "Mom? Mom, are you home?" Joy hollered.

"Hi, baby," a voice called from the kitchen. "I'm in here."

Joy entered and she stifled a gasp. The small wall-mounted television was on a shopping show. There were bake trays everywhere. A cake was cooling, a pan of brownies was waiting to be cut into squares, and there were two cookie sheets in the oven. A notepad was next to her mother. Joy stepped closer. It was a Christmas shopping list. "Hi, baby, hey, step to the side. I want to get the code for those earrings. Your cousin Jenny would love those."

"Mom, you left the vacuum on, and the television in the living room," Joy said.

"Oh, I did? I'll get it. I thought you and your dad would like a cake, and then I realized that we had all these boxes of baked goods and they'd been in the pantry forever, so they would probably go bad if I didn't go ahead and make them. Plus, if we have any leftovers, I thought you could take them to school. I remember when I was in school and how much we loved it when kids brought in baked things. Honey, you're in front of the television again."

Joy turned around before her mother could see the tears threatening. She fought the burning pain that had seized her heart and went about turning off everything her mother had turned on. She shut the vacuum off last, returned it to the hall closet, went into her room, and called her dad.

"Hey," she said softly.

"What's wrong Joy?" her father asked.

"It's Mom. She's off her meds."

"Up or down?" he asked.

"Up, way up." Joy wiped her eyes. "She's baking everything in the house. And she's buying Christmas gifts on *The Shopping Network*."

A heavy sigh on the other end, and then, "Okay, listen, I'll leave right now. I've got to call the bank and put a freeze on our cards first. You going to be all right with her?"

"Sure, Dad. You know, she's a blast when she's high, a real blast."

"I'm so sorry, honey. She's…" he hesitated, "she's been good for a long time now. I don't know what happened. But don't worry, we'll get her back on her medications. Hopefully before she cycles down, okay?"

"Okay, Dad."

"Bye, honey. I'll be home as soon as I can, okay?"

"Sure. Bye."

She sat down on her bed.

"Joy," her mother called. "Come tell me about your day. I want to know all about it."

Joy checked her cheeks; the tears were already drying. "Okay, Mom. I'll be right there."

Chapter 25

The boys, or—more truthfully—young men, swarmed the kitchen like a locust invasion. "T-man, this place is stocked! My mom never has jack to eat," Fred announced. "Check it, is this roast beef?"

"Take it out of the fridge, dummy," Larry replied, "along with anything else in Tupperware."

"Brah," Fred said as he knelt down to pray in front of the refrigerator, "you've got to come home more often. *Oh my God*, it's pie! What kind of pie is it?"

"I don't know, open the container," Larry replied. "I just got here, too."

Fred popped the lid off and smelled, "It's, it's…purple pie! My favorite!"

Larry went to get the rest of his laundry from the garage, glad his buddies had arrived—he missed them. He missed being T-Man and living for the next set of waves. He found his mother in the laundry room behind the kitchen already starting his first load of clothes. "Here, Mom, I'll do it."

"Dump it out. You'll throw it all together and it needs to be separated," she instructed. "Have you done any laundry at all since last month?"

"Oh, absolutely," Larry lied, "but you know. I go through a lot of clothes."

"Uh huh, go see if your brother has any more to add since I'm doing this anyway."

Larry walked around the growing pile of leftovers Fred was stacking on the kitchen floor and went to find his little brother. He knocked on the closed door, careful not to invade his brother's sacred space without permission. He heard a bang instead of a reply, so he poked his head in. His other friend Ramone was sitting on Justin's chest and poking him in the ribs. "Oh, hey brah. I haven't seen your little sis here in months."

Justin tried to buck him off, "I'm not a girl, you vacuum-brained, moron. Get off me!"

"Not until you say 'sorry'."

"For what? You're crushing me."

Ramone poked him in his ribs again, "For not sharing the love, little brah. And for generally being a twerp. Oh, and for insulting my awesomeness!"

"Mom—"

Ramone clamped his hand over Justin's mouth, "Shh, you tell, and I'll have to move your stuff around like this." He reached over and pushed Justin's laptop. "And I know you don't like your things moved."

"Off Ramone," Larry said. "You'll get him all freaked out. Mom wants to know if you have any clothes for the wash, Justin."

Justin angrily shook his head no and pushed his way past the laughing Ramone. "Dude, I was only playing. Don't be so bleak."

Justin stormed out of the room, past his dad in the family room, and into the garage. Ramone shrugged, "Whoa, what's up? I always mess with him."

"Ah, don't sweat it, brah," Larry replied. "He's, like, maybe getting too old to tease like that."

"Oh, dude, you mean like the big P, like puberty?"

"Huh? No, I don't know, maybe. He's, getting a little more sensitive about being messed with. And you know how he doesn't like his stuff touched."

Ramone nodded, "I got it, brah. You're right, I mean, like this room hasn't changed at all. He's still baggin' bugs."

Ramone had moved over to Justin's computer, drawn by the pretty bouncing lights on the screensaver. "What's SETI?" he asked as he hit the space bar.

"Brah! What are you doing? That's private," Larry said.

"Huh, oh sorry, man. You're right, I was being nosey. Ew, hey, check it, brah, look at this."

Larry moved to look over Ramone's shoulders. "Yeah, so? He's chatting with someone named, Dragongirl. Well, that kind of figures."

"No, dude, it's like you said—puberty. Maybe she's his v-i-r-t-u-a-l girlfriend."

"Maybe you're a d-o-r-k. Even if she is, it's none of our business. Come on. If he comes back and finds you snooping in his computer, he'll explode. Besides, Fred's gonna eat all the food."

"Yeah, yeah, I know, Fred's a pig. Hey, check it, this doesn't sound like puppy love chat," Ramone said pointing to the screen.

Larry stopped and read the page more carefully. Then he reached around and scrolled up. It looked like his brother had kept all their conversations. He moved Ramone over some more and reread the conversations. "This is weird stuff. It's like this girl is pumping him for info."

Ramone reached into his pocket and produced a hair tie. As he started to pull his long, brown hair back into a ponytail, he added, "If it's a Barbie."

"What do you mean?" Larry asked.

"I mean, like, what if Dragongirl1 isn't really a girl at all. It could be some old, fat perv. You know, like some creepy old guy eating a chicken leg and watching—"

"Brah," interrupted Larry, "you are foul, yuck, okay, quit."

"Oh, wait, foul, like fowl...I get it. You going all college-like, making puns?"

"Huh? Oh, no, brah, total accident," Larry looked over the emails again. Larry's first guess seemed to be correct, though; the whole exchange looked as if someone was trying to get info from Justin. He had to talk to his brother. "Hey brah, go graze in the kitchen with Fred while I find Justin."

"Yeah, brah." Ramone agreed, "This could be bad news. You don't know what kinds of sickos are out there."

"Okay, go. I'll see you in a few."

Larry found his brother in the back yard kicking the side of the house. "Brah, I mean Justin. Hey, don't let Ramone get you down. He didn't mean anything. That was his way of saying he misses you." Justin ignored Larry and continued punishing the house. From years of experience, Larry knew it was almost impossible to talk to Justin when he was like this, but he had to try. "Listen, this is important. Can you stop kicking the house?"

Justin didn't, so Larry continued anyway. "Okay, fine. Now, don't get upset. Oh, never mind...anyway, Ramone, I mean Ramone and I accidently saw what was on your computer."

Justin stopped kicking the house. He turned and looked at his brother. He had turned so red that Larry thought he was going to pop. Through gritted teeth, Justin said, "You stay away from my room and my things. You keep your homeless, trashy friends away from my room. And I'm telling Mom and Dad!"

Larry held up his hands in surrender. "I know you're angry right now. It really was an accident. And I think it's a good idea to tell Mom and Dad. Listen, there's something about who you're talking to. This Dragongirl—"

"It's none of your business. She's my friend, not yours. You shouldn't even be here; you're supposed to be at college, not sneaking around in my room."

Larry continued, "Whoever that is, it's like they are trying to get information, stuff about the dragon maybe. Do you have any idea who this person is?"

Justin hissed back, "She's my friend. You don't know anything about her so get out of my business."

Larry knew enough about his brother to realize that this exchange wasn't going to solve anything. He'd have to tell his mother and let her handle it. He didn't care if she yelled at him about snooping. It was more important to protect Justin. "All right, sorry. I'll, make sure to stay out of your room, okay?"

Justin went back to kicking the house and Larry retreated to the front yard.

From across the street, Shou sighed. She'd listened to the entire exchange, one of the benefits of dragon senses. Ah, what to do, what to do? She contemplated going on over and trying to straighten Justin out about Berit's deception, but after what she had overheard, it might be too much for the poor boy right now. Maybe she could figure out some other way to deal with Dragongirl 1. She had other problems as well: the dragon's time was getting close, Steve could be in danger, and Berit was obviously growing bolder.

She needed to be in several places at the same time. Unfortunately, splitting herself in halves or thirds wasn't a power she possessed. She could form a little link between the mortals, however. Not Steve, no—with his new talent that could backfire. These older boys, Justin's brother and his friends, they were special. They were surfers and that meant that the only thing on their minds was catching the next wave, and girls, and food, and bad music...Okay, they had a lot on their minds, but the wave thing, the call of the ocean, that was what had made them immune to the demon Mammon's influence. That might be enough to keep them safe from Berit and her friends. With scarcely a touch of her magic, maybe they'd be able to see through Berit's deceptions and act as her eyes and ears while she returned to the dragon. It was worth a try. As for Steve and his friends, she'd have to trust that Roger could keep them safe, at least for a little while. Plus, she might be able to provide a few more allies of her own. With her mind made up, she crossed the street to have a quick chat with Larry.

Chapter 26

"That's it!" Berit fumed. "No more subtleties, no more light fingers. Shou had her chance, and she spurned our efforts. You are completely free to wreck this town if it will bring its dragon down."

Halldor squirmed as Berit glared at him and Brita, but didn't say anything. He rarely did, especially when Berit was exploding, which was happening more and more. He glanced sideways at his partner, who had nothing to say for a change. "First, stay away from that boy—"

"You mean Steve?" Brita suggested.

"What? Of course, I mean Steve, you buffoon. By the Great Dragons, were you hatched yesterday?"

Brita smirked, "I wasn't hatched at all. If I had been, I'd be sleeping now and letting all you underlings go about changing the world."

Berit clenched her fists and the fireplace burst into a roaring flame. But she stopped. Brita was doing it again, intentionally goading her, trying to get under her skin. "Well, I suppose you are correct, technically. Anyway, stay away from Steve. We'll have to deal with him in another way. But his friends, his family, this whole town, it's all fair game. Stir things up, wreck a few houses, sink a few boats."

Brita stood and approached the fireplace. She knelt and ran her hands through the large flames. "Berit," she said in a smooth voice, "do you have authorization for this? Do we risk exposing ourselves?"

Once again, Berit thought, *Brita felt the need to question her.* This time, however, she was right to do so. The humans had grown strong with their little technological toys. If it became common knowledge that dragons truly existed, that they had an agenda, and that agenda included suppressing the human race, would they now be powerful enough to fight back? It was worth considering.

Berit took her time answering, "Yes, I am not acting without guidance. If, no matter how unlikely, Shou's dragon were to prevail, it would give her and her friends an enormous advantage in this part of the world. Right now, she and hers are barely an annoyance to us. She must not be allowed to cultivate another great dragon partial to the human race."

Brita stood, her tall elegant human form towering over Berit's human disguise. She pulled a bit of the flame from the fireplace and flipped it between her knuckles like a magician's coin. "No, it would be a colossal failure on your part if that were to happen."

Berit didn't react to the dig. Instead, she smiled and the tiny flame darted from Brita to land on her open hand. Gesturing with the other, Berit grew the flame, molding and shaping it. First, it was a boat, then a building, then a group of children, then a highway; the fire shifted from one scene to another. When she was finished, she looked to her assistants, "Understand?" Words were not necessary.

Brita nodded and Halldor started for the back door. "Where are you going?" Brita asked.

"Thought I'd grab a smoke. All the flames kind of made me hungry."

Chapter 27

"Does he have to keep winking at us?" Steve asked.

"Huh, what?" Justin asked. "Who?"

Steve inclined his head toward the tall man restocking books in the non-fiction section. "Anthony, you know, my dad's best friend, over there. No, don't look…"

Both Justin and Joy turned to see Anthony pushing a rolling cart full of books. As soon as they turned his way, he looked left and right and then gave them two thumbs up.

"This is my dad's great idea to keep an eye on us?" Steve asked, cheeks red. "I can't believe they cleared him to volunteer here." Neither of his friends responded; both seemed lost in their own thoughts. "What's wrong with you two? You guys haven't said anything all morning."

Before either could answer, a squeal echoed across the room from a table of girls seated next to where Anthony was working. Mrs. White rushed over to shush them—their teacher was busy scolding a group of boys who had managed to turn a stack of printer paper into four sets of paper claws. One of them was holding a pair above his heads like a pair of horns, and another was pretending to have spider pincers. The teacher demanded they turn over the entire lot and the boys reluctantly complied.

For a moment, the claws made Steve think of his dragon, but this thought was quickly interrupted by another peal of laughter. Some girls had stopped Anthony to ask about one of the tattoos that ran across his forearm. Steve knew that each one had a story—often more than one. Anthony had hundreds of stories and used the tattoos as props for most of them. Of course, Anthony would have stood out anywhere with his nearly albino coloring and tall height, but to a bunch of middle-school girls, his tattoos were like bubblegum to ball players.

Steve watched Mrs. White approach the crab fisherman and say something to him. He nodded enthusiastically and rolled down his sleeves. He also gave Steve and his friends a big wink before rolling on to the fiction section. "I'm doomed," Steve lamented.

"It's not a big deal, Steve," Joy replied. "Everyone is trying to keep you safe."

"Yeah, but—"

"No buts. It's wonderful that you have people who care that much, and Anthony would probably rather be somewhere else," Joy retorted.

Steve looked at her, "What's your deal? I just don't like having people baby-sitting me."

"You need to be appreciative, that's all," Joy responded.

"Yeah, at least you don't have your brother's friends digging into your stuff and physically assaulting you," Justin blurted out.

"What are you talking about?" Steve asked.

"Nothing!"

"You brought it up," Steve said, "so, obviously it's something."

"Fine," Justin boomed. "Larry came home last night and brought Fred and Ramone. Besides eating all our food, they always eat all our food, Larry and Ramone were snooping on my computer and looking around my room. It's my room! They have no respect for my personal property…or for my personal space either."

"Did you tell your mom and dad?" Joy asked.

"I didn't have to," Justin replied. "Larry told them what was on my computer, and then everyone came and read through all my emails, all my personal stuff." Justin's leg was bouncing like a jack hammer.

Joy and Steve looked at each other, "Justin," Joy asked calmly, "what stuff? Who were you talking to?"

Justin's face suddenly got very red, but his leg stopped moving. "No one, a friend on a website. It's nothing."

Before Joy could ask any more questions, the assistant principal, Mr. Johnson, entered the library and approached their table. Johnson was his name, but that's not what kids called him. To a generation of kids, he was Mr. Baldhead, or Mr. Potato Head, or Mr. Clean, or Mr. Skydome, or Humpty Dumpty. Because he was bald, and because it was middle school, and because he wasn't one of those nice bald guys, kids always called him creative things behind his back. "Good," he said, "you're together. Grab your things, all of you. You're coming to my office." Then he yelled across the library, totally violating the quiet rule, "Mrs. Righter, I'm taking these three to my office."

As the whole room made the obligatory "Ooh" noise, Mr. Potato Head pointed to the library sign next to the exit and yelled that it was a library and they should be quiet, without a hint of irony. Steve almost got up and started walking and then remembered he was supposed to be on crutches. He reached back to grab them, pretending to hobble on one leg. As he did, Justin turned and asked, "What do you think he wants us for?"

"Shh," Mr. Johnson scolded, "you're in trouble. No talking." He led them down the hall to his office and opened his door, which was located right across from the head principal's. He told them to sit, but there were only two chairs, so they waited for him to huff past them and grab one from the office lobby. "There, now sit down. Now, why don't you tell me why you three have been bullying the new girl, that one from Sweden."

"Iceland," Justin corrected.

"Yeah, Iceland, whatever. You know who I'm talking about, Barry—"

"Berit," Justin corrected.

"Quit being a smart-aleck, young man," Mr. Johnson scolded. "You know the school's policy against bullying; it will not be tolerated. Because of your actions, her parents have taken her out of school."

"Mr. Johnson, what are you talking about?" Joy asked.

"Bullying, bullying, you know, picking on someone, repeated abuse!" Johnson pointed at each of them. "You, you, and you were identified by name by Mary's parents!"

"Berit," Justin corrected again.

Mr. Baldhead slapped the desk, "That's enough! This is serious! We take this very seriously; you three could be looking at a suspension!"

Thankfully, Mrs. Wren was walking into her office and heard Mr. Johnson's outburst. She leaned into the room. "Mr. Johnson, what's the trouble?"

"Huh, oh, when you were over at the district office that new girl's, the one from—"

"Iceland," Justin suggested without expression.

"Yeah, the new girl from Iceland," Mr. Johnson continued, "her parents came in complaining about these children bullying their daughter."

Mrs. Wren walked in and looked at the three kids. "That seems a little out of character for this group. Mr. Johnson, how were these students bullying her?"

Mr. Johnson turned around his yellow tablet of paper and pointed, "Her mother said that they were saying things behind her back, you know, the usual bullying stuff, teasing. She said they'd called her and were nasty on the phone. Oh, and she brought in this."

Mrs. Wren took the page. It was copy of a Facebook post started by Joy and joined by both Steve and Justin. In it they were saying some terrible things about Berit. Mrs. Wren showed it to the children, "Look familiar?"

"That's not mine!" Joy exclaimed. "I never wrote that. I've never bullied anybody!"

"M-m-me either," Steve agreed. "Mrs. Wren, I'm n-n-not even on Facebook!"

"No one is," Joy added.

"What was that?" Mr. Johnson asked.

"No one our age uses it," Joy explained. "It's for our parents."

"This is obviously a setup!" Justin announced. "Definitely, someone wants it to look like we were bullying Berit. I wouldn't bully Berit, she's…" Justin stopped himself, suddenly embarrassed.

Mrs. Wren looked again at the paper and then at each of them. "Well, this is pretty strong evidence, and we can't ignore the accusation. I'll need to call your parents and tell them what is going on. Are you sure you had nothing to do with this?"

"This is stupid. Just because someone says we did something, and because that someone is an adult, then it's automatically true? My parents don't need to be bothered by this right now. You suspend me, or whatever; that's fine," Joy answered, "but you need to leave my parents out of it."

Joy's response caused Steve to look sideways at her. Joy was the calm one, the level-headed one; she didn't normally react like this. "Yeah," Steve added, "why are we automatically guilty?"

"You can call my mom, or dad," Justin added. "They've been all through my computer, looked at my bookmarked sites, read my favorite blogs. They probably—"

"Justin…" Steve prompted.

"Yeah well, point is you can call my mom and she'll tell you if I was bullying Berit. Go ahead, she won't lie to you."

Mrs. Wren frowned, "Okay, children. Mr. Johnson, can you write them a pass back to class?"

"But—"

"I'll follow up with this one, Mr. Johnson. Since Berit's parents removed her from school, I need to speak with them anyway. Okay children, you can go back to class as soon as you get your pass. But I am going to research this, and if I find that you've been lying, there will be serious consequences."

Steve took the pass that Mr. Johnson angrily scribbled and the three left the office, each looking a little dumbfounded about what had happened.

Mrs. Wren shut the door. "Chuck," she said, "you've got the girl's file?"

He handed it over. Mrs. Wren pointed to the phone on the desk, "May I?"

"Sure. But I wrote everything down already," Mr. Johnson complained.

"Oh, I know you did, Chuck," she replied as she dialed the number in the file. "But I can't have a student removed from school because they were bullied without speaking to the parents. Hmm, no one's answering and no voicemail is set up. That's strange. Any other numbers? No? Okay, I'll wait to call these other's parents—"

"I can call them," Chuck replied.

Mrs. Wren hesitated and then seemed to come to a conclusion. "No, Chuck, let's do a little background checking first. I know Joy's father, and I've known Joy since she was a baby. For her to react like that is not normal. I have some serious doubts about this whole scenario. Can you see what classes Berit had and talk to her teachers, see if they heard anything? We might have to call in some of the students as well, but maybe the teachers can help identify which ones."

Mr Johnson reached into his file cabinet and pulled out a brand new yellow tablet. "Got it!"

The three friends slowly made their way back to the library. Fortunately, the crutches provided a convenient excuse to creep back to class. The trio crawled along, eyes open for the attentive adult or habitual hallway malingerer.

"What the hell?" Justin voiced for them all.

Joy shook her head in confusion, "Why? Why would they bother doing this? It's stupid."

"Yeah, why would Berit do that? She's—"

"Hey, you're walking normal. When did that happen?" Justin asked.

Steve suddenly remembered that Justin hadn't been there when Shou cured him. He didn't know who Berit actually was or how his leg had healed. And worse yet, Justin kind of had a crush on Berit. He thought Shou was going to go to Justin's house, so he assumed that Justin knew everything. "Shou did it after you left. I guess I had siphoned all this dragon magic from, um…" Steve hesitated. He had to tell him the rest, but not here, not at school. "Anyway," he continued, "she helped me focus all that magic on my knee and I was healed."

Steve could see the wheels turning in his friend's head, so to head him off from asking more questions he put his uninjured leg back on the ground and held out the crutches. "I hate these things; can't wait to get rid of them."

Joy seemed to be lost. "Huh, oh, yeah, sorry, guys. We didn't do anything. It's all a bunch of crap."

"But why would Berit leave?" Justin asked. "It doesn't make any sense."

"Justin, didn't Shou go over to your house like she said she would?" Joy asked.

"No, huh, you know I completely forgot. Oh, my God, I mean when Ramone and Larry got into my computer, I was so mad…"

"Justin, look," Steve started, sighed, then continued, "there's a bunch of stuff Shou told us last night. About, about why I'm blowing stuff up, and maybe why Berit left too."

Suddenly, Joy spoke up, "I've heard enough about Berit. I don't need this right now!" She started to walk off, but Steve touched her arm, "Joy, what is it? What's going on?"

Joy didn't respond.

"It's your mom, huh?" Steve asked, after searching her face for a moment.

Joy nodded once, but wouldn't meet their eyes.

By now even Justin had noticed what was up. "What, what happened to your mom? She stop taking her medication?"

"Will you shut it?" Joy hissed. "God, don't you know how to whisper. I don't want people to know my family's business."

"It's nothing to be ashamed of. Mental illness is very common and lots of people go off their medication."

Joy slugged him in the arm.

"Ouch! Hey, what did you do that for?" Justin yelled.

"Why do you think, you moron? Can you shut up about it?" Joy insisted.

"Fine," Justin announced, "but you didn't have to slug me…again. You ever heard the phrase, 'use your words?'"

Joy looked to the ceiling for patience, "Sorry. It's, it's not, I'm not mad at you. You're so darned loud sometimes."

"So, what's your dad doing?" Steve asked.

"He's been staying at home, dealing with it, but he has basketball practice to run, so he has to go to Eureka. Maybe he can talk Mom into going back to her doctor. I don't know…"

"But you don't need to be worrying about this too," Steve finished her thought. "Joy, I'm sorry. This all has to do with me and my family." He looked around before whispering, "And with the stupid dragons."

"That's what I've been saying! There have to be dragons involved in this whole thing," Justin exclaimed.

"Look, weirdo, my mother refusing to take her meds has nothing to do with dragons."

Justin bit his lip in thought, "Are you sure? I mean, she's fine for two years and suddenly, when this stuff starts happening to Steve, your mom stops taking her—"

"Stop it, Justin," Joy almost shouted. "My mom is sick. Dragons didn't make that happen."

"All I'm saying is, why now?"

Even at a glacial pace, they had arrived back at the library. Steve stopped walking normally and slipped the unnecessary crutches under his arms. Heading back to their table, they got several quizzical glances. An undertone of curiosity zipped through the room. "What'd he want?" one of Joy's friends whispered once they sat down. Joy shook her head and mouthed, "Nothing. Tell you later."

Chapter 28

Halldor boldly walked up to the front door and knocked. Berit said it was time to shake up this sleepy little town and see if they could interrupt that great dragon's rest. When no one answered, he twitched two fingers and stepped into the unoccupied home. All the furniture was covered, waiting for summer. From the kitchen, he retrieved a roll of paper towels and wadded them up in his hand. He started to say a few words and then stopped himself. He smiled and pulled out his lighter, "No use in wasting magic when you've got one of these." He flicked his Bic and started a neat little flame. When it nearly consumed all the towels, he dropped the flaming bundle onto one of the tarp-covered couches. He took a final look around to appreciate the cute house. What a shame. And then he left.

After Brita had unenrolled Berit and filed the bogus complaint, she headed for the iconic lighthouse on "A" Street. A relic of older times, Battery Point Lighthouse still operated and helped the local fishermen navigate the perpetual fog in the area. Off-season meant there were no tours, so there was no one about and, because it was low tide, the skinny concrete walkway was accessible, though this was unnecessary for Brita. Her eyes followed the pathway up the hill to the house. She stared at the trees, whose branches hung along the edges of the building and hesitated—these trees were real, not manmade abominations; Brita liked trees. But, for the greater good, some sacrifices had to be made.

She took a quick look around to ensure that there were no witnesses and then began a deep garbling noise in her throat followed by a trance-like swaying. The cloudy, grey haze in the air started to coalesce. A wind picked up and spun the clouds in a circle. A black, swirling cloud began to form above the lighthouse. It grew to cover the entire islet before there was a loud crack of lightning. The bolt split the nearest tree and sent it tumbling onto the roof of one of the smaller buildings on the point, far short of her intended target. Brita stomped her foot in anger for missing so badly. Oh well, she resolved, it seemed more sacrifices would have to be made.

Berit wasn't Berit any longer; or rather, Berit no longer looked like an Icelandic princess. Right now, she resembled a grizzled, old sailor, or perhaps a retired logger. She wore a pair of heavy rubber boots, a red and black flannel shirt, and a ball cap with the bill bent so tight it almost looked like a tube. She squinted out to sea and, occasionally, spat a long brown stream of chewing tobacco. Some of it dribbled down her chin and into her scraggly brown beard. "Huh," she mused aloud, "sometimes it can be fun to dress up!"

Berit closed her eyes and listened. The gulls were squawking and the breakers were slapping at the rocks. A pair of sea lions were courting, their guttural love language audible above the surf. That blasted foghorn sounded, then again, and again, every ten seconds. The cars and trucks rumbled back along the road, as ever-present as the irritating horn. Humans, polluting everything, even sound.

She opened her eyes and there it was, a dot way off in the distance. Berit knew what it really was, though: a massive pile of floating junk. Thanks to a powerful tsunami in Japan a few years ago, bits and pieces of trash had been hitting the West Coast, from California to Washington, for months. But this was special, a flotilla of debris, a small island of garbage, and it did not take a great dragon's magic to coax it here.

Berit almost clapped when she saw a rusted refrigerator bob into the marina and smack a crab boat. More junk followed: shampoo bottles, tires, soccer balls, shaving cream cans, a whole trawler section. She smiled, feeling quite smug: a floating dump, a little natural ocean current, a dab of dragon magic, and voila, a homemade disaster! She giggled in a little girl's voice, which made people turn and stare. A crowd started to form around her, "You see that? What in the world? Where's it all coming from?" No one paid attention as the grizzled old man turned and walked away, laughing to himself, "Idiots, they don't even watch their own news."

Chapter 29

Shou sat in the entrance of Dragau's cave watching the cold rain pour down the hill in dozens of tiny rivers. She thought it ironic that the children had started calling this dragon by that name. It was, in fact, the name of the dragon who gave it life. When she looked up, everything seemed washed out, like a grey and white watercolor painting. It was not sight, however, that she depended upon most. She closed her eyes and sniffed. Then again, and again. *Damn, damn rain,* she thought. It was so heavy that it doused her strongest sense. She could still smell the pine trees, and some of the oil on the highway, and some bear scat—a fancy term for poop—but she had lost completely the three young men she had tasked with keeping an eye on Berit. That was the source of her connection with them; if she could keep their scent, she could maintain a kind of telepathic link—more like snippets of thought really—but the pouring rain was blocking the signal.

Well, scat...wait a minute, she wondered. *Could it be?* She stepped out into the cold monsoon and sucked in all the air her lungs could hold. *By the Great Dragon! It is!* She started to call, but then worried that she might disturb the dragon within. Already its sleep was tumultuous; its time was fast approaching, and something was bothering its dreams.

Shou followed the scent, first of the droppings, and that, eventually, led to the black bear himself. She found him lying on his back underneath a trio of large boulders that served as the entrance to his den. As Shou got closer, the reclining bear stopped reading its magazine and looked her way. "Hey Boo, wondered when you'd show. Trees were whisperin' that you was on yo way."

"Thaddeus."

"TJ, that's my new *nom de plume*, my nickname, if you will. What's up, my sista. Welcome to my crib!"

Shou approached and the bear rocked a couple of times to its side before sitting up on its butt. "You look like you're about to burst," Shou observed, "close to hibernating?"

TJ rubbed his belly, "Still room for a few more nuts and berries, but yeah, it's almost that time. Come on in out of that rain, dawg."

Shou bent down and entered under the large slabs of rock. She shook her hat and placed it by her side, then picked up the magazine the bear was reading. It had a beautiful African-American woman on the cover. She noticed a small pile of magazines, *Essence, Black Men, XXL Magazine.* "Thaddeus," Shou began, "why the sudden interest in…?"

"Hip-Hop culture?"

"Sure."

"They my dawgs, Boo, my people!" the bear replied.

"Thaddeus, you're a dragon."

"Who chooses to be a bear," TJ corrected. "A B-L-A-C-K bear, Boo, you smell me?"

"Of course I smell you. I smelled you from the road!"

TJ laughed, "No, no, I mean you get me? You understand? Shou, you need to get out. You be needin' some culture."

"Where in the world did you get all these magazines?" Shou asked.

TJ rolled back over on his back and shimmied back and forth to scratch himself, "So I was kickin' it at one of those RV parks with some of my dawgs, waiting for some choice scraps, when I found this really nice RV unoccupied and unlocked. So I went shoppin'. Had me some pork chops, and Funyuns, and…never mind, anyway, some magazines caught my eye, so I took a couple to the bed in the back and got comfy."

"You got them from the RV?"

"These? Naw, not these. When them folks came back, they got all freaked out and started screaming, so I had to roll on outa der without my mags. I got these down in Oakland from a 7-11."

Shou raised an eyebrow, "You went all the way to Oakland to fetch a couple of magazines?"

"Let me break it down for you, Boo." TJ replied. "I heard of this phat krunk club on the East side and had to check it out—"

"Thaddeus—"

"TJ" he corrected.

"You went clubbing? Thad...TJ, how'd that go?"

The bear sat up with its hind legs poking out in the rain. He sighed and his large head kind of sank down into his shoulders, "It was whacked! Dawgs jus ain't ready for true interspecies relationships; had to roll on outta there in a hurry. Okay, enough 'bout my trials and tribulations. Why is you here?"

"Haven't you sensed the great dragon nearby?" Shou asked.

TJ nodded. "Then," Shou continued, "you should know that its time is almost near."

"Yeah, so? What's that got to do with me? You be fightin' the good fight, moving with the shakers and movers of the dragon and human world. I chose this elegant and sexy form. Keeps me outta trouble, ya dig?"

"A choice that you are completely satisfied with?" Shou asked.

"Wuz, I wuz for a long time. I guess things be changing and it's hard to block the human world out now. But it don't matter none, sleep's a callin', and I like my long naps. S'all good."

"Well, I need you to postpone your nap for a little while. The dragon's time is near and the other side is trying to sap his strength before the battle. If they succeed, they'll have another breeder and our side will be that much weaker."

"Shou, I don't pick sides, yo. It's why I'm a bear. I roll along season to season, eat my berries, catch me some salmon, got a little honey bear up near the Oregon border. You know how it is. Life's good."

"Which is why you're traveling all the way to Oakland for magazines, and dance clubs? TJ, I worried about this from the time you made your choice to be a bear all those years ago. You could have chosen a human form; you could have interacted in the human world."

"Yeah, but while you're always globe trottin' looking after mankind, my brothers and sisters here needed protectin'. Nothin' wrong being a bear."

"No, there's not, and you've done a wonderful job of looking after all the lesser dragon spirits in these woods. But you wouldn't be clubbing in Oakland if you didn't care about the humans," Shou insisted.

TJ considered a long time before answering, one of the advantages of operating in bear time. "What do you want me to do?"

"There's a group up north and their efforts are disturbing the dragon's rest. I have some young humans trying to help out, but they can't do it alone, and I need to be here to try and ease this dragon's sleep. I need you to help them stop, or at least slow down the mischief the trio of dragonettes is causing. And I need a couple of special human children looked after."

TJ looked longingly at his cave. "All right, but can you get me a subscription to *Vibe Magazine* when I get back? It's hard out here for a bear," TJ admitted, looking down at his claws and wiggling them, as if hoping thumbs might sprout.

Chapter 30

"Come on, man. Let me look," Ramone begged.

Larry handed the binoculars over, but pulled his friend down when he stood up to use them. "Dang dude, will you get down? We don't want her to see us. What's she doing now?"

"Brah, she is bangin'. Think I should ask her out?"

Larry grabbed the binoculars back, "Give me those, you freak. She's a dragon thingy. That's not what she actually looks like."

Ramone sighed, and then brightened, "No, no, brah, it's like make-up! You know how Betties look when they're surfing, no make-up, I mean they look nice in their bikinis, but, you know when it's time for prom, bonus, they get all made up. It's like that."

Larry stared at his friend. "No, brah, it's nothing like that."

Suddenly, the sky got very dark and a lightning bolt split the air. "Dude, check it, she knocked down that tree! How can she knock down trees?" Ramone shouted.

"Keep your head down!" Larry shouted back. "She's a freakin' dragon, dude, no matter what she looks like. Wait, she's leaving. Go, no, wait a sec. Okay, go check out the lighthouse and make sure everyone is all right. I'm going to see where she's goes next."

"Okay, naw brah, how come you get to follow the Bettie?"

"Because it's my van! And she's a dragon, not a female."

"Brah, she could still be female."

Larry started the van. "Call 9-1-1 if anyone's hurt in the lighthouse. I'll follow her and check on Fred."

Ramone raced across the beach and up the path, and Larry crept the van as stealthily as a GMC Safari could creep until the woman got into her black rental car. Larry hit Fred's number as he followed.

"What?"

"Brah, it's me. What's going on?" Larry asked.

"Call ya right back," Fred replied.

Larry put the phone in his lap and continued to shadow the car, lingering a half block behind. It had turned on Front Street and looked like it was continuing around the marina. From out of nowhere, a police car zipped by, running lights and siren. Another followed. Larry thought he heard other sirens, but the woman ahead was undeterred. She turned onto the Redwood Highway heading south. Larry hoped she wasn't heading out of town; he wouldn't be able to follow her if she got too far out. Fortunately, she only went as far as Citizens Dock Road and pulled into a parking lot. Deciding to risk it, he pulled around the car as it parked and watched as a scraggly looking dude climbed in. Then, it took off again. Larry started to follow when his phone beeped at him.

"Sorry, brah, I was busy putting out a house fire," Fred announced.

"What, where?"

"It's cool, chill. Check it, one of those dragon goons walked right into this house and lit it up," Fred explained. "But the donk didn't wait around so as soon as he left, I went in and got it under control. Found a fire extinguisher under the kitchen sink and no problemo. I am so grand. All bow to me."

"Uh-oh."

"What's wrong, brah? I do something wrong?" Fred asked

"Huh, no, no brah. Hang on a sec!" Larry had gotten too close to the car ahead which had stopped at an intersection. Suddenly, the passenger was no longer an old, straggly-looking guy, but a pretty blond girl, and she was looking right at him. Larry watched as the older woman tilted down her mirror and smiled.

"Brah, what's going on?" Fred called.

At that moment, a fire truck came screaming down "I" Street. The car ahead waited until the truck was almost upon them and then cut in front of the speeding vehicle. It locked up its brakes and started to slide. Larry watched in horror as it came his way. He jammed his shifter into reverse and hit the gas right as the tail end of the fire truck swung in front of him. It narrowly missed swatting him like a bug, but it continued to slide, jumped the curb, and then slammed right into the side of the nearest building.

"Brah, T-Man, Larry, what's going on?" Fred called from the phone.

"Holy…dude, I almost got blasted by a fire engine. It smashed into a building."

"What?"

"Chill, brah, I want to see if everyone's okay." Larry got out of the van and ran over to the fire truck. The firemen were already out, checking for injuries. Fortunately, it looked like their vehicle had only scraped the side of the building. The firemen did a quick assessment of their truck and jumped back in. "Back up, son," one of them yelled at Larry as he climbed onto the rear of the fire engine. With a thud, the large truck plopped back down on the street and hit its lights and siren.

"Brah…You okay?" Fred asked.

"Yeah, yeah, I'm cool. Ah, man!"

"What's up?"

"All my tires! The dragons popped all my tires!" Larry stepped out into the street, but the car he'd been following had vanished.

Chapter 31

About the only advantage Steve could see having Anthony babysit him and his friends at school was that they got to ride home in Moby Dick. That was Anthony's name for his monstrous Ford F-250. The four-wheel-drive truck sat perched way up on three-foot-tall tires that made almost as much noise pounding the road as the massive motor did. The massive truck couldn't fit in Joy's driveway, so Anthony idled it in the street next to her house.

"I'll wait, Joy, while you see if anyone's home," Anthony yelled as she opened the door and climbed down to a safe jumping distance.

Steve watched her go to the door and use her key. A minute later she returned, "Mom's not home, but she left a note saying she'd be back soon. Dad's running practice in Eureka. He'll be home around seven."

"You want to stay at my house?" Steve asked.

"Naw, it's fine. Go ahead."

Anthony leaned across the seats, "Listen, why don't you go on over to Steve's?"

Joy stepped up on the runner and poked her head into the cab, "No, you guys go on. Mom's note said she'd be back soon. I'll lock the door, and I have my phone."

Steve wanted to argue, but he knew Joy was upset about her mother and being accused of bullying. "Okay, but call me after a while, okay?" he asked.

Joy nodded, dropped back down and went into the house. Anthony looked at Steve, "We couldn't change her mind, could we?"

Steve shut the door, drowning out a little of Moby Dick's metallic breathing. "Not really. Joy's not a change-her-mind kind of girl."

Anthony roared, "Ha, you're smarter than half the male population if you can already figure that out about women." He sobered almost instantly, "But you're worried, aren't you?"

"Yeah, a little. Her mom said she'd be back, but..." Steve hesitated.

"But you're worried she's off being all manic and everything," Anthony continued.

"Yeah, how'd you know about that?"

Anthony put Moby Dick in drive and the truck lurched forward. "It's a little town, Steve, and Joy's mom's been pinging all over it for a couple of days now. But not to worry, after we get Dani and I drop you all off, I'll come back here and keep an eye on Joy's house until her dad gets home."

Steve perked up, "That would be great."

Anthony looked into his mirror, "What about you, Justin? Am I taking you to Steve's or your house?"

Justin didn't immediately answer, "Did you know that Edgar Allen Poe, Florence Nightingale, Ludwig Van Beethoven, Vincent van Gogh, and Russell Brand all have bipolar disorder?"

"Even Russell Brand?" Anthony asked a little amused.

"Uh huh."

Anthony chuckled to himself, "Russell Brand and Beethoven."

"What?" Steve asked.

Justin passed over his phone from the back seat, "Look, see, a bunch of people have mood swings. Maybe Joy's mom will do something to make herself famous."

"Like Russell Brand?"

"Or Beethoven," Justin replied. "I got a book from the library too, but our books are stupid. This one was written in the 90s, totally out of date. But it's got some excellent pictures."

"Justin," Anthony interrupted, "what about dropping you off? Your house or Steve's?"

"Oh, mine is fine. Mom and Dad are working from home today and Larry hasn't gone back to college yet, so someone'll be home."

Justin was Googling more information about manic depression and bipolar disorder when Anthony pulled up next to his house, and Steve almost had to take his phone to get his attention. "Hey, dummy, you're home," Steve announced.

"Hmm, what? Oh, yeah, okay," Justin absently replied as he climbed down from the truck. Without even waving goodbye, he disappeared into his house, still thumbing along on his cellphone.

"Kind of focused, huh?" Anthony asked.

"Yeah, when it's something new or something important, he gets like that," Steve replied. This time Steve was grateful for his friend's obsessive behavior. He wouldn't have to explain everything to him right now. He hadn't even had to explain why they were catching a ride with Anthony. Most importantly, he hadn't had to break his best friend's heart.

Anthony turned around, went up and over the curb, and bounced the truck back down again. "Next stop, Dani."

Chapter 32

Joy reread the note her mother had written. It was a grocery list which had turned into a "to do" list followed by a note that she was going to run some errands. Joy sighed and checked the house to make sure nothing was left on that shouldn't be. She was satisfied that this time, at least, her mom had managed to turn off most of the house's electronic and heating devices.

Joy forgot that she had her book bag slung over her shoulder, so she dropped it on the kitchen table alongside the past week's mail, some of her dad's manuals, some extra glasses, keys, you name it. The table always became the dumping ground until someone found time to put everything where it belonged. Joy started to pull some books out, but then shoved them back in. She went into the entryway closet and grabbed a basketball; it wasn't her sport of choice, but slapping a volleyball against the garage wouldn't work, and she needed to let off some steam.

One advantage of being the only child of a basketball coach was having excellent fundamentals. Joy dribbled, left-handed and right-handed, through her legs, and through her imaginary opponents. She drove in hard, stopped, pivoted, and shot—swish! She dribbled back out and shot a dozen close in. Then she backed out all the way to the street and made about half of her three-pointers. She moved and moved and moved because, if she stopped, she had to think, and she didn't want to think.

Eventually, she slowed down. She dribbled slower, her shots started missing, her mind drifted back to her mother. Everything always came back to her mother. Maybe it was because of her that Joy was so good at sports. Her mom's illness had pushed her toward her father, and since he hadn't had any boys, Joy had become the next best thing—better, in fact, considering she'd taken to competition like a duck to water. But Joy was still a girl, and remembered her mother dressing her up when she asked, combing her hair and braiding it in the mornings, even showing her how to put on just a touch of makeup so the other girls—the ones who thought being pretty meant being grown-up—would stop teasing her.

Feeling tired, Joy dropped down and sat with her back to the garage door, rolling the ball underneath her legs, wondering what craziness her mother would come up with tonight. She also thought about the bogus bullying accusation. Fortunately, her folks knew about Dragau, so all she had to do was explain how three evil dragons were harassing her and her friends. That worried her far less than her mom's latest episode.

Now that she had stopped moving, Joy started to cool down, even to get a little chilled, but she didn't want to go inside; it was too easy for thoughts to crowd in once she went inside. Besides, it was early and wouldn't get dark for a while. Joy decided she would sit and watch the clouds, the neighborhood, the post lady...

"Huh" Joy remarked to herself, "she usually doesn't get to our house for another hour."

As Betsy approached, Joy thought about getting up and saving her the trouble of sticking the mail in the box, but Joy knew Betsy liked to talk, and Joy didn't much feel like talking right now. When the postal carrier got to Joy's house however, she didn't stop at the mailbox. Instead, she turned to walk down the driveway. For a moment, Joy remembered that she was supposed to be inside with the door locked. But she told herself that it was only Betsy. That thought should have suppressed the tiny shudder she felt, only it didn't. Joy was starting to rise when Betsy reached down to give her a hand up.

Hesitantly, Joy took the hand, but suddenly, it wasn't Betsy anymore, it was a tall Nordic-looking guy. Joy started to jerk back, but the guy held her hand firmly. "Don't be frightened. I'm not here to hurt you. I only want to have a word with you about your mother."

It was his mention of her mother that kept Joy from screaming. Joy stood, slightly trembling, but she held the man's gaze, determined not to be intimidated. His height didn't bother her; she was always the tallest kid around, and her dad was even taller than this guy. But his eyes, which were so blue they almost looked black, kind of freaked her out. Still, she got her courage up to ask, "What about my her?"

"Do you know who I am?" he asked, ignoring her question.

Joy nodded. "I know what you are, too!"

The tall man smiled, "You're smart. That's good. Listen, we can help your mother."

"Can I have my hand back?" Joy asked.

As soon as he let go, Joy started toward the door, but a long, powerful arm moved quicker and blocked her way. "Wait, just hear me out. Don't you want her to get better? No more ups and downs, no more unattended appliances, or crazy lists. No more locking herself in her bedroom for days at a time."

Joy was getting angry, "How do you know about that? Why do you care?"

Slowly, the man lowered his arm and stepped back. "We are not your enemy. We have not come here to harm any of you, not even your friend, Steve. You are all unfortunate bystanders."

"What does any of this have to do with my mother?" Joy demanded.

"You aren't listening. I told you, we can help her. We can make it so she never has to endure those awful mood swings ever again—we can make her normal."

"Why would you do that?"

"Because I, we, need your help. It's simple, really; you and your friends are caught up in a battle that has been going on since your species emerged. Your kind is fragile, and, while it's possible that what you do might influence the outcome, few leave a battle without getting hurt."

"Is that a threat? You want me to betray Steve," Joy accused. "You're afraid of what he might do, aren't you?"

He looked at her and a shadow crossed his face. He hesitated before answering. "Your friend is an unknown in all this. I don't know what he can or can't do to hurt us. But think about it—if he stays away from us, it's obviously best for us to stay away from him. I'm not threatening you, and I don't want you to betray anyone. I simply want you to stay out of it. Stay away from your friend for a while."

"How does that help you?" Joy asked.

"Me? It doesn't. But this way you won't be helping the other side, either, you see. You'd be neutral. And, in exchange, we would help your mother, and leave you be."

"What makes you think I would do that?"

"You wouldn't? Not even to help your mother? You would let her continue living like this, like she's a human roller coaster? And her dark days, you would condemn her to that emotional suffering when all you need do is stay away from a boy for a few days?" He let the question hang in the air.

"I don't believe you. How could you help her?"

A tiny hint of a smile, and the man continued, "Tonight, your mother will come home. She will be completely normal—not medicated, but truly herself. She will never need medication again, unless...unless you contact Steve before this conflict is decided. Then, she will be exactly as she was." He turned and started to walk away, again the pleasant postwoman Betsy. Joy ran after him...her...it. "Wait, how can I trust you? What happens when you get what you want? You could just change her back."

Betsy turned and looked at her with the man's dark blue eyes. "You have my oath that the magic will not go away, that your mother will not relapse."

Joy nodded, somehow knowing that he was telling her the truth, which made it that much harder.

Chapter 33

Justin's parents shared an office in the house, when they weren't swimming through forests of marine algae, or teaching post-graduates how to find shy sponges. Sometimes when Justin was younger, he went along and played in the sand, so long as one or the other of his parents could keep an eye on him. As he got older and it became clear that he had not inherited the family's passionate love for the ocean, he stopped going.

Although both his parents were attached to Humbolt State's Biology department, they were almost never on the main campus all the way down in Arcata. Justin asked them how they could be college professors and not teach and was told that they were primarily researchers and their salaries were mostly funded by grants. Justin wasn't completely sure what that meant until he looked it up. Mostly, it meant that his parents conducted research with a rotating group of students who worked on their projects and that, therefore, they did not do much classroom teaching. Additionally, it meant that they were pretty much left alone until money got tight. Then they had to hustle for funding.

In a way, Justin liked the arrangement. His mom and dad were always around if he needed them, and yet not the kind of parents to hover over him. This meant when he burst through the front door and headed right for his room, eager to find out more about Joy's mother's condition, he wasn't surprised to hear his mom yell hello from their office. He poked his head in the open door and said he was home. Neither parent looked up from the computer they were crowded around, but his mom told him he had a snack in the fridge, and his dad briefly waved. His dad never said much.

Justin skipped the snack and went directly to his own laptop. His phone was handy, but slow. If he really wanted to dig something up, he used his home computer. He hung his backpack on the hook on the door where it would remain all night. He never had homework because he always got it done in school. The only reason he bothered bringing a backpack home was because his parents kept bugging him about not having homework, so it was easier to use it as a prop and just pretend.

The computer was already on and active, running his search for extraterrestrial intelligence, the SETI program. It was a University of Berkley program that borrowed his computer when not in use to join with thousands of other computers to search through data for weak alien signals— basically, it was his screensaver. Justin watched the graphics a bit, knowing the colors were meaningless, but still mesmerizing. They were better than watching fish to put you to sleep.

After a minute, Justin tapped his mouse and the program slipped down to a tiny rectangle on the bottom of his screen. He was about to start researching bipolar disorder when his computer beeped at him. Someone had messaged him.

> ➤ Hey, I need to talk to you (Dragongirl 1)
> ➤ Are you there? It's important! (Dragongirl 1)
> ➤ Hi, what's up? (DragonKeeper)
> ➤ Justin, is that you? (Dragongirl 1)
> ➤ Huh? How do you know it's me? How do you know my name? (DragonKeeper)
> ➤ Because it's me, Berit. Please listen, I'm so sorry for deceiving you, but I had to. (Dragongirl 1)

Justin didn't reply; he didn't do anything. He couldn't believe it. How could this be Berit? Was it a coincidence? *No,* he thought, *because he had been talking to her for months. And if she knew who he was, why not say anything at school?* All of the sudden, his conversation with Steve and Joy that morning made sense. They knew something about Berit, something Shou was supposed to talk to him about. Maybe Larry was right, or maybe this was much worse. He reached for the delete button.

➢ Justin, are you there? You have to listen, you've been lied to. (Dragongirl 1)

➢ By you! (DragonKeeper)

➢ Yes, and I'm sorry. But now you know the truth. There are other dragons out there and they need your help. I need your help. (Dragongirl 1)

"Oh my God," Justin whispered to himself. "She's a dragon; she's a freaking dragon. All this time…"

➢ Why should I help you? You lied to me and you tried to get us in trouble at school. (DragonKeeper)

➢ That was a mistake. My friend thought she was doing the right thing, but it was a mistake. Listen, you only know part of the story, only what Shou has told you and your friends. It's not the whole story. Can I talk to you in person, so I can explain? (Dragongirl 1)

➢ No, you keep away from me. You're a liar. Leave me alone. (DragonKeeper)

➢ Justin, I am sorry I lied to you, but so has Shou. I am here to protect all dragons. I know they are important to you. Shou wants them all to be like her, powerless and hidden. I want dragons to be a part of the world. I want the world to believe in magic again. You want those things, Justin, I know it. Your friend, Steve, you've said he doesn't even want to talk about dragons anymore. Why does he deserve dragon magic if he doesn't even want it? Justin, you can be a guardian, like your friend, only a better one! You can use the magic to protect us. You can show the kids at school that you're special. (Dragongirl 1)

Justin read the message once, and then again. Shou was his friend and he trusted her, and Steve was his best friend. He wasn't jealous of Steve. Steve was a good soccer player and had more friends, but that didn't matter. And he had Joy; even though she liked to tease him, he knew she was his friend. But the other kids? No, other kids didn't like him; he didn't like them much either.

> Justin, Steve doesn't deserve to be a dragon's guardian. He doesn't appreciate it! All he wants to be is normal. Well, you don't! You love dragons; you would protect dragons. You deserve the magic, not Steve. (Dragongirl 1)

> What do you want? (DragonKeeper)

> We don't want you to do anything to hurt your friend. All we want is for you to stay out of the way and let the great dragons battle. (Dragongirl 1)

> I can't do anything. I'm not a guardian. Why are you telling me all this? (DragonKeeper)

> Because your friendship with Steve is a kind of magic. Just as Dragau has given Steve power in the past, the dragon also draws power from Steve's friends. Without you to lean on, Steve will be alone. It will weaken his dragon. (Dragongirl 1)

> I don't want to weaken the dragon. Why should I help you? (DragonKeeper)

> If your dragon wins, the world will never know. It will be just another secret dragon hidden away from the world, practically useless. If we win, there will be magic to spread around, more minor dragons, more magic to share with your kind. Justin, you could work with us; other humans do. (Dragongirl 1)

This wasn't right. Justin knew this wasn't right. She was asking him to betray his friend, and he knew she was a liar. He thought he should delete her and call Steve or Shou. But what if she was right? What if Shou hadn't told them everything? And Steve? Steve should have told him about Berit. All Steve ever did was shush him when he wanted to talk about the dragon, and now he didn't know what to think.

Justin couldn't make up his mind—did he actually want to be part of the dragon world? Could he do magic? This is something he should call Steve about, only he couldn't. What if

Steve got angry, or what if Shou was lying to them, and Steve told her about Berit's offer?

> Justin, it's started. The battle has already begun. My friends and I have to start some mischief, nothing to hurt anyone, just to create problems for your friend's dragon. It's necessary. Stay away from your friend, please. And Justin, I want you to do one other thing, please, as a token of my friendship. I want you to have a taste of what magic, real magic is like. Take one of your brother's surfboards to the water. You'll see what it's like to be on our side. Trust me. (Dragongirl 1)

Chapter 34

Steve stood beside Anthony's truck, planning to intercept Dani on her way home. He saw her come out of the school building with a gaggle of her friends and he waved. He knew she saw him; how could she not standing next to Moby Dick? But she turned away anyway, obviously ignoring him. She must still be upset about not having any special dragon abilities, he decided. Well, that was too bad. There was nothing he or anyone else could do about it, and she'd have to get over it. Besides, it wasn't all it was cracked up to be.

With a sigh, Steve started to walk toward her, but remembered he was supposed to be injured. He reached in the backseat and grabbed his crutches. "I've got to go grab her. She's being a pain," he told Anthony and hobbled over to where his sister and her friends were moseying along the sidewalk. "Hey, Dani, come on! Anthony's giving us a ride home today."

Dani tilted her head and gave him her best quizzical stare, "Why?"

"You know why, so quit being stupid. Come on!" he instructed.

Dani began to walk away, forcing Steve to hop around and get in front of the group. "I mean it, Dani. Mom and Dad set it up with Anthony. You need to come on."

Dani addressed her followers, "Sorry, ladies, I better go before my big brother has a seizure! Alison, I'll call you as soon as I get home."

One of the girls pointed to the monster truck, "You get to go home in that?"

Dani smiled, "Oh sure, no big deal. We ride in it all the time."

Steve huffed, "Dani...."

Dani hugged each and every girl like she was going away forever, while Steve stood there powerless to move her along any faster. When she was done, she turned and started to the truck, "Are you coming?"

Steve opened the door to Moby Dick and started to help Dani up, but she pushed him off. From the ground she yelled up, "Hey Anthony, can I ride in the back?"

"No can do, baby doll. It's illegal and if you fell out you'd crack your head open. Plus, your mom would kill me," Anthony answered.

"Okay," she replied, "go ahead, Steve, I want shotgun."

"No way, Dani. I'm the oldest. Get in."

"So what? That gives you special privileges? I'm not getting in." She crossed her arms.

"Guys, you need to work it out," Anthony prompted. "Steve, remember, I need to go back to Joy's."

"What about Joy?" Dani asked. "Did something happen to Joy?"

"Nothing happened to Joy," Steve snorted. "Here, get in and I'll trade you places."

Dani smiled while Steve helped push her up into the cab and then he climbed in and shut the door. Before Dani could complain, Steve switched places with her and got in the middle. For the 50,000th time, he wanted to punch her.

Anthony looked around to make sure he wouldn't crush any vehicles and started to back up when his phone went off. He answered it one-handed, "Hey, what's up? Oh my God, you're serious. Okay, I'll be right there. Listen, kids, I've got to run over to the marina."

"What's wrong?" Steve asked.

Before Anthony could answer, his phone received a text, and then another. Anthony tried driving and reading the texts at the same time, which meant that he drifted a little bit, causing a woman in a brand-new SUV to almost run off the road. "Dang it, here Steve hold this. Call your dad for me. He's under 'Favorites.'"

Steve hit his dad's number and waited. "It's his voicemail."

"Yeah, he's probably in class," Anthony said, clearly frustrated. "Okay, tell him you guys are going with me while I check out what's happening at the marina."

"What's going on at the marina?" Dani asked.

Anthony rolled up to an intersection and barely slowed before moving on. "Huh, oh sorry, Dani. A bunch of garbage and junk is heading in toward the boats. Steve, look up your mom's number and give her a call. Let her know where we're headed."

As they got closer to the boat moorings, Steve heard the sirens, some in the direction they were headed, and some behind, too. "Hi, Mom. Anthony got a call that something was happening at the harbor. We're heading there now...I'll ask."

"Hey, Anthony, she says she's leaving work now. Should she meet us at the docks?" Steve relayed.

Anthony nodded, "That's fine." As he turned a corner, he saw Larry and Ramone standing next to their van. Anthony rolled down his window. "Hey, you guys all right?"

"Yeah, we're cool. All my tires, splat, all at once—" Larry started to explain.

Dani jumped over Steve, "Hi, Larry!"

Larry waved back, "Hey, Dani. Hi Steve."

"How come your tires are all flat? Hey, look," Dani pointed to the building across the street. "Someone smashed into that building."

Ramone blurted out, "Oh, dude, check it, the firemen hit the building. Like skid and smack, you know?"

They all looked. Anthony turned back to the two surfers, "You guys need any help?"

"Naw, we're cool," Larry replied, "My dad's going to pick us up—"

"But the craziness has started man," Ramone interrupted, winking at Steve. "The giant dragon showdown."

"We don't know that," Larry interrupted. He stepped up on the truck's runner and looked into the cab. "There is a lot of stuff going down. Fred put out a house fire. Something happened to a tree at Battery Point. These dragon people, I guess you'd call them hybrids, are running around causing all kinds of, you know, destruction and stuff."

Steve leaned across the seat. "You know about Berit and her friends?"

"It's the dragons!" Dani yelled.

Larry said, "Shou told us all about it last night."

"We're like her shock troops, brah," Ramone added. "First responders against the evil dragons."

"Look, we probably all need to compare notes," Anthony said. "But right now I need to get over to the marina. We've got two boats docked and they're in danger of getting crushed by a mountain of floating trash coming in with the tide."

"It's cool, brah, head out, we're good," Larry explained.

"Yeah, we are on it!" Ramone exclaimed. "The old lady dragon gave us a mission and we are all over it!"

Anthony pulled into a parking lot off Citizens Dock Road where dozens of cars were already crowding. There were emergency vehicles as well, including a fire truck and several police cars. "Kids, stay put," Anthony directed. "I need to check on my livelihood." He jumped down from the truck and went off to find his brother.

Steve scooted over to the driver's side to roll down the window and listen. Dani immediately started to complain, "I'm not a baby. Why can't we get out and see what's going on?

"Quiet," Steve shushed, "I want to hear what all the commotion is about." He watched Anthony stop and talk to a fireman and then jog on down to where he kept his boat docked.

"I can't see anything," Dani griped.

This time Steve agreed. "Hey, let's climb in back. We're still in the truck, but maybe we can see what's happening."

The siblings guiltily opened the door and dropped down to the ground before going to the back of the truck and lowering the tailgate. Steve helped his sister up and the pair had a pretty good view of all the chaos. Everyone was moving toward the moored boats. Steve followed with his eyes and saw what was concerning them, tons of junk had drifted into the harbor, some of it already smacking into the boats. As Steve continued to scan the area, he had a moment of panic—the bait shop! Had anything happened to it? He couldn't see it.

"Dani, stay put. I need to check on The Worm Hole."

"No way, I'm coming with you!" she announced.

"No! I'll be right back. I mean it, Dani, you stay right here!"

He jumped down and looked back to make sure his sister hadn't followed, remembering again that he was supposed to be on crutches. "How long am I going to have to keep this up?" he wondered. However, everything was total chaos and he didn't recognize too many people. He'd have to chance it. After a quick check, he sprinted around people to get to where the family business was located.

The bait shop should have been closed and locked, waiting to be opened on the weekends. With his dad in school, it was the only time to do any business. They made less money that way, but it still helped. As Steve approached, he saw that the building was intact. But his relief was short lived as he got close enough to see that the padlock had been picked.

The Worm Hole had a side door, which is the one Steve used to get in. He used the key attached to the lanyard around his neck with his school ID on it, slid inside, and took a quick look around. The place was cleaned out! No tackle, no crab traps. Even the refrigerator was missing. *This is horrible,* Steve thought. *Where'd they take everything?* Then he remembered the mass of garbage floating a few feet away in the water. *No, no, they wouldn't throw all the equipment away!* But if they did, they were screwed—Steve and his family would never get it back.

Steve walked back to the truck, his eyes down at his own feet. "Watch out, kid," someone hollered. Steve looked up, remembering that everyone here was in danger of losing valuable things.

Steve had gotten tired of working at the shop, but he knew how important it was to the family finances. Besides that, however, Steve knew the place meant a lot to his dad—Steve was very worried about how his dad would take the news. He was thinking about the loss when he came up on Anthony's truck. Dani was nowhere in sight. "Oh, God, what now? Where's she gone?" Frantically, Steve began to climb back up in the truck for a better look when heard a familiar voice, "Steve, over here!"

He turned around and saw his mother waving at him, Dani standing beside her, clearly upset. His heartbeat slowed considerably. He hurried over. "Mom, it's the bait shop—"

His mother grabbed him in a bear hug, "Oh, you're okay. Good, with everything that's happening, I was afraid."

"But Mom, The Worm Hole. Someone stole everything out of it. They broke in and they took everything—even the old fridge."

Jeanie held him at arm's length and asked, "Everything?" She looked tired, but less frantic than he thought she'd be. "Never mind the shop, it's okay. You guys are all right, and that's what's important. Let's go find Anthony. I don't want him worrying about you, and then we'll go get your dad."

Securely holding her children's hands, Jeanie led them toward the docks. "Mom, let go," Dani complained. "I can walk by myself."

"Not now, Dani. You hold on to me," she scolded. Steve didn't even bother to try to break free. They found Anthony standing with two of his brothers, all tall, skinny, and blond, and only slightly less tattooed. They were staring helplessly as tons of debris sloshed in and around all the boats in the marina. Occasionally, some large object banged into someone's boat, and a series of inappropriate curse words filled the air.

Jeanie interrupted the brothers, "I'm so sorry, Anthony. Are your boats going to be all right?"

Anthony turned and shrugged, "Don't know. Coast Guard's been notified. Some of this mess will go out with the tide and we might be able to put up something to block it from coming back in. A couple of folks have tried to idle their boats out, but there's too much junk."

"Someone broke into the bait house," Steve announced.

"It was the dragons," Dani announced.

Everyone looked at her. "Well, it was! This was probably the dragons' fault too."

Anthony's brother smirked, "Hon, this is all from that Japanese earthquake a couple of years ago. No dragons created all this."

"Uh huh, how come it all showed up now?" Dani asked.

"Dani, shush, it doesn't matter right now," Jeanie chastised.

Anthony looked out over the mess, "She might be right. This floating dump has been tracked for a couple of years and whenever it's supposed to wash up, there's been plenty of warning. This just showed up. And it's a pretty big coincidence that your shop was broken into on the same day, not to mention all the other stuff going on in town."

"I don't know. It's...I don't know what to think about any of it," Jeanie started. "Anthony, I'm going to take the kids back home. Do you need anything? Is there anything we can do?"

"Naw, we'll figure it out," Anthony replied. "Be real careful. This is like a war right now, and I've got a feeling it's gonna get worse. Tell Roger I'll swing by later."

Steve wanted to stay, but knew there wasn't anything he could do; it didn't seem like there was much anyone could do right now. He followed closely as his mom half-dragged Dani back to their pickup. People were hurrying back and forth, and a few more police cars showed up. His mother waved at several people, but didn't stop to speak to anyone. No sooner had they gotten into the truck than Jeanie's phone rang.

"Hey, Mrs. Batista? This is Ramona, you know my mom, Florence. We own the Tastee Freez."

"Hi, Ramona," Jeanie answered. "Is something wrong?"

"Yeah, my mom asked me to call you. We got a boy that works for us who volunteers with the firefighters who got a call to head out to your Granny's place a little bit ago. Seems like they needed extra help dealing with it. So, I guess maybe there's a fire out there? Mom thought you should know."

"Is she all right?" Jeanie asked in a panic.

"Oh, right, well Mom went on up there along with everybody in town, but I'm supposed to hang around here. So, um, I really don't know."

"Okay, thanks, hon," Jeanie said before hanging up. "Hurry up, you two, and buckle up." Jeanie repeatedly dialed Granny's house, but got no answer. She tried her husband's phone with the same result.

Weaving through the mess of people and cars, Jeanie kept trying the numbers. "Mom, what's going on?" Steve asked.

"There's a fire at Granny's, and she's not answering her phone. I can't get your dad either." She handed Steve her cellphone, eyes a little wild, "Here, you keep trying so I can concentrate on driving. If he answers, tell him we're on our way to get him."

Chapter 35

The mountain shook for the third time in as many minutes. Birds soared out from their trees and then alighted back on familiar branches; squirrels scampered up their trunks and then down, not knowing which was safest; and Shou held on tight inside the dragon's lair. When the shaking stopped, Shou worked her way back, ignoring the billowing smoke issuing from Dragau's nose and mouth. Shou took a deep breath; it was good to share the air with a great dragon again and its heat seemed to revitalize her tired bones. "No," Shou admitted to herself, "it is not my bones that are wearing down, but my spirit." Seeing this dragon reminded her of the creature whose magic gave it life. That dragon was also named Dragau and, over three hundred years ago, Shou had retrieved its magic from its corpse and sent it away to the New World with one of Steve's ancestors.

That had been the last great dragon Shou had called friend, and the last still alive willing to help her. She had such hopes for this dragon, whose love for humans was even greater than his predecessor's—but, now, that was the problem.

More heat poured off the slumbering giant, forcing Shou to assume her real form. The intense heat would have scorched her human clothing. She moved with a snake's grace to the back of the cave, where she stood on her hind legs to peer at the tormented dragon. Its breathing was shaky, its eyes, behind their lids, shifted back and forth. Shou was worried. This dragon needed to conserve all its strength, all its magic. Something was upsetting it, getting into its dreams. She knew what that something was: Berit and her friends.

This dragon had spent over a century sharing its magic with every living and non-living thing in the area. It bathed the community in good luck and it felt the presence of every man, woman, and child; of every fly, worm, and pinecone; of every seagull, beaver, and banana slug. While Shou found that connection admirable, it also could be potentially disastrous. This dragon, more so than any other Shou had known, could not seem to shut himself off sufficiently to prepare his egg. Whatever Berit and her friends were doing was causing the great beast pain. Berit hadn't only stepped up her assault; she had declared war. All she had to do to thwart Shou was continue creating as much chaos as possible and their side would win, again.

Shou hoped that TJ and the surfers could help a little. She caught glimpses of what the boys were dealing with, but so far, no one was seriously hurt, and TJ was almost there. She hoped he could help. It was a long shot. Berit had eons of experience in bringing human beings down. She seemed to be playing by the rules for now: she hadn't killed any people. It was an agreement that she and Shou had struck decades earlier at the end of a war that had threatened to not only wipe out mankind, but take a good part of the green earth with it.

Even with that stipulation, Berit was causing enough hardship to break through Dragau's rest. If it woke up prematurely, then it would stand no chance in its upcoming battle. An elder dragon from Berit's side would appear from the North and defeat Dragau, taking the magic that might have become another dragon friendly to humans and instead creating more beings like Berit and her posse.

Shou squeezed closer to the slumbering giant and began to sing a song older than the trees on these mountains. It was nothing a human would understand, or even hear, but the dragon could. As the song reverberated throughout the cave, the dragon stopped thrashing. The smoke that jetted from its mouth slowed to a trickle and its breathing eased. Shou continued until she sensed that it was resting peacefully; she had to keep it asleep for as long as dragonly possible. As the cave began to cool, Shou considered changing back to her human form, but the chance to luxuriate in her dragon skin was too good to ignore; she loved her humans, but sometimes it was nice to be herself. Besides, if she knew Berit, Shou was certain she would have to sing to the dragon again before long.

Chapter 36

Granny had her hose out spraying down everything she could long before the Gasquet Volunteer Fire Department even sounded an alarm. She had been visiting with one of her friends when she had suddenly looked up from her deck of cards. "What's the matter?" the elderly woman across the table had asked.

"Call 9-1-1, dear," Granny had instructed, "I think someone has set my house on fire!" Then she'd ran out the door, hurrying down the dirt road between their houses. She saw the smoke almost immediately and caught its smell at about the same time. She'd jogged as fast as her 74-year-old self would allow, wishing she had the vitality that had disappeared with the dragon. At least, occasionally, there was still a glimmer of the old magic—maybe that was what had warned her that her house was on fire.

Only it wasn't her house; it was the unattached garage next to it, she realized. She'd run to her porch and turned on the water. She had a good well with plenty of pressure and hoped that she could slow the fire until real help showed up. She'd uncoiled the heavy, faded pink rubber hose and run it up to the garage—a garage that held a lifetime's accumulation of junk and memories. She started spraying everything in sight.

Gasquet's only fire engine showed up a few minutes later. The four volunteers who heeded the call jumped down and went into action. Two of them undid their own heavy collapsible hose, while another worked the truck to prepare it to shoot its limited water supply. "Estela, you all right?" George, from over at the American Legion, asked.

"I'm fine," Granny managed, though truthfully all her recent activity had been a bit much.

"Hey, George, this is going up fast. Look at those trees!" another part-time firefighter pointed.

Both Granny and George turned. Sure enough, flames were starting to lick the lower branches of one of the many dried pines that surrounded Granny's property. If one tree caught fire, the whole yard, including the house, would go up next; it might even jump to the neighbor's and beyond if they didn't get a handle on it.

"Estela, take that hose back and start spraying down everything around your house," George instructed. "Focus on your porch and your roof. Terry, get on the radio and call the forest rangers. If this gets out of hand, we could have a major disaster."

Granny dragged her hose back, looking forlornly at the back of the garage as it caught fire, burning the mural Steve and Dani had painted a few summers ago. Suddenly, the heat made one of the old windows blow out; Granny realized that she might lose her home.

A car careened into the yard: two more volunteers had gotten the call and left work to fight the fire. They were in their street clothes, but ran to the back of the fire truck to retrieve the mandatory helmets and heavy fire-resistant jackets. They ran to George who was the acting fire chief while Lucy was in the Bahamas on her honeymoon. "Start clearing out any brush from around this building."

A loud pop made everyone turn. It was probably a can of something flammable. George went over to where Granny was looping a stream of water on her roof. "I don't understand it, Mrs. Batista, we've got enough water on that building and it's not that big. It should be out by now. Is there anything especially flammable in there to keep this heat up?"

Granny turned and looked back at garage; the flames were shooting upward from the roof now. "No, well, maybe," she answered. "Could be some old paint, or chemicals I've forgotten about...But I can't understand how it started in the first place."

Meanwhile, Steve's dad was rushing with his family as fast as his little pickup could handle the curvy mountain road that led to Granny's place. Steve's parents were speculating about the fire, but they didn't have much information. Dani kept saying it had to be the dragons again, and Steve wondered if she was right. There was too much crazy stuff going on not to at least consider it a possibility.

His pulse started racing as they hit the straight stretch of highway that made up Gasquet. As they passed the Tastee Freez, he had a brief flashback featuring the demon Mammon—he hadn't gotten an ice cream there since. He didn't have time to dwell on it, because he could already see and smell the smoke.

Only a bit further, they turned onto his grandmother's dirt road. His dad parked their vehicle behind the growing number of cars and emergency vehicles and started to tell Steve and Dani to stay put, but thought better of it when he saw Dani's panicked expression. "Okay, Dani, take your mother's hand, and Steve, come with me."

There were strangers running around everywhere, along with a few neighbors Steve recognized, some in fire gear. The big fire truck was blasting the garage with a steady stream of water. Everyone turned as a green forestry truck arrived, followed by another fire truck. The chaos grew as more firemen started pulling hoses to get more water on the garage. Suddenly, one of the trees near the building lit up like a giant matchstick.

Roger and Jeanie worked their way around to the house, the smoke starting to make everything a bit hazy. They found Granny speaking to someone from the forestry service. A neighbor had her hose and was wetting down her porch. "Mom," Roger yelled, "are you all right? What happened?"

"I have no idea," she answered as she wiped the sweat and soot from her forehead. "How'd you find out about this?"

"Ramona from the Tastee-Freez called," Jeanie answered. "This looks bad. Are they going to be able to save the house?"

A guy in green interrupted and introduced himself, "Hi, I'm Tom Sample, with the forestry service. We're putting a lot of water on that building and the surrounding grounds. We should have it under control soon."

Steve stared back at the garage. He felt a deep sense of loss knowing what was in there: a treasure trove of old saddles, rusty iron tools, elk antlers, and hundreds of things left undiscovered. Another tree suddenly went up, and everyone turned. The forestry service guy, Tom, ran off yelling for people to get more water on all the trees.

Besides the knot of sadness Steve was feeling, there was something else bothering him. The fire wasn't right. It shimmered in a way that didn't make it look like a normal fire. *It was almost like...no,* Steve thought, *it couldn't be.* Steve moved closer, ignoring Dani when she asked him what he was doing. He found himself drawn to the flames and didn't notice when his parents yelled at him to come back. He had his hands stretched out in front of him; he could feel the heat, and more. A realization shook him, these weren't natural flames—this was dragon magic.

Steve knew that they weren't going to put this fire out; no amount of water would douse it until the magic had consumed itself. He should tell someone, anyone. But what could they do? Steve thought he heard something, like a whisper. He turned around and didn't see anyone. There it was again. He might as well have been chasing an echo. *That was it,* he thought. *It was like an echo.*

Granny suddenly appeared by his side. She was looking at him in a strange way. And then she looked around. "You hear it, don't you, boy?" He nodded.

"It must be our dragon's magic," Granny said. "It's like what protected us when Mammon tried to get in. It's weak, but it—"

"No," Steve shook his head, "I mean, yeah, I can sense it, but this isn't Dragau's."

Steve focused real hard, trying to block out everything except the whispers. Berit had been here, and the one called Brita. He could not actually see them, but somehow, he could hear them talking almost like their voices were being carried from far away. Steve found himself repeating bits and pieces of their conversation to himself. He didn't even notice that he was walking forward.

He no longer saw the flames. Instead, he watched the swirling vortex of color as it consumed the garage. It was beautiful, seeming to be made of a hundred colors all at once; and it was violent—magic meant to destroy. Yet, it drew Steve so strongly he wanted to touch it. Steve barely resisted the urge, but he knew he had to do something or the magic would not stop with this building. It occurred to him that maybe he could do what Shou done with his knee. Without weighing the consequences, Steve let himself repeat Berit's echoes and at the same time, pictured himself drawing the magic away.

Almost at once, he knew it was working. He experienced a rush as the magic hit him, and just as quickly, he knew he had made a terrible mistake. There was nowhere for it to go. Like iron to a magnet, the magic poured into him. He felt it enter him; it felt like getting the flu all at once—his body suddenly heavy and achy, his skin hypersensitive, his stomach cramping.

Everything went black.

Chapter 37

TJ was puffing hard, his tongue drooping outside his open mouth, and his feet hurt. Crescent City was not far now, perhaps only a few more miles to the north. He could hear the commotion that humans made, and he could smell civilization. But he was pooped. He stopped and sat back on his mighty behind and started licking his sore toes. *This stinks!* TJ thought to himself, *I chose to become a bear for a reason, and it wasn't to march my happy self all over the country. Bears need their downtime.* TJ was not built for speed; he was built for playing in rivers, picking berries, and napping.

He'd thought he could make the trip relatively easily. He had a tried-and-true system when he traveled: sneak into a truck stop, figure out which driver was going the direction he wanted, work a little dragon magic, and climb into the sleeper behind the cab. Sometimes his nature got the better of him, though, and he fell asleep. That turned out to be the one flaw in his travel plans; his snoring alerted the driver, and, after a big to do, he had been forced to walk.

He'd known that he needed to stay awake, of course, but the trucker had been transporting satin sheets—satin! It wasn't TJ's fault, really. *I mean, come on,* TJ thought to himself as he rested, *who could resist satin sheets?*

Still, that poor driver had been thoroughly freaked out. *Never thought I'd wake up to a 300-pound grown man screaming like a little girl,* TJ mused. He'd tumbled out of the sleeper in time to see the trucker jump out of his truck and run away. TJ had contemplated driving the rest of the way himself, but figured he'd attract the wrong kind of attention.

That had been a couple of hours ago, and TJ had been forced to waddle through the forest along the coastal highway. He could have transformed into his dragon self, like Shou sometimes did, and make a lot faster time, but once he'd decided he was going to be a bear, well, by the Great Dragon, he was going to be a bear. That had disappointed Shou, at first. Maybe it still did; she would rather he help her in her quest to save mankind, seeing that he was really a very powerful minor dragon.

Truthfully, it wasn't that TJ didn't like humans—he did. In fact, he attributed his life philosophy to mankind's greatest writer: "This above all, to thine own self be true." Of course, that was only half the quote, but it was the part that resonated with the big bear. No, TJ felt that his place was in the woods, looking after the other less powerful magical creatures and taking his long winter naps. Even his newest obsession, Hip Hop, wasn't enough to get him to change his ways. But he owed Shou this one, he figured. Without her, he'd have ended up under the claw of one of the Great Dragons bent on destroying humanity—TJ had it on good authority that those minor dragons didn't get to take many naps.

With a heavy sigh, he set off again, paws smarting with each footfall. From off in the distance, he thought he heard a car engine, something he recognized. Yup, it was the high-pitched whine of an old Volkswagen—he recognized it from the short period when he thought it'd be fun to roll with the hippies. When the 70s beetle rounded the corner, TJ twitched his shoulders a bit and the car's tiny motor conked out. The driver coasted to the side of the road to see what was wrong. TJ watched as a young guy got out and said something to the female in the passenger seat. The guy went around to the rear of the car where the air-cooled motor sat and lifted the trunk, which was actually the hood, considering that was where the engine could be found. He pulled on a couple of wires and then got back inside.

TJ coolly approached the vehicle with a little magic-induced stealth and climbed up on the roof. If the car could grunt, it would have, but the roof held, even if the tires were mashed down a couple of inches. The car started right up and continued north. To anyone looking, except for the little girl in the rear car seat, all they'd see was a little VW bug loaded down with luggage strapped to the roof. The toddler, on the other hand, enjoyed playing several dozen rounds of peek-a-boo with a big, goofy bear.

Chapter 38

Larry's dad picked him and his friends up not long after they saw Anthony and the kids. They managed to coax the van over to the curb where it would have to sit until they could get four new tires on it. His dad was furious, at first—four ties flat at the same time. However, Larry's dad knew all about Steve's dragon, and when Larry explained what happened, his dad promised to take them for a new set of tires after he finished his work for the day.

Once they got home, they pulled into the garage and piled out of the little SUV. Ramone and Fred were already inside when Larry stopped. "Whoa, hey, Dad, I'm missing a board!"

His father poked his head back into the garage, "What's that?"

Larry pointed to the wall that held his surfboards, to where a tri-fin thruster, slightly under six feet, was missing. That he would even notice it gone among all the other single and multiple finned boards was a testament to his life's passion. "My board, Dad, look, it's gone."

"Well damn, kid, what do you want me to do about it?" his father exclaimed. Apparently, he was a little more miffed about the tires than he'd let on. "You sure you didn't leave it in your van or back in Santa Barbara?"

"Negative, no way, Dad. I only took one board down there, and the rest should be here."

"Well, I don't know, Larry. Why don't you check with Justin, maybe he's seen it?"

Ramone and Fred stepped back into the garage while Larry's dad went back to work. "Look around guys, I love that board."

"Could have gotten moved," Fred offered.

"Or you may have totally angered the surfer gods by leaving us here to go to college and this is your punishment," Ramone suggested.

"Whatever, brah, you guys look around would yah? I'll ask if Justin's seen it." Larry said.

Larry left his buds searching while he went to find his brother. He poked into Justin's room and found it empty. He roamed the house, hollering his brother's name and got no reply. He entered his parent's office and asked them, but they were so engrossed in some science stuff that they barely acknowledged him. Larry went out on the deck in the backyard. Fred and Ramone were down on the grass kicking around an abandoned soccer ball. "Dudes, what are you doing?"

Ramone looked up, "Huh, oh, yeah, yeah, we're looking for your board, brah." Then he rolled the ball behind him like it really wasn't there. However, Larry wasn't paying attention any more.

Their deck had a magnificent view of the ocean—there was a specific spot with a nice, constant break in view. It was a spot that Larry and his friends discovered when they were in middle school, and still one that they hit if they were forced to walk to surf. Lots of afternoons after school, the trio had trekked the quarter mile down the road and then slid down the treacherous trail to the bottom of the cliff. Once there, they found the tiniest sandbar, not big enough to attract sun worshippers, but large enough to hide a few things among the rocks, and then they'd hit the waves. Larry stood, staring out towards the ocean, then immediately ran back into the house and into the garage where a pair of binoculars hung on a rusty nail.

He bounded back on the deck and trained them on the lone surfer. "Oh, no, no, no!" he shouted.

"T-Man, what's up?" Ramone asked.

Larry pointed, "Oh, hell, check it! That's Justin out there!"

All three surfers were now on the deck, each one taking a turn with the binoculars. "Brah, when'd he start surfing?"

Larry shook his head, "He doesn't. I don't think he can even swim. How the hell did he even get down there?!"

Ramone had the binoculars, "Brahs, check it, those waves are cookin'! If he tries to catch one he's gonna get cranked!"

"Come on, we gotta get wet!" Larry bolted back inside with his two friends right behind him. With speedy efficiency, they all stripped down, and each threw on one of the wetsuits that hung in the corner. They each grabbed a board and sprinted out of the garage. "What's that kid thinking?" Fred asked. "He can't surf; he can't even..." Fred trailed off, racking his brain for any memories of Justin doing anything even remotely athletic, "Brah, can he even ride a bicycle?"

"Barely, he's not very coordinated," Larry replied. "We got to get him before he drowns."

"Or smacks the rocks," Ramone interjected. "Don't forget about those gnarly rocks!"

"Got it, brah," Larry agreed. "I know!"

They got to the spot where a narrow path started down the cliff to the water below, a drop of close to eighty feet. That path had been owned by three sets of feet for so long that no plant would dare try and grow back. Larry took the lead, half sliding down, holding his board over his head. He kept one eye on his brother and another on the trail in front of him. So far, Justin hadn't moved; he was straddling his board, looking back as each set of waves came in.

"Dudes, check it, there's a cruncher," Ramone pointed.

Larry looked up and saw a single line in the water running toward the shore. If Justin took that wave, he'd be munched, lacerated, or worse. He tried yelling, but knew it was pointless. There was no way his brother could hear that far out. He watched in horror as Justin turned, facing the shore and started an easy paddle in front of the swell. He was going for it!

The wave started to crest, producing a six-foot face. Larry screamed at his brother to duck it, his voice lost beneath the sound of the waves as they hit the shore. Justin paddled forward, miraculously ending up in just the right spot to catch the wave. Larry watched as his little brother pushed the nose of his board down with his weight a little forward and popped up on two feet. Larry froze, and the two other guys ran into his board.

"Brah, why you stopping?" Fred asked, then looked over Larry's shoulder. "Whoa, you seeing this?"

Justin had not only managed to stand up, he was now shredding, executing crisp turns back and forth.

"Check it, that is not your brother!" Ramone exclaimed.

Larry didn't know what to say. It was Justin, only this Justin was a kamikaze wave rider, and not his nerdy, dweeb, little brother. He'd tried teaching Justin to surf a dozen times and the kid couldn't even ride a foamer on a long board—he'd given up in less time than it took to say "cowabunga". Larry marched forward to get a better view of the imposter, wondering the whole time how he was going to break the news to his parents that a group of aliens had abducted his brother and replaced him with a surf ninja.

"Oh man, look," Fred cried. "He's heading toward the breakers!"

Larry looked south. Fred was right; Justin was getting dangerously close to a bunch of jagged rocks. It was one reason this spot wasn't surfed much and especially not by novices. If Justin didn't bail soon, he'd wreck on them. At the last second, he kicked out and made his way back towards the shore.

"Yes!" Larry yelled, fist pumping. "Did you see that?"

"Brah," Ramone said, "I'm so glad your brother didn't die."

"Me too," Larry whispered.

Chapter 39

Joy put the math homework aside. She had erased a hole in the paper trying to solve the problem and knew her head wasn't in it. Math was usually easy for her, but not today. It was starting to get dark out, and Joy wondered where her mother was. She'd probably come charging in with her arms full of unnecessary stuff her father would have to return the next day. Or she might slip in like a shadow and head straight for her darkened bedroom. Or, maybe, if the Nordic guy was telling the truth, nothing would happen, just normal Mom—whatever that looked like. Joy got up from the coffee table and went looking for something to eat in the kitchen. She stood in front of the refrigerator and forgot why she was there; she wasn't really hungry. She looked at the clock again, wondering where her dad was, too.

It was the key in the lock that woke Joy up; she didn't even remember laying down on the couch. She stood groggily as the front door opened. "Oh, hi, baby," her mother said. "I'm sorry I'm home so late. I—I had a bunch of things to return." She walked into the kitchen with a gallon of milk. "Are you hungry?"

Joy followed her in and sat down on a bar stool. She shook her head no, not trusting herself to talk. Her mom put up the milk and walked around to hug her, "I'm sorry, Joy. I'm so sorry."

"It's okay, Mom. It's not your fault."

Her mother sat on the stool next to her, looking down at her hands. She didn't say anything right away. "This was," she hesitated, "I stopped taking my medication, like I always do eventually…when I don't think I need it anymore. This time, this time I was really high, felt like I could do anything. You know, baby, you know how I get." Joy nodded while her mother continued, "And then, I stopped. I was right in the middle of driving to that little *Things Remembered* store all the way in Brookings to buy a birthday gift for your Aunt Sara. Her birthday isn't for six months! Insane. Suddenly, I knew how crazy it was, and I turned around."

Joy reached over and grasped her mom's hand, not ready for words. She was so torn about what to do, what to say. Her mom wasn't manic; she wasn't depressed. She was exactly as the dragon-man said: normal. Joy smiled at her mom, who was beautiful, despite the running mascara. Joy got up and wet a paper towel and dabbed at her cheeks. "It's going to be all right, Mom."

By the time her dad got home, mother and daughter had dinner almost done. Nothing fancy or over-the-top—a salad, spaghetti, and some garlic bread. Joy's dad came in slowly, tentatively, like he wasn't sure what he'd encounter. Joy knew why. When her mom was off her meds, her dad never knew what he'd have to deal with. She wondered sometimes how he did it, how he managed to love her still. Mostly she was glad he stayed; Joy had friends whose parents had split up for things a lot less serious than this.

As he dropped his jacket and briefcase on the couch, Joy's mom turned to him and they smiled at each other. Their love for each other was unmistakable. Joy set out plates, confident in that moment that her dad would never leave her mom.

Chapter 40

"What's wrong with him?" Dani asked.

"Try it again," Roger told his wife, ignoring Dani's question.

Jeanie dialed Shou's cell for the fourth time. "Roger, I keep getting her voicemail. Dani, go get another wet washcloth from your grandmother." Dani stomped off to the kitchen to get another rag. Granny was dumping ice trays into a large salad bowl full of tap water. "What? Oh, here you go, child."

Dani hesitated, "What's going on, Granny? What happened to Steve?"

Granny frowned, looking out her window. The garage fire was nearly extinguished. The fire crews were just being cautious now, raking through debris and dousing any lingering hot spots. One group from the forestry service had already left. Dani asked again, "Granny?"

"Oh, sorry, honey. Whatever made that fire was magical, Dani. Steve made it stop, but it's making him sick. Here, you take that rag and I'll bring over this bowl of ice water."

Steve lay on the couch with a rag placed over his forehead. It was already nearly dry, even though they just put it on him. He had finished having another violent seizure, his third in the last ten minutes. Granny pulled Steve's shirt off and started a sponge bath with the ice water. "Isn't there anything you can do, Mom?" Jeanie asked.

Granny kept wiping the feverish boy. "I'm doing it, dear."

"We need to get him to a hospital," Roger insisted. "It'd be quicker than waiting for an ambulance. He pulled the thermometer from Steve's armpit. "Damn, 105, we've got to do something; that's heat stroke temperature and with the seizures…I don't know."

Granny nodded, "You're right. I don't know if a hospital can help him, but we're sure not doing much good."

Roger ran out and grabbed one of the local volunteer firemen and explained that Steve had to get to the hospital in a hurry. He ran to his truck and got on the emergency radio. Because of the fire, there were all kinds of emergency responders close by. In a matter of minutes, a sheriff's car arrived, closely followed by a highway patrol cruiser. The deputy recognized Roger, "Hey, good God, Roger, what else is going on today?"

"It's my boy, Steve. He's unconscious and seizing, with a 105 temperature. We've got to get him to the hospital."

"They've already dispatched an ambulance from Sutter, but we might make better time meeting them on the way," the officer stated. "Go ahead and get him in my car."

As they attempted to belt Steve's prone body into the back seat, he began thrashing violently. "Here, help me," Roger said as he tried to keep Steve from hurting himself. Once the episode subsided, Jeanie strapped herself next to Steve. Roger climbed up front with the officer. Dani only mildly complained about not riding in the patrol car before hopping into the family's pickup with Granny. The highway patrolman ran lights and sirens ahead of the deputy sheriff's car, and they made it through the canyon and almost to Elk Valley Road before meeting up with the ambulance. The EMTs swapped Steve into their vehicle and took off toward the hospital while everyone else continued in the patrol car. Granny followed behind in the truck.

The ambulance pulled into the emergency room drop-off and they got Steve right in. Despite Roger's EMT training, he was told to wait with everyone else. "Any luck?" he asked Jeanie.

"Nothing, voicemails," she replied. "This is horrible. What if they can't get his temp down?"

Roger paced. "Come on, think, think," he told himself. "What are you doing?" he asked his wife, who was wandering back towards the lobby.

"I'm trying his friends. Maybe Justin or Joy knows something about Shou's whereabouts."

Granny took Dani and led her over to a window. "Is Steve going to die, Granny?" she asked.

"No, child, he's going to be fine," Granny replied.

"He didn't look fine," Dani said. "The fever's because of magic, huh?"

Granny nodded, "I think so."

"I'm not getting either one," Jeanie said. "Do you think they're all right?"

"You said Anthony dropped them off," Roger answered, "so I'm sure they're fine."

Just then, a doctor walked in. "We're doing all we can to lower his fever. So far, nothing is bringing it down, but it's not going up. Fortunately, he has not had another seizure. Now, I want to try and understand what might be causing this. The EMT said you came from a fire. Was he inside? Did he get dehydrated fighting it? Anything?"

Roger looked at Jeanie, who answered, "No, doctor. We had only just arrived at the fire and he wasn't dehydrated. He hasn't been bitten by ticks or any other normal ailment. It's…" Jeanie broke off and rubbed furiously at her forehead.

"What? Here, ma'am, why don't you sit down."

"It's going to sound crazy, doctor. And it is, but I promise we're not," Jeanie answered. "You can run every test you want, but Steve was fine, right up until…"

"Until what?" the doctor asked.

"Until he took in the magic that caused the fire," Roger answered for her. "Look, doctor, you're not from here and I'm sure this sounds crazy. But Steve is storing magic right now, and he has to get rid of it. We're trying to get someone who can help."

The young doctor had only arrived a few months ago. He liked the town and the fact that there were all sorts of outdoorsy stuff to do. People were nice, if not overly friendly, and these people certainly didn't look like nut jobs. He decided it was possible they were all suffering from heat stroke, or some other kind of mass delusion. Maybe the fire had caused some sort of chemical reaction—metals in the air, or something. So, with a coaxing nod, he responded, "Uh, okay, well, I think I'm going to test him for Lyme's Disease, and maybe a few other things, if that's all right?"

Roger sighed, "Sure, go ahead. We'll be right here."

Jeanie kept trying phone numbers.

Chapter 41

The VW drove into town and the first thing it passed was the marina. TJ could smell dragon magic all over the place. At a red light, he eased himself off the roof of the car, tapped the back window to say goodbye to his new friend in the back seat, and stiffly waddled toward the boats.

The sun was sinking on the horizon, coloring the sky a brilliant orange, red, and pink combo. Shadows began coming out. Whenever someone came too close, TJ would slip into one of them and disappear. On the few occasions that he couldn't find one, he'd strike some silly pose and pretend to be a stuffed bear—Northwest people were used to stuffed bears.

As he got closer to the water, he could see the lingering use of magic hovering in the air. He stopped in the shade of a large building before attempting to sneak across a parking lot full of people. There were dozens of humans milling around, many staring into the bay. Unless he wanted to completely transform himself, there was no way he could get near enough to see what was going on. However, he did have a bear's nose, and used it to detect all the debris and garbage that had invaded. He concluded that Berit and her friends had done something to clog the marina.

There wasn't much he could do at the moment with so many people about, so he decided to move on and see what other mischief had occurred. Before he left, he took one last, good sniff on Shou's behalf; the two of them had made a strong mental connection before he left, so at least now she'd know what had been done to the harbor. When he cleared the parking lot, he did manage to get close enough to the water to get a good look. It was as he suspected: mountains of trash and junk had swamped the moored boats.

He headed north, tracking the scent of magic as he went. He passed a convenience store, but hesitated besides a dumpster full of exquisite treats, and only with supreme effort did he keep going. His belly grumbled angrily. Occasionally, he had to come out into the fading light where someone could see him. He didn't stress over it; there were black bears all over this area, and by the time animal control arrived, he'd be long gone. When he arrived at the lighthouse, he again found the presence of powerful dragon magic. Thankfully, the damage looked to be confined to an empty building and a single tree. He moved on, but the scents were getting stronger now as he made his way toward town.

He leaned up against a nearby wall, standing on his two hind legs, and scratched his backside while he considered what to do next. Sooner or later, if he kept chasing down these smells, he'd run into the three dragons. Still, he supposed he would have to cross that bridge when he came to it. His nostrils flared as he dropped back to four paws; more magic, northward and not too far. He loped in that direction.

Chapter 42

The four boys were stripping off wetsuits in the garage, relating their latest epic rides. "Brahs, did you see me carve that wave? It was sick!" Fred exclaimed.

"As if, Justin totally ripped it," Ramone replied.

"Naw, brah, I shaved it, man." Fred argued.

Justin unzipped his suit like a blue banana peel and tried to conceal his excitement. After their initial shock at seeing him surf proficiently, the trio had joined him, and they'd spent the next couple of hours putting on a surfing clinic for the seals and seagulls. In between sets, Larry and his buddies peppered Justin with questions about when he learned to surf so well. Justin evaded their inquiries by smiling or shrugging noncommittally. What could he tell them, that his ex-crush had given him magic surfer powers?

Fred and Ramone were still going on about the quantum surfing, so Larry sent them inside to ask his mom if she'd spring for pizza. When they left, he asked his brother, "Okay, truth. What happened? You and I both know you can't surf."

Justin tried to lie, "Maybe I've been practicing while you were at college. Did you consider that?"

"Yup, but that's not true, is it? Justin, the way you surfed today, no one just picks that up. It takes years to get that good. So, what's going on?"

Before he could answer, a large black bear with a particularly large rear end lumbered up the driveway and into the light of the garage. Justin's eyes grew big as saucers and Larry started to ease back and reach for a kayaking oar. The bear, however, was unconcerned. It plopped down and started licking it paws. "Chill, dawgs, we ain't got no beef!"

Larry dropped the oar and fell backwards. "What the hell, you talk! Justin, you hear him?"

"What?" Justin asked. "Are you nuts?"

"Brah, check it out! It speaks!" Larry yelled as he pointed at the bear.

With a huff, TJ broke up the exchange, "Listen, my brother, don't diss me. I am not an 'it'; I am a he. You can call me TJ."

"See! See, there it goes again! It's talking. Justin, you can't hear that?" Larry asked.

Justin shook his head, but now he was less concerned with the bear than he was his brother, who had obviously suffered a head injury or something. "No, Larry...all I see is a bear."

"He can't comprendo, my friend," TJ interjected.

"Huh?" Larry replied.

"The boy! Man, Shou didn't tell me you were slow!"

Larry approached warily, while Justin yelled for him to get back. "You know Shou?"

"Shou? What about Shou?" Justin blurted out.

"You know any other talking bears, dawg? Geez, I thought you'd be down with all this." TJ got up and leaned on the car. "Shou sent me to help you out."

"So, why can't he understand you?" Larry asked pointing to his brother.

"Because he wasn't the one Shou assigned to look after everything here—you were. Well, you and your 'brahs.'" He chuckled.

"What's he saying, Larry?" Justin asked.

"Hang on," Larry answered. "Okay, so what—"

Ramone and Fred came barreling through the door into the garage. Fred was first, but Ramone knocked him down and climbed over him. "Mommy-O says all right on the pizza...What the heck is that? Check it, brah, you got a bear in your garage!" Ramone yelled.

TJ rolled his eyes, "Oh my God, not again! You tell 'em. You all's wearing me out!"

"Whoa, check, brah, you got a talking bear in your garage!" Ramone corrected.

"You can understand it, too?" Justin asked.

"Not an it," TJ corrected again. "I'm a he—and I got feelins'." Turning to Larry, "Talk to this boy, would you? Tell him why you can understand me and he can't before he has a conniption."

Larry explained what he thought was going on. Justin got angry. "And you didn't tell me? Shou is my friend and so is Steve, and it's his dragon and…"

TJ folded his arms and looked at Justin, who suddenly stopped talking when the bear gave him a dirty look. TJ turned to Larry, "Why don't you ask him why he's covered with dragon magic?"

"Who?" Larry asked.

TJ smacked his own forehead in frustration and then pointed at Justin. "Him, the little one. He's the reason I found you all. I followed the trail of dragon magic being left all over town. First the marina, then that lighthouse, and then booyah! I smell me some more magic, and it's all over that boy."

Larry moved closer to his brother, "He says you've got dragon magic all over you. Maybe you should tell us how you really learned to surf?" As Justin started to explain, Ramone pulled out his cell phone and pulled Fred closer to TJ. "Fred, go stand next to the bear so I can get a pic."

Chapter 43

The house was dark; the only light seeping beneath the bedroom door came from a laptop. Berit was waiting for a reply from Iceland. Everything was going as planned. Halldor and Brita were out creating mayhem while she awaited instructions for her next move. Not that she needed any; Berit was used to acting autonomously. She knew a cargo ship left Iceland two weeks ago—a very special cargo ship. The resting dragon in its hold would not be disturbed until the boat crossed from the Atlantic to the Pacific and traveled far up the western coast of Canada. Only then, away from most populated areas, would the great dragon wake and fly the rest of the way. Berit was tracking the ship's progress. She had two, perhaps three days.

Things were going well; they were making life miserable for people around here, and she felt reasonably confident that she had temporarily isolated the boy from his friends. The only hiccup was that Shou had not interfered thus far That part bothered her, somewhat. What was that old crone up to? Berit didn't fear much of anything, but she had a healthy respect for her ancient adversary.

Berit was also frustrated that they hadn't found the young dragon. Of course, they wouldn't have attacked it directly. It was against the rules and—depending on how powerful it had become possibly suicidal. They might have woken it up, though. Now, they were forced to disturb it in an indirect way by harassing all the things it cared for. "Ah, sweet revenge," Berit sighed. Shou had stolen this dragon away when it was only a ball of magic, but their rivalry had existed for millennia; it was Berit's turn to win.

Still, she knew better than to rely on luck, and she expected Shou to make her presence known at some point—probably when it was least convenient. As long as Berit kept her attacks within reason and avoided casualties, Shou would have little cause to step in directly. She would focus instead on the dragon.

It was a good plan, Berit decided—especially the part about severing Steve from his friends. Berit loved manipulating humans; it was her forte. Blowing things up, causing fires…those were for the young ones like Halldor and Brita. They'd revel in destruction; blasting humankind back to the stone ages was as far as their imaginations could take them. Berit's approach was subtler: a little lie, a little favor here and there, and mankind would walk itself into obscurity.

She considered contacting the boy again to see how he liked his new self. By now, he would have discovered what it meant to be agile, coordinated, and normal. He'd soon discover that being able to surf was the smallest part of the gift he'd been given. Now, he'd know when to say the right thing; he would be able to pick up on social cues, not be such an outcast. She'd gone further than perhaps she needed to—she'd tweaked that part of his brain, that unique part that made him memorize everything and that allowed him to focus on tiny details for hours. *Normal,* she mused. *What a disgusting idea.*

Berit felt so good that she got up from the desk and pirouetted around the room. When she passed the mirror, she stopped. A thousand faces appeared in her mind, all the beautiful men and women she'd been and all those silly fools who had fallen in love with them. How many hearts had she broken? Justin was another in a long line of poor, lovesick dolts she'd duped over the centuries, and he wouldn't be the last. Not until she put these humans back in their place—back to the caves from whence they came. Only this time when they crawled out, the dragons wouldn't make the same mistake. This time the dragons would know better than to give them fire!

Berit took a step closer to the mirror. Her tiny perfect pearl white teeth elongated, and her nose flattened and flared out. Her eyes grew wider, changing to the color of flame. She stopped the transformation midway with her neat little bob of blond hair perched on her head. Then she smiled and curtsied for the mirror. "Love this, you silly fools," she laughed aloud, her teeth sharp and gleaming beneath the soft light of a computer screen.

Chapter 44

Larry dropped Ramone and Fred off at his van. "Brah, aren't you gonna wait and see if it works?" Fred asked.

TJ rolled down the rear window and assured them that, if they followed his instructions, the van would be fine. Larry shrugged, "Brahs, we gotta go. I have to get these guys to the hospital. Good luck."

From the back seat, Justin said, "Hurry, Larry. He could die!" And less loudly, "It's all my fault."

In the backseat, TJ reached over and patted Justin with a large paw and shook his head. Meanwhile, Larry drove as quickly as he could. Justin leaned forward, willing them to get there faster. He was miserable.

Justin had been right in the middle of telling everyone how Berit had gifted him with super-human surfer powers, when his mother barged in with news that Steve was in the hospital. When she saw the bear, Justin thought she'd freak out, but TJ had quickly reassured her with a little wave that he was housebroken. Fortunately, everybody knew about Steve's connection to the dragon, which had saved precious time. With only a bit more reassurance that the black bear was on their side, Justin's mom agreed to let the boys take the car with a promise that they'd call as soon as they found out anything about Steve.

When they finally arrived at the brightly-lit hospital, Larry pulled into the circular drive in front of the emergency room. "What are you doing?" TJ asked.

"What do you mean?" Larry asked. "I thought you could do some magic stuff and go right in."

Even though he didn't understand the conversation, it was Justin who answered. "He can't use magic around Steve. Just park somewhere and let me go in."

Larry looked back in the rearview mirror. "You sure, little brah? You know what that will mean."

Justin nodded. "Yeah, I do." He jumped out of the car and ran into the hospital, momentarily exhilarated by how fast he could move. He juked past an elderly couple and booked it towards the hospital lobby. Giving all this up would be hard, Justin knew, but the choice between his best friend and his newfound skills was an easy one; Justin would do anything for his friend. He did feel guilty, though, for enjoying himself as much as he had.

If Steve hadn't gotten sick, would he have stayed away from him to become a surf god like his brother, or to not be such a social cripple? Maybe, Justin realized, and that's what made him feel so awful. Still, he could apologize later. First, he had to know what was happening.

He found Steve's family in the emergency room lobby. Mrs. Batista ran over and gave him a big hug. "We've tried everyone. Do you know where Shou is?" she asked.

Before he could reply, Dani jumped up and looked at him. "You look different." Granny came over, as well. "She's right. What's going on, boy?"

Justin sighed, "It's nothing." He smiled and gave Dani an affectionate nudge, "Don't worry about it, kid. It won't last."

Dani cocked her head, rubbing the shoulder he'd willingly touched, her mouth rounded in surprise. Before she could say anything else, Justin squared off with the rest of the family and answered Mrs. Batista's question. "She's with the dragon. What happened to Steve?"

"It's a long story, and we need to get hold of her as soon as we can," Jeanie replied.

Justin shook his head, "I don't think that's possible, but if you tell me what happened I might be able to help."

Everyone looked at him. Justin was an amazingly smart kid, but what could he do to help? And why was he so calm and confident? Something wasn't right. "Please, we don't have a lot of time," he continued. "Tell me what happened."

Roger stepped forward and filled Justin in, adding little possibilities as he went.

"So, you think it's like before, then, when he absorbed that magic in the classroom?" Justin asked.

Jeanie answered, "That's what we think, except that the fire was huge, and Steve might have absorbed way too much of it. It's burning him up."

"Shou sent someone to help," Justin announced. "He's with me, but we might have a problem. Any ideas how we might get a bear in here?"

Chapter 45

There were two voice messages and at least a half dozen missed calls from Steve's mom on Joy's phone. Joy had just returned to her room, and had only checked her phone as an afterthought. Why was Steve's mom calling? Joy was worried. She stared down at the phone. Could she listen to the voicemail? Did that count as contact with Steve? If it was Steve's mom and not Steve, then was Steve in trouble? Was he hurt? She didn't know what to do.

A soft knock on her door startled her. "Honey, it's Dad. You okay?"

What should she say? "I'm okay," she answered.

Her dad came in. "You don't sound okay. What's the matter?"

Joy's parents knew all about Steve's dragon and Joy's part in that story, but she hadn't gotten around to talking about the latest venture into the magical dragon world. She suddenly felt the urge to explain it all to her dad. She needed someone to help her decide what to do.

Her dad took her silence as hesitation, "Come on, Joy, you can tell me anything. Is it about your mom? Or maybe about school? Friends?"

"I'm scared, Dad," she finally blurted out. "A man told me today that if I stopped talking to Steve for a while, Mom would be okay. And she was, is—"

"A man? What man?" her dad asked.

"No, Dad, he wasn't actually a man," Joy struggled to tell the story without having to explain everything. "Dad, do you remember Shou? The old lady who brought Justin back? Well, she's like this half-dragon and—"

"What? Jesus, Joy, what's going on?" her father demanded.

"It's okay, really, it's just that there are these sort-of dragons who look like people. Shou is one and she is trying to protect Steve's dragon—"

Her dad interrupted, "I didn't think anyone has seen his dragon in a while."

Joy nodded, "They haven't. That's because it's, like, going to have a baby, or an egg, or something. So anyway, there are these dragon people and one of them told me that if I stayed away from Steve for a while, then Mom would be all right."

Her dad stood up, a worried look on his face. "And you think that's why your mom is better now?"

She nodded.

"I wonder how they knew about her…being sick. When did they get to town, again?" he asked.

"I wondered that, too," Joy admitted, catching his drift. "That's part of the problem. It's like, she was doing fine until they showed up. When she came home tonight, acting normal and without any medication…"

"I don't know if what they did cured your mom or not," her dad added, "but, even if they did, what makes you think you can trust them, or that she would stay this way once they have what they want?"

Joy pulled her knees up and wrapped her arms around them. "I don't know that. And now Steve's mom is calling. I think something bad is happening, but—"

"But you're worried if you answer, you'll hurt your mother. Oh, baby…no one should have to make a choice like that." He sat down next to her on the bed and put a large arm around her.

"I don't know what to do, Dad," Joy admitted.

He sat there with her for a long time, neither speaking. Joy wondered if he'd know what to do. Eventually, Joy's mother hollered from the other room, asking if everything was all right. "Fine, babe," her father yelled back. "We'll be right out."

As he stood, his phone vibrated in his pocket. He pulled it out and looked at the screen. "It's Jeanie. If she's been calling all of us, it's probably important." It buzzed again and then went to voicemail.

Joy's dad gave her a sad smile. "Joy, listen, with this magic stuff, I don't know what's real or what can be changed...but if your friend is in trouble, then it's not right for these people, things, whatever, to hold your mother hostage. I want your mom healthy as much as you do, but not with strings attached. What do you think?"

"I want Mom to be okay," she started. "But if Steve needs me, then I think you're right."

He handed her his phone.

Chapter 46

Roger held the door open at the side of the hospital—the door his classmates had used to sneak out for a cigarette when they'd observed at the hospital. The doctors and nurses knew about it, too, but, luckily, no one was about.

Three forms slunk from an SUV, first Larry, then Justin, and finally, a large black bear. Larry slipped behind one of the trees that surrounded the parking lot and motioned for the others to hurry. Justin and the bear were almost across when a car pulled in, sweeping them in its headlights. Somehow the driver missed them and pulled into an empty parking slot; he must not have been paying attention.

Roger stepped out when the coast was clear and motioned for them to hurry up. "Come on, quick," he whispered.

The brothers rushed in while the bear lumbered past on all fours. They all blinked in the brightly-lit hospital hallway. "Mr. Batista," Justin said, "this is TJ."

Roger started to extend his hand and then retracted it; maybe offering up a perfectly good arm to a bear was not a good idea. But TJ stood up on his hind legs and scooped him up in a big old hug. "You, my brother, are a dragon-keeper; we's practically blood, baby!"

After he dropped Roger back to the floor he continued, "Okay, so enough parlayin', where's the boy? I can feel dragon magic oozing everywhere."

Unfortunately, Roger hadn't been given any of Shou's magic to understand TJ, so all he heard was the bear growling. Larry loosely translated for TJ, "Ah, he says hello."

TJ raised an eyebrow, "Hello?" and then started to waddle down the hall, but Roger hissed, "Wait, tell him to wait."

"He can understand you; you just can't understand him. Neither can Justin," Larry explained.

Justin shrugged.

Roger pointed to the mobile hospital bed, "Okay, then, ah, TJ can you climb aboard?"

TJ looked like he was going to protest, but Roger quickly added, "It's made for obese patients, rated to hold 1,000 pounds." He looked again at the bear, head tilted a bit. "I think it'll hold him, maybe."

"Hmm, don't be hatin' on the bear's weight. Hibernation is celebration," TJ replied, as he climbed up on the contraption, which groaned, but held. He flipped one way, and then another, and finally settled on his stomach. Roger threw a white sheet over him and then pulled out a thin pair of scrubs, what all hospital staff wear, from under the gurney. He slipped them on over his clothes and said, "You boys go on back to the emergency waiting room. If someone sees me, I know my way around enough to come up with something."

Roger set off with his unusual patient as the boys returned the way they had come. The brothers barely rounded the corner when a young woman almost ran them down. Roger heard her and quickly positioned himself so she couldn't tell that the patient was completely covered. The young woman stopped and barely looked up from her phone. Roger greeted her with a tentative hello, and TJ started to compliment her choice of footwear—she wore a pair of comfy-looking Chucks—but Roger kicked the gurney. The woman smiled and made her way past them.

Justin followed his brother into the emergency room and found the rest of Steve's family. Steve's mom was getting off the phone when they entered. "Hey boys, that was Joy. I was trying to see if she knew where Shou was."

Larry answered, "Not here. That's why she asked me and my compadres to help out. She's dragon-sitting."

"Oh," Jeanie replied, "well, alright. I guess that explains why I can't reach her. Thanks?"

Larry smiled, "No problemo, happy to serve. Ramone and Fred are out de-magicing, or magifying, or whatever—they're undoing some of the bad dragons' magic."

Jeanie looked at Justin, "She also said one of them tried to keep her away from Steve, tried to make some kind of deal with her."

Justin blushed. "Yeah, sorry, Berit—"

Jeanie waved it aside. "You came, so whatever happened doesn't matter; you're here."

Dani strolled up and gave Justin a little push, similar to the one he'd given her earlier. When he didn't recoil, she eyed him suspiciously, "You're different. Something is different. What'd you do?"

"Nothing, I swear," Justin explained. "Berit promised a whole bunch of stuff if I stayed away from Steve, but I didn't."

Dani look dubious, "Maybe, but you seem weird."

Justin knew she was right, of course. He wasn't his normal spastic self. He didn't feel compelled to blurt out the first thing that came into his head, and he still felt, well, coordinated, like he could walk and chew gum at the same time. Whatever Berit had done to him hadn't been undone.

Yet.

Chapter 47

Fred and Ramone loitered in front of the disabled van, which sat on the side of the road. Crescent City's foghorn blared every few seconds and the street light only partially lit up the vehicle.

"What are we supposed to do again?" Fred asked.

Ramone looked down at the pink plastic sand bucket and the little blue shovel inside. "Check it, brah, you were there. You know, we're supposed to use this stuff and make the magic disappear."

Fred answered, "Yeah, I got that, but, like, how much?"

Ramone looked in the bucket and accidently got a whiff of the concentrated bear poop. "Whoa, God, smell this!"

"No way, Jose, I trust you. Go ahead and try it."

Ramone took the little shovel and scooped out a bit of what the hunters called bear scat, which was hunter talk for poop. He stood in front of one of the blown tires. "Dude, you think I should smear it on, or just kind of fling it?"

Fred cocked his head in deep thought. "You should smear it. If that doesn't work, then you should like rub it on like finger paint."

"You're a donk," Ramone answered, but he took the shovel and spread a little of the disgusting stuff on one of the wheels. Nothing happened. "Ah, man, this is weak. I can't believe—"

The tire began to slowly inflate itself, then another one started and finally all the rest. "Righteous! Check it, Fred."

"That's some potent poop, brah!" Fred exclaimed.

Ramone handed the bucket to him. "What's up? Why you handing that to me?"

"Because, brah, I'm driving, so you get to hold the bucket."

Reluctantly Fred reached for it. "Check it, I'll just put it in the back."

Ramone shook his head, "No way, brah. You want that to spill all over the van?"

"This is whack," Fred grumbled, but climbed into the passenger seat anyway.

For the next hour, Ramone drove them around town, and whenever they thought they saw something out of the ordinary, Fred would jump out of the van and fling a little bear poop on it. Of course, not everything they stopped to fix was the result of dark dragon magic, but it was better to be safe than sorry. Besides, so what if a few people got up the next day to find their mailboxes covered in animal poo? Maybe they should have less silly-looking mailboxes.

After making several runs through town, Ramone pulled over. "Can you think of any place we left?"

"Naw, brah, we've been all over," Fred answered. "Wait, what about the marina? It's a wreck!"

"How much poop we got left?" Ramone asked.

Reluctantly, Fred tilted up the bucket and peered inside. "We're almost out. I don't think we have enough. See?"

"Ah, dude, get that out of my face! It stinks," Ramone exclaimed.

Fred put the bucket back down on the floorboard between his feet. "Okay, so what do we do next?"

"I don't know. Why don't you call Larry while I head over to the marina? Maybe we can mix that stuff with water and still use it."

"Ah," Fred replied, "yeah, like my mother does to the dish soap."

"You add water to dish soap?" asked Ramone.

"Brah, you've been to my house. We add extra water to everything—it's free!"

Chapter 48

Roger entered the emergency room, leaving TJ in the hall and hoping no one would come by and discover him. It wasn't busy. Only a couple of the curtained areas were closed with patients inside. There were two, no, make that three, nurses going back and forth. Roger saw that the curtain surrounding Steve was open and two physicians were with him. There was no way he could get the bear in here, or Steve out. Confounded, he returned to TJ.

Roger lifted the sheet. "There are way too many people in there. I can't get you in. We'll have to think of something else." He pulled out his phone and started texting his wife to see if she had any ideas.

The next thing Roger knew, the bear had thrown off the blankets and dropped off the gurney. Standing on his hind legs, TJ twisted left and then right, cracking his back. "What are you doing? Someone will see you." TJ growled something Roger didn't understand and then walked boldly into the emergency room.

For a second nothing happened; everyone stopped and stared. Black bears were a common site around the area, but a novelty in the emergency room. Sensing the moment slipping away, TJ roared and pushed a medicine cart across the room. That had the desired effect. One of the nurses screamed while another one ran out of the room. The two doctors in attendance jumped behind one of the beds and got on their phones. TJ was trying to herd them all out front into the waiting room. Most had taken the hint, even the two patients, neither of whom had injuries as serious as those they might end up with after being mauled by a black bear. However, when TJ got in front of Steve's curtain, one brave nurse grabbed a clipboard and started swatting at him, yelling for him to shoo.

TJ snatched it, careful not to hurt the woman, and bit it in half. That was enough to scare the brave nurse out of the room. In the meantime, Roger slipped in and ran to Steve. He was all hooked up to IVs and wrapped in ice packs. Roger expertly disconnected his son and started wheeling him back to where they had entered the building. Once Roger had a good lead, TJ dropped down on all fours and galloped through the waiting room and out the front door. He was hiding behind Larry's SUV before the hospital's aged security guard even made it to the ER.

The commotion out front allowed Roger to roll Steve to the back door and slip him out. When he saw the black bear waving at him across the parking lot, he lifted his boy and carried him to TJ. Reluctantly, Roger handed Steve over and then jogged back to the waiting room to join his family and the frazzled medical staff. A siren announced the arrival of a sheriff's deputy, who jumped out of his car and burst in with his gun drawn.

One of the nurses asked the officer, "Did you see any bears out there? We had a crazed bear here a minute ago!"

Roger spoke up, "Yeah, I did. Here, I'll show you where it ran." Roger took the deputy out and pointed in the wrong direction, away from TJ and Steve. As everyone else crowded outside, Roger leaned over to his wife, "I'll go with Larry and the bear. Go ahead and follow with everyone else."

A few minutes later, Larry drove out of the parking lot, with Roger and Steve up front and TJ occupying the entire back seat. "Where are we going?" Roger asked.

"Head to the marina, boo," TJ replied. "We can siphon off all that magic and do some good at the same time."

All Roger heard was, "Growl, growl, growl," so Larry translated.

"Okay, but hurry. He's burning up!"

Chapter 49

The cave was heating up again. Shou had not had a chance to revert to her human form; the hazardous conditions in the cave were more than her other form could handle. Waves of hot grey and white smoke streamed from the dragon's nostrils, making it impossible to see more than a few inches. The slumbering beast inhaled and exhaled like a giant set of bellows. Every few minutes, it kicked a leg out and rocked the whole cave.

Shou looked up, not completely sure that the dragon wouldn't bury them both. This was Berit's doing. Whatever she and her friends were accomplishing was causing this dragon tremendous distress. Shou's song was no longer working; Dragau was going to wake up, and it wasn't going to be days from now, it was going to be hours. For the time being, though, there was nothing she could do about that, so she bounded out of the cave on her powerful rear legs.

The cool autumn air stung after the oppressive heat inside. Shou zigzagged her way through the trees and up the ravine to a relatively open spot where the night sky poked in. There she rose to her full height and spoke to the woods.

Chapter 50

The docks were busy. Powerful floodlights had been brought in to supplement the existing lighting. Some industrial-sized backhoes and other heavy equipment were being used to try and push larger piles of debris from causing further damage. Many emergency vehicles remained, and there were half a dozen cop cars parked nearby. Larry approached warily, looking for somewhere they could park and do whatever they were supposed to do without being seen. He eventually found a large metal building with no lights on one side. Jeanie pulled in right after him.

As soon as they parked, TJ informed Larry what had to be done. He needed to sit with Steve and help the boy expel all the pent-up magic inside, all the magic that was eating him up. "Unfortunately," TJ said, "it might not be safe for y'all non-magic folk, so y'all need to clear out and leave me with the boy."

Jeanie didn't want to leave her son's side.

"Shou sent him to help us," Roger reassured everyone. "He's going to be fine. I know he'll be fine," he repeated.

"Sure he will," Dani agreed. "It's just like when Shou did it back at the house."

"He wasn't this sick back home," Jeanie replied. "This seems so much worse."

Granny hugged her daughter-in-law close. "He'll be fine. The longer we stay here, the more danger he's in."

Justin stood a little apart. He still felt different, both mentally and physically, almost like he had been a bunch of wires all knotted up and something had straightened them out. He wondered how long whatever Berit had done to him would last, or if it would disappear once TJ helped Steve. Knowing there wasn't much he could do, but still feeling guilty despite

Jeanie's reassurance that he wasn't at fault, Justin moved toward the warehouse door to keep watch. No one paid him much attention, though Jeanie mumbled something about being careful as she and Roger walked past.

When he got to the door, Justin tried a couple of things. First, he stood on one leg, balancing for a while—too easy. He tried a cartwheel and was pretty sure he did it correctly. *Weird,* he thought. Then he had an idea, something that he'd seen his brother do a hundred times. Justin leaned down and placed both hands on the ground. Then he kicked up his hind legs using the forward thrust to keep his balance. He was walking on his hands. "Wow! Oh, wow!" He couldn't believe it. It wasn't only a couple of steps, either; he was so balanced that he began hand-walking in a circle. He was going around for the second time when he saw two pink-and-white colored Sketchers. Still balancing, he said, "Hello?"

Dani bent down and tilted her head up at him. "What are you doing?"

"Oh, it's you. Hey, Dani," Justin managed.

"Why are you walking around on your hands, Justin?" she asked. "Also, how?"

Justin collapsed his arms and dropped down on his behind. Even that was done with some grace.

"What's going on, Justin?" Dani demanded. "How come you can magically walk on your hands all of a sudden? Oh, wait, wait a minute. Magic. What have you done? What's going on? You better tell me."

Justin put his hands up in surrender, "Really, Dani, I haven't done anything. It's kind of a long story."

Dani pointed her finger at him, "See, like that. You don't even sound like you!"

Before he could explain further, a van blaring music turned the far corner and headed their way. "Hey, look, it's Ramone and Fred," Justin announced.

"Uh-uh, no you don't," Dani said. "You better tell me."

"Hold on a sec, Dani. They've got to turn down that music," Justin announced and ran to meet the van. Larry also came running over.

"Brahs," Justin said as reached the van. "You're making too much noise. Someone will see us back here."

"Brahs? Did you say Brahs?" Larry asked.

Justin turned to his older brother, "What, I can't say "brahs"?"

Ramone poked his head out. "Only if you're in the women's section at Macy's," he laughed and high-fived Fred.

"Yeah, you're hilarious," Justin replied.

"No, really brah," Larry continued, "you know, you aren't a guy who says 'brah.' You know what I mean."

Justin did know. His brother was right; he didn't talk like Larry or his friends. Was he turning into one of them? Sure, now he could surf, but what else did Berit change in him? Without another word, he walked off.

"Hey, where's he going?" Ramone asked. "Brah, I was only kidding. You can say 'brah.' It's cool."

"Leave it, brah, it's got to do with whatever that dragon-chick did to him," Larry explained. "Any luck?"

"Check it, brah," Ramone said, "we've been all over town and graffitied anything weird with bear dookie. See?" He held up the almost empty sand pail.

"Eww, that stinks. Cool. Go ahead and park behind the—"

A bright flash stopped Larry from finishing his directions. He turned and saw that the light had come from his parents' SUV. "I hope that's a good sign," he said.

Chapter 51

Justin moved off by himself, far enough away to avoid any more questions, but close enough to see the light emanating from their car. *Good,* he thought, *maybe TJ is doing what Shou did earlier.* Ramone had been right. *Brah? What was happening to him?* He didn't talk like that, he didn't know how to surf, and he couldn't walk on his hands. He needed to talk to Steve, but that wasn't possible right now. That left Joy, and, even though they were friends, Justin realized he usually didn't talk to her about truly important things without Steve present. It had always been like Steve was the nucleus and Justin and Joy circled around, interacting, but not really in the same orbit. For some reason that bothered him now in a way it never had before.

The light from the SUV continued to shine, and Justin was about to go back when his phone rang. It was Joy. "Hello, Justin, you there?"

"Yeah, it's me."

"It's Joy. I tried calling Steve's mom, but there's no answer. How is he? Is everything alright?"

"I'm not sure," Justin admitted. "Everyone's at the marina and TJ is trying to help him, like Shou did earlier."

"Who is TJ?" Joy asked.

"It's a long story, but basically TJ's someone Shou sent to help. He's a dragon like she is."

"God, how many are there?"

"Several, hey, listen for a minute," Justin asked. "I, I don't know how to explain this…"

"Go ahead," Joy urged, though she sounded confused, as if Justin being at a loss for words were like hearing that the floor was actually the ceiling.

Justin told her everything, about the chatting, about liking Berit, about suddenly being normal, no…better than normal. And about feeling very guilty. "I swear, Joy," he continued, "I wouldn't do anything to hurt Steve."

"Don't you see, Justin? You're there. You haven't done anything wrong."

"Yeah, but—"

"No, you listen, you can't help what Berit did to you," Joy said. "You haven't betrayed anyone." And then, after a pause, "I guess, I haven't either."

"What do you mean?" Justin asked.

"One of Berit's friends offered to cure my mom if I left Steve alone. And I did. I didn't answer when his mom called at first."

"That's not right, Joy," Justin said. "How can you be expected to make a choice like that? These people, these things suck. I mean it. I wish I had never heard of dragons." Justin paused, startled by the intensity of his anger. He took a deep breath. "Anyway, what are you going to do? Wait a minute, you've already decided, didn't you? That's why you talked to Steve's mom."

"I talked to my dad. He says it wasn't right to have to make a deal like that."

"Has your mom, you know, reverted?" Justin ventured.

"No, not yet," she answered. "I thought that as soon as I called she would change, but she hasn't."

"Me, neither," he replied.

"You do sound different," Joy admitted, "less…I don't know…"

"Geeky?"

"No, that's not it," Joy said. "You know how you get, going off on certain things, forgetting that you're still in the middle of a conversation. You, sometimes stop connecting with people."

Justin laughed, "Yup, that's me, the distracted robot."

"It's not funny."

Justin sighed, "No, it's really not. It's not only how I'm communicating; I can walk and chew gum. I could probably walk, chew gum, and do somersaults at the same time." He paused, "But it's not me. I know that. It's like someone put me back together, but I didn't know I was broken." Before he could continue, Justin heard someone calling for him. They were probably wondering where he was. Justin began walking back toward the group and then stopped. For a minute, he had to cover his eyes as a brilliant stream of white light poured from his mom's car. It wasn't just a flash this time. It lit up the entire rear of the building they were parked behind.

"Justin, what is it?" Joy asked.

Justin tried to open his eyes by looking down, but bright blue dots appeared so he shut them again. "There's a blinding light," he started, "it's so intense, I can't see anything right now. I hope it means that Steve is going to be okay."

"That's what happened when Shou helped him last time," Joy explained. "I'm going to get my dad to bring me out there," Joy announced.

Before he could answer her, Justin heard someone hoot, then another, then more hollering. He cracked open his eyes and saw that the light was gone. Still seeing spots, he ran to where TJ was administering to his friend. "Hold on, Joy. Let me see what's happening."

The small group was hovering around the SUV. TJ lumbered out of the side door and flopped on the ground. Lying flat on his back, the exhausted bear growled something that Justin didn't understand and waved everyone to the car. Justin approached more cautiously and saw that Roger and Jeanie had reached in for their son. Dani pushed between all, "Is he all right now?"

"He's not hot anymore," Jeanie said. "His fever is gone!"

Justin could see that he was still out. He turned to find Larry speaking to TJ. "Larry, ask him why he's not waking up? What's he saying?"

Larry turned around and answered, "He says he's tired right now. He'll be fine. Come on, TJ says to go and check out what's happening in the bay."

Larry ran off with his two best buds in tow. Dani started off as well, but Granny told her to hold on a minute. "It's okay, Mom," Roger said. "Go ahead and take her. We'll be right here."

Justin followed closely behind and then remembered that he had Joy on the phone. "Hey, you there?"

Apparently, she had gotten tired of waiting and hung up. Oh, well, he'd call her back as soon as he knew what was happening. He rounded the corner of the building and saw everyone standing around and pointing. He heard things like "It's a miracle" or "I can't believe it!" He found where his brother and friends were and headed toward them.

"Brahs," he heard Ramone say, "check it, we don't even have to get the bear poop!"

Justin saw what had everyone's attention. The giant crush of trash, metal, and miscellaneous junk was heading back out to sea. To anyone looking, it might have seemed only to be the tide, but it was clear to Justin that the trash was magically being swept out. People down by the marina started taking video and pics from their phones, which reminded him to call Joy back.

"Hey, sorry, I kind of got sidetracked," Justin apologized.

"It's fine, but how's Steve?" Joy asked.

"He's good, and guess where all that magic he was holding ended up?"

"No clue," Joy answered.

"Okay, so he magically shoved about a million tons of garbage back out into the open ocean," Justin explained and then he added, "Well, he may not have done it; It might have been TJ using the extra magic. I'm not sure."

Joy was quiet for a minute. "Can I talk to Steve?"

"Can't yet. He's still out of it, but his fever is gone. I'm actually not near him right now anyway. You want me to go and see if he's awake?"

"No," Joy answered. "Don't wake him up for me. I'm a little worried. That's all."

"Why?" Justin asked. "He's going to be okay and it looks like he's saved the marina."

"If he can undo all that magic," Joy started, "isn't he going to make someone really upset?"

"Yeah, you're right. I didn't think of that."

Chapter 52

Dragau was waking too soon. Shou skittered around the collapsing cave as rocks tumbled around her. Hot jets of fire and smoke exploded from the groggy dragon. When a giant wing broke completely free of the cave, all Shou could do was get out of the way. Like a determined lizard, she scrambled up the ravine and clung to a spot above the destruction.

Only hours earlier, she'd put out a call to all the magical beings in the region: there were many. Since she had found this beautiful, isolated place centuries earlier, she'd brought many minor dragons here. A few were strong, intelligent personalities like TJ—though without his power—and some were simple souls like her tree friends. Shou watched with sympathy as the dragon broke out of his home of the last two years. She could only imagine the poor beast's confusion. A dragon's regular sleep was normal—its mind remained active and aware—but this was the breeder's sleep, and it was supposed to be so deep that nothing disturbed it. That he would wake up disoriented was normal. That did not overly worry her; rather, Shou was concerned because a dragon awakened prematurely may not have had enough rest to be ready to fight.

Shou didn't try and communicate with Dragau, not yet. She knew from experience that he wouldn't be capable of understanding. He would spend the next several hours slowly becoming more aware. Unfortunately, he would suffer during that time. His magic was condensing within him, concentrating itself to a single point for the creation of new life. This process left the dragon with almost no magic of his own, and it hurt. The pain made the animal fierce and ready to fight. But, if the battle didn't start soon, Dragau would start destroying things. Shou knew this was Berit's plan. Wake this one early and let him weaken himself and then a stronger, older dragon would come and defeat him. Unfortunately, Shou had seen this strategy too many times to doubt its effectiveness. What was worse, this dragon was so connected to his land and people that disturbing Dragau's slumber had been even easier than usual.

A sound brought her back to herself. She turned and saw a doe approach through the trees. Soon, other disguised dragons started arriving. There were a pair of rabbits and a red fox. From the air came a turkey vulture and a great blue heron. This wasn't all of them; many magical spirits were immobile, having taken the forms of giant trees or boulders. Others were insects who could not overcome the distances to get here. And there were those who wore human forms like the Modoc medicine man living near Happy Camp. But he and she had a falling out years ago, and she wasn't sure he would come. Finally, a blue squirrel appeared. "Do I know you?" Shou asked.

"You mean, am I one of yours?" it answered. "Course not, but I heard your call. So here I am." It then started picking something under its arm.

Shou hesitated a moment.

She'd thought she knew every minor dragon in this part of the world; she had in fact, deposited most of them. However, it was entirely possible that the squirrel had recently arrived, or perhaps avoided her radar. Before she could contemplate it further, the newcomer said, "My friends call me Jackie."

Shou nodded, "I'm—"

"Shou, I know. Heard lots of good things about you."

"From whom?" she asked dubiously.

"Oh, you know, here and there. That's not important." The squirrel craned its head to eye the thrashing dragon in the background and pointedly stared, as if reminding her to focus on the task at hand. "Why don't you tell us what you need?"

To Shou, all the animals appeared as they truly were, creatures of magic, minor dragons all. Some were larger and some were smaller and all were wingless and sinewy like her. None, however, were as powerful as she was; few dragonettes anywhere were; Berit was an exception. Shou drew them all away from the awakening giant to a spot where she could prepare them for the coming trials.

In her dragon tongue, Shou showed them Berit and her friends and gave them visions of past battles between great dragons. The ground shook in the middle of her explanation and they all turned as one.

Dragau had completely broken out.

Shou realized she was pressed for time. She needed to send some of these creatures back out, to reach those who could not come and explain what was happening. The rest, she would keep with her to help her prepare.

The odds were long, Shou knew. Younger breeder dragons capable of growing an egg rarely defeated the older, more powerful ones. And yet, there was something special about this one; she felt it in her bones. This one had a chance; Dragau was closer to its humans than any dragon she had ever known, and this place was special, too. From the first time she had come here centuries before, she'd felt it, felt the magic of this place. It was why she'd started bringing minor dragons here, and, even as the world became covered in concrete—its magic capped beneath human feet—this place remained pristine, admired by the humans, but not overrun. That was part of her plan, in fact; she had brought so many minor dragons here, it was like she had seeped the area in even more magic. If she could give Dragau time, he had a chance—they would all have a chance.

Chapter 53

The Crescent City miracle was all over the news. When the junk from Japan first landed, it warranted 30 seconds on national television. Now that the giant mass of debris had inexplicably reversed itself and headed back out to sea, reporters had returned to the little town on the northern coast for a more extensive follow-up. Steve woke with a massive headache and plodded into the kitchen where his mom and dad were listening to the reports on the radio.

"Hey, look who's up," Roger greeted him.

"You want something to eat, sweetie?" his mother asked and then added, "Maybe something light like a yogurt, or some oatmeal?"

Steve started to shake his head, but it hurt too much. "No," he croaked.

His dad pulled a chair out, "Here, sport, sit before you fall down. How you feeling?"

"I'm okay, but my head hurts."

Jeanie approached with a glass of water and a couple of Ibuprofen. "Here, take these."

"Why aren't you guys at work?" Steve asked.

"Not today, son," Roger replied. "I've got a feeling that we all need to stay together today."

"What time is it?"

"Almost ten."

Granny came in the back door with Dani right behind. "Well, it's good to see you alive and kicking, boy. How're you feeling?"

Steve groaned. Was everyone going to keep asking him that? Before he could answer, his sister ran over and crushed him in a hug. "I'm so glad you didn't die, jerk!"

Steve winced, but didn't complain. "I'm all right. What happened?"

"Oh, you almost died," Dani began, "and then we had to take you to the hospital, only that didn't help. So, TJ came, he's a bear, then we broke out. We took you to the boat docks and, oh, Justin, he can do cartwheels now which is really weird—"

"Dani," Roger interrupted, "I think you're confusing him."

"Come on, Dad, let me tell it," she continued. "So, TJ helped you get rid of the magic that was making you sick and you saved the marina."

"Dad?" Steve asked.

Jeanie and Roger looked at each other and smiled. "Well, yeah, son, I guess that pretty much sums it up."

"What?"

Something on the radio caught Roger's attention. "Shh, listen a minute. Never mind, I'll check the TV."

Roger went into the living room and searched for the remote. After removing a couple of pillows, he found it stuck between two couch cushions. He flicked it on and found a news station. Though they were talking about an upcoming folk celebration in Brookings, a streamer across the bottom announced that a freak hurricane had mysteriously formed off the coast of Canada and was moving south. He flipped around and found a channel that was talking about the strange weather phenomenon. A tropical cyclone had somehow completely caught weather scientists by surprise, and, additionally, it had somehow formed over cold water, which was essentially impossible: normally cold water killed hurricanes and typhoons. One expert was speculating that perhaps an El Niño had occurred and carried enough warm water north to account for the abnormal event.

"Roger, what is it?" Granny asked from the kitchen.

"Just a sec," he hollered back. The freak storm was rated a category one with winds above 74 miles per hour and very small in size, barely over 60 miles in diameter, but it was noteworthy because of its sudden appearance in the north Pacific.

Roger returned to the kitchen with a worried look on his face. "Did you catch the thing about an unusual storm forming off the western Canadian coast? They're calling it a category one hurricane."

"Roger," Jeanie replied, "that's impossible—"

"Yeah, it is," he cut her off. "It's small, but it's heading south, paralleling the coast about 50 miles per hour."

"And you think?" Granny asked.

"Yeah, I do," Roger answered.

Steve was looking back and forth between the exchanges. "Will someone tell me what you're talking about?"

Dani blurted, "It's a dragon, dummy."

"Dani! Knock it off. Leave your brother alone," Jeanie scolded.

"Yeah, but it is, isn't it? Am I right?"

Roger shrugged, "Maybe. It is a strange coincidence, if it's not somehow related. We need to find Shou."

"It's not our dragon," Steve said.

"No," Roger agreed, "I don't think it is."

"How long, Dad?" Steve asked.

"What?"

"How long until it gets here?"

"I think they showed it just north of the Washington border. That's, let me think a minute, maybe 600 or 700 miles? If it's coming south at 50 miles per hour, then…"

"Then it's 12 to 14 hours away," Steve finished before Dani could do the math. She gave him a dirty look.

Jeanie spoke up, "That's not long. Steve, if you're feeling better, we need to go to Justin's house. That's where TJ is staying and he might be able to get in touch with Shou."

"Who is this TJ?" Steve asked again.

"I told you," Dani almost yelled, "he's a bear! Don't you listen?"

Chapter 54

Justin walked into the living room and had flashbacks of when his brother was in high school; Ramone and Fred were both stretched out on opposite ends of the large sectional. They used to fit in Larry's old room when they were younger, but had outgrown the space after middle school. Justin used to think they were homeless; he even asked his mom about it once, but she'd laughed and said that strays were welcome.

Justin walked into the kitchen. There was a note on the counter and some scrambled eggs covered up in a big skillet on the stove. Justin didn't bother reading the note, figuring it was his mom telling him she and his dad were out. Justin could smell the coffee remaining in the pot, which had now gone cold. He tried the stuff a couple of times, but unless he loaded it with sugar and creamer, he couldn't stand it. Plus, his parents didn't want him to have the caffeine because he was already screwed up. Well, that's not what they said, but it's how it is, or was. That made him stop and question whether he was still enchanted. He was tempted to grab a surfboard out of the garage and test it, but with everything going on, it probably wasn't a good idea. Was he still different?

A muffled sound got his attention, and he proceeded out of the kitchen and back the way he'd come. Listening, he heard it again coming from Larry's room. The door was shut, but unlocked, so Justin slipped in. The window was open and the room itself was freezing. Larry had his head sandwiched between two pillows and all his laundry dumped on top of his bed for insulation. Snoring away, half in and half out of the closet, was the large black bear. Every once in a while, TJ moved and banged against the sliding door, which was the sound that Justin had heard earlier. Quietly, he backed out of the room and shut the door.

Justin returned to his own room and checked his computer again for correspondence from Berit. It wasn't that he wanted to hear from her; it was more like he was waiting for the other shoe to drop. She had to know that he didn't keep his end of the deal and wasn't going to stay away from Steve, right? He honestly half expected something nasty from her assuring him he would revert to his uncoordinated, socially-bumbling self. But there was nothing. He did notice that his phone had a missed call. He tentatively picked it up and was more than a little relieved to see that it was from Steve. He was about to call back when the house phone rang. They kept one, more out of habit than anything else.

It was Steve's dad. "Hi, Justin, it's Roger. Is TJ there?"

"Yeah, he's sleeping in Larry's room."

"Okay, do me a favor and don't let him go anywhere. We'll be right over."

"Mr. Batista, is everything okay? Is Steve all right?"

"He's fine, sorry to freak you out," Roger apologized. "It looks like we might be in for some more trouble and we need his advice. We should be there in a bit, okay?"

"Okay, bye." Justin hung up. What was going to happen next? Suddenly, he thought of Joy. If things were going to get crazy, then he thought she should know. He dialed her number and it went right to voicemail. *Darn,* he thought. *Well, hopefully, nothing will happen that will blindside her.* He stood in the living room staring down at the two stray boys, debating who to wake up first, when she called back.

"Hey, what's up?"

"Joy, Steve's dad called and said he thought there was going to be trouble. I wanted to make sure you knew, and uh, you know, to watch out."

There was a pause, "That was really nice of you, Justin. I'm at Denny's with my folks. Hang on a sec." There was a brief pause, and then Joy spoke again. "Sorry, I didn't want to talk right at the table. Mom's got an appointment with her shrink later. She's going to start back up with her meds."

"So she's back to normal? Or, well, you know what I mean." Justin said.

"No, she's doing well, but we talked it out this morning and she agreed that if this is some kind of spell or dragon magic, then it isn't real, so while she's got a level head we should plan on it going away."

Justin thought about that for a second. Not real. Would that include him too? If this new person wasn't real, then what did that make the old Justin?

"Justin? Hey, are you there?"

"Oh, sorry, Joy. Something you said made me think, that's all. Anyway, so you'll be with your parents?"

"No, I don't think so. I already asked if they could take me to Steve's house before they went to the appointment. Dad wasn't for it, but Mom talked him into it."

"Well, they're all headed to my house, so you might want to get dropped off here if you're leaving soon."

"Yeah, we're almost done. I'll see you in a few."

"Okay, bye."

"Bye, oh, and thanks, Justin," Joy added.

Chapter 55

Brita and Halldor pulled into the drive, but didn't immediately exit the car. Halldor moved first, slowly opening his door and stepping out. He took a couple of shuffling steps before he stopped and remembered to shut the car door. He looked at his companion and motioned for her to follow him. Brita nodded weakly and followed.

Berit heard the car and went to greet the pair. As soon as she opened the door, she knew something was wrong. Both young dragons looked exhausted. Brita's normally perfect exterior was off, disheveled. Some of her hair had slipped out from its proper place. Her normally rigid posture was bent. Halldor looked even worse. It appeared as if he had slept in his clothes. Berit started to ask what had happened, but hesitated. Something else was wrong.

She had expected to hear sirens, to smell smoke, to see panic. Instead, it was a wonderfully bright, cheery day. Birds chirped, a lone dog barked, an elderly man out for his morning stroll waved from across the street. "What's going on?" she demanded.

Neither answered immediately. "We've been—"

"Wait," Berit hissed, "inside."

As soon as she shut the door, she demanded, "Well, what have you been doing? I expected this town to be going insane by now."

Brita stiffened, pulling a stray clump of hair from her face. "We were doing our jobs! We lit fires, we blew things up, we caused some minor car wrecks on the highway, I, I don't know—"

"We even ran off a bunch of cows north of town." Halldor added.

"You ran off cows?" Berit tightly repeated, "Cows? You were supposed to create a war zone and you ran off some cows?"

Brita glared at Halldor. "Not just cows. Come on, Berit, we know our jobs. We messed with about everything we could think of. The cows were congregating by the road, so we let them out."

"Then something's wrong. You two get yourselves together. I'm going out for myself to see what's happening. Be ready when I get back. Our dragon is on its way."

Berit burst out of the front door and stomped to the car. She yanked open the door and sat in the front seat. In her present disguise, she could barely see over the steering wheel. She pounded the dashboard in anger. She was about to adopt another human shape when she heard the deep thwop, thwop of a large motorcycle. As the cyclist rounded the corner, Berit made a snap decision. She jumped out of the car and stepped out in front of the bike. The rider locked up his brakes and skidded to a stop right in front of her. The biker put his big booted feet down to hold up the enormous Harley Davison. He jutted his bearded face forward, ready to scream at her, but Berit cut him off with a wave of her hand. She was in no mood for niceties.

"Off," she demanded.

Without another word, the confused man lowered the kickstand and swung off the bike. Berit pushed him out of the way and climbed up on the chrome motorcycle. She needed to stand on the pegs to reach the ridiculously high handlebars. The bike kicked over and tilted itself upright. Berit twisted the throttle and skidded off down the road. The big man stood in the middle of the street and began to cry.

Chapter 56

Justin's whole house seemed to wake up the minute Steve and his family arrived. Everyone gathered in the large kitchen that opened onto the family room. Dani had made it her mission to wake up Ramone and Fred by jumping on them both. Jeanie insisted on calling Justin's parents to let them know what was going on and why they had invaded their home. Everything stopped when TJ waddled into the room. Wiping his sleepy eyes, he stood on his hind legs and approached the stove. He removed the lid from the frying pan and took a deep breath. "I thought I smelled eggs. Yum, yum," and then he scooped the whole batch into his mouth. He was chewing joyously when he stopped and turned around. "Oh, my bad. Did any of y'all want some?"

Ramone and Fred understood what he was saying, as did Steve, but to everyone else it was "growl, growl," chomp, chomp, "growl." Larry finally came in looking pretty haggard. He reached for a mug to pour himself some coffee and took a big swig before he realized it was cold. "Are you kidding me? Who let the coffee get cold?" Only then did he realize he had a house full of people. "Ah, what's up?"

While Roger started explaining, Steve found Justin and pulled him into the garage away from the crowded kitchen. "What's been happening? Dani said you're not you anymore. What's she talking about?"

Justin reddened and looked down. "It was Berit. She did something to me, made some of my quirks go away, and I'm a lot more coordinated."

"But why? Why would she do that for you?"

"It was to hurt you," Justin answered. "I was supposed to stay away from you. I guess she thought that if we left you—"

"We? Who's 'We'?"

"Joy and me. I'm sorry Steve—"

"You agreed to help her?" Steve asked.

Justin quickly shook his head, "No, I told you. I didn't agree to anything."

"I don't understand," Steve replied. "If you didn't help her, how come you can, you know—"

"What, like surf? Or act normal?"

"That's not what I meant," Steve answered uncomfortably.

Justin stepped closer, "Yeah, but it's true, isn't it? And why didn't you tell me about her?"

"Who, Berit? Man, I'm sorry, but I didn't want to hurt your feelings. I knew you kind of liked her."

"You let me have a crush on a dragon," Justin pointed out. "Plus, she said Shou lied to us. That all she wanted was to keep hiding dragons. Berit said her side wanted to bring dragons back out into the world."

"And you believed her? Come on."

"I never said I did," Justin replied defensively.

"What about Joy? What did she promise Joy?" Steve demanded.

"You should ask her, but it has to do with her mom," Justin answered. "She's on her way here."

Steve was utterly confused. Why would Berit try and make deals with his friends? What was she afraid of? And Justin said she tried to promise Joy something about her mom. It had to be about her mental illness. "I don't get it. If you're here now, then you broke your deal with Berit—"

"I never made a deal with her," Justin insisted. "All I did was try some surfing and then I found out you were in the hospital; I came as soon as I found out."

"Okay, okay, I didn't mean that you did anything wrong," Steve reassured him. "How come you didn't return to how you normally are when you came to the hospital?"

Justin shrugged, "No clue."

The door suddenly opened and Steve's grandmother poked in. "Oh, there you are, boys. Steve, you can't wander off. You need to stay where we can keep an eye on you."

"I wasn't going anywhere, Granny, just out here to talk to Justin."

"It doesn't matter, Stevie. If that dragon is coming here, then you might be in a lot of danger."

To Steve's surprise, Justin groaned and seemed more than a little frustrated. "There's a dragon coming here?" He glanced at Steve, "Is it yours?"

Steve shook his head no. "Everyone thinks there is a different dragon coming from up north. Well, it's really a hurricane, but everyone thinks it's a dragon."

"Crap! Of course, it's headed here," Justin said with a sneer.

"It could be, or it could be going to find our dragon," Granny continued, "If it's a dragon. Either way, we all need to talk about what to do next. So come on inside."

Justin followed Granny, immediately, but Steve hung back a bit. His friend's shoulders were straight, his hands tucked in the pockets of a new pair of jeans. From behind, Steve realized he would never have been able to pick him out of a crowd.

Chapter 57

Shou and her allies had done their best to support the fledgling dragon. Shou sang, while they all focused their magic on Dragau, trying to keep him calm and ease his pain. While Shou tried to soothe him, she also tried to help him understand what was happening. Unfortunately, there was no way for her to know if she was getting through, to know if he understood what was happening to him.

Eventually, Dragau became fully aware; his need to find and engage the other great dragon became too strong. Shou knew he would be functioning instinctually, reacting to his own pain and the need to fight, so, as soon as it took to the air, Shou scrambled her troops, sending north those who could fly. The rest she loaded in her Honda. The deer had not been too pleased about having to be strapped to the hood like a trophy, but there was only so much room in the compact car.

She drove with the window down, trusting her nose when she lost sight of her dragon—she had begun thinking of him as hers. *And why not?* she thought. *If not for her, none of them would even be here.* She hoped he would head out to sea; if he'd understood her, then he would. In his pain, he would lash out at anything, but if he traveled over the ocean, then he might not turn that ferocity on any people.

Shou turned her head to answer one of the more vocal critters riding in the back seat; the blue squirrel with the horrible attitude chirped incessantly about how someone should have told him what was going on earlier, so that he could have helped. Shou caught movement ahead and barely swung the little car back into her lane to avoid the eighteen-wheeler blaring its horn at her. Momentarily frazzled, Shou almost lost her own temper, but took a deep breath and remained calm.

The highway started heading inland as Shou followed the dragon's powerful scent. She pressed on the gas and pushed the little car as fast as she dared. Fortunately, the coastal road made mostly sweeping turns, so she could keep her speed up. It was beautiful, with trees everywhere climbing up rocky mountain passes and down into lush green valleys. There'd been a reason Shou kept coming back here all these years, and it wasn't only to give minor dragons a home.

Shou had little time to appreciate the scenery, however, especially not after a bunny hopped up from the floorboard onto the passenger seat to get Shou's attention.

"What is it, Henrietta?"

The rabbit nosed Shou's purse and flipped it up on the seat. Inside, her cellphone was buzzing. Shou kept one hand on the wheel and reached into her bag with the other. She started to answer it, and then realized it was all of her missed calls coming in at once. She must have moved into an area where her cell service returned. She had to pull over for a minute because she wasn't good enough with human technology to check phone messages, drive, and track the scent of a flying dragon. Almost all the messages were from Jeanie, Steve's mother. Shou was concerned at first, but fortunately, later messages said the boy was all right. The last one had come this morning. They thought a dragon was headed for Crescent City and it would be there by nightfall.

Shou pulled back on the road and pushed hard on the accelerator. She was a few hours south of Steve and his friends. The best Shou could hope for was that the great dragons would meet out to sea and no humans would be hurt. If they fought anywhere near the coastal town, the battle could wipe it out. Shou had done all she could, resting the dragon, helping it to conserve its strength. *Would it be enough? And what about Berit? What would that conniving dragonette do to tip the scales?* Shou huffed at her own pun. "Dragon, scales, I must be getting senile," she mumbled aloud. The bunny in earshot wisely said nothing.

Chapter 58

Berit pulled into the driveway of a house and got off the bike to take a closer look. Sure enough, a corner of the meager little dwelling was completely black, but something had kept it from burning all the way to the ground. She sniffed and walked around to the side, where she saw a splattering of some animal's waste. She found it speckled all over the vinyl siding. She stomped back to the bike, which had waited obediently upright for her to climb aboard. She whipped the Harley around, spinning the rear wheel, and raced into the street before she skidded to a smoky halt. She yelled something over the deep throttle of the motor and every window in the house exploded outward.

Berit was livid. Everywhere it was the same: no fire, no destruction, no mayhem. It wasn't Brita's and Halldor's fault, though she desperately wanted to blame them. Berit could smell every single spot where they'd used their magic. Unfortunately, she could also smell every single spot where someone or something had wiped bear excrement to counter the magic. *"Bear crap? Really?"* she thought. There was a dragon masquerading around as a bear with enough excrement to undo all their hard work—and worse, it was powerful enough to do it!

Heedless of who saw her, she roared right through the middle of town back to the docks. Everywhere she turned, humans were going about their normal business with no sense of urgency, no panic. When she arrived, her jaw dropped; she saw nothing of the destruction she had set in motion. Where was the small island of junk she'd sent to choke the bay? This was a disaster. Everything she had been sent to do was unraveling. This had to be Shou's fault. That old lizard was the only one who had ever beaten her. Obviously, she had enlisted someone, a bear of all things, to assist her.

Berit was standing on the bike, lost in the angry rant in her head, and didn't even notice the police car pull in behind her. The officer got out, took one look at the little girl straddling the huge motorcycle and immediately call to her, "Hey, kid, what the heck are you doing?" When she didn't answer, he walked right up to her and reached over to turn the key off. When that didn't work, he tried the kill switch with the same effect. "What's going—"

Berit screamed something at the young man and sent him flying through the air. Lucky for him, his own car kind of broke his fall. The next thing he knew, the kid was riding up the front end of the squad car and he had to roll off the hood to get out of the way. He didn't have enough air left in his lungs to say a thing when the little blond devil stopped on the roof and proceeded to smash it down with the front end of her motorcycle.

Berit only quit when she saw another policeman turn into the parking lot. Grinning, she rolled down and collapsed the trunk before hitting the ground. She gave the motorcycle full throttle, popped a wheelie, and went up and over the approaching car. The shocked driver cranked his head around to watch her screech away and promptly rear-ended the police car in front of him.

Chapter 59

"Joy, hey everybody, it's Joy," shouted Dani at the door. Everyone was huddled in front of the large flat-screen TV in the family room. The phenomenal weather system had suddenly picked up speed and was heading in a straight line down the coast. Joy followed Dani into the room. "They're watching for another dragon," Dani explained matter-of-factly. "I was the first one to figure it out."

Joy, however, wasn't really listening. "Um, why is there a bear lying on the floor? And why is it eating a bowl of popcorn?"

"Huh? Oh, yeah," Dani nodded. "that's TJ."

"But, that, that's a bear," Joy pointed.

"Sure is. He doesn't like to be called an 'it,' though," Dani corrected. "His name is TJ and he's a friend of Shou's. Come on in. I'll introduce you."

Dani pulled Joy through the room, walking around everyone who was gaping at the television. "Oh, hey Joy," said Steve who was sitting on the floor behind the large black bear. "When'd you get here?"

"My mom and dad just dropped me off."

Dani poked her brother with her toe, "Move, I want to introduce her to TJ."

"You move, you little creep," Steve replied. "You can't even understand him."

"Says you. He understands me, and I think I'm picking up bear."

TJ handed the bowl to Steve and rolled over to face the quarreling siblings. "You two need to learn to get along, you know what I'm sayin'? You brother and sister and stuck together fo' life. Oh, hey, waddup, young lady?"

Joy stared as the bear growled at her and then extended a large paw, clenched like a fist. She looked to Steve who said, "It's okay. He's saying hello."

Joy reached out to shake hands, or paws, "Um, it's nice to meet you?"

"Naw, girl," TJ said, wiggling his paw, "You gotta bump it."

"He wants you to do fist bumps," Steve explained, then shrugged in response to Joy's expression.

"Um, sure," Joy said, before tapping her knuckles against his fur.

The programming interrupted their exchange; an announcer was hurriedly saying that another weather anomaly had formed along the California coast and appeared to be heading north. Ramone pointed to the TV and hollered, "Check it, you seeing this, everybody? This is tense!"

In the next few milliseconds, the entire room erupted. Roger and Jeanie were arguing with Granny about what to do next, while the surfers tracked along another line of thought. "Brahs, that's two weather systems," Fred said. "If they meet, like it's a convergence, man—"

"I'm so stoked, brahs, that means like—"

"It's gonna be a fat wave fest, man!" Fred continued.

Larry shook his head, "No, brahs, it's gonna be two giant dragons trying to kill each other."

"Yeah, yeah, we got that part, but it's gonna also be—"

"Two giant dragons trying to kill each other."

"No, but—"

"Maybe right over our town," Larry pointed out.

Fred opened his mouth to say something, but closed it. Ramone looked like he was going to cry. All three surfers needed a moment of silence.

Joy had recovered enough from meeting TJ to talk to Steve. "Hey, I know this is a bad time, but I need to tell you something."

"Justin kind of did already," Steve said. "It's okay."

Joy looked for Justin who came across the room. "What?" he said.

"No," Steve corrected, "he didn't—"

"I didn't what?"

"Tell him about me and my mom," Joy answered angrily.

"No, I didn't, not really."

"Not really?"

Steve stood up, "No, s-s-stop and listen. Joy, he told me what B-B-Berit did to him and th-th-that something happened to your mom. I don't care, I mean I care that your mom is all right, but I don't care if you had to do something to protect her."

"Honest, Steve, I wouldn't have done anything to hurt you," Joy explained. "One of them told me to stay away from you and my mom would be all right; she'd be cured, and she had stopped taking her pills again…I didn't know what to do."

"It's ok-k-kay," Steve started. "Is she, you know…"

"Hiding in her room or bouncing all over town?" Joy shook her head, "Nope, no change. She's completely normal which is—"

"You're stuttering again," Justin interrupted. When Steve did not say anything, he continued, "Follow me outside a minute will you?"

He led them out the back door on to the deck. They started to jump for him when he climbed up on the rail and faced them. "Relax, watch this." Then, still facing them, he did a perfect back flip off the high deck and landed gracefully on the ground below. Steve and Joy bounded down the stairs after him. "Don't you ever do that again!" she yelled.

Justin moved to the side and did a nice cartwheel before landing a handspring. "See, it's pretty obvious that I'm still magical as well."

"W-W-What's w-w-wrong with you?" Steve stammered.

"I wanted to show you that the magic hasn't gone away. Which means it's probably the same with Joy's mom."

"Yeah, well, no kidding," Joy said. "But maybe warn us next time. It is like you said earlier, though, isn't it? It's not only the super gymnastics?"

Justin tapped his head, "Yup. I think my wiring is still normal too."

Steve joined them, "What does that mean?"

"No more quirks, obsessions, and stuff, I guess."

"B-B-But," Steve hesitated. Justin was right; he was stuttering, and badly. *What did it mean?* he asked himself. He tried again very slowly and deliberately, "That's who you are. I mean, it's h-h-how you've been your whole life."

Justin nodded, "I know."

"What's going to happen when it all goes away, if it goes away?" Steve asked.

"No more backflips, I guess."

"That's not what he means, Justin," Joy interjected.

Justin smiled and shrugged, "I know what he means. Seriously, I didn't have a problem with who I was. Part of me misses it…" Justin paused, reflecting for a moment on the other part of him, the part that let him express himself this way to his friends. He shrugged, then glanced up at Joy, "It might be different for your mother though."

"That's what I'm afraid of," Joy answered. "Would you miss it?"

"You mean that I might not get chosen prom king?" Justin asked with a grin, "Naw, I've got you two, and a whole lot of other things that make me happy."

Joy stared at him.

"What?" he asked, searching her face.

"Nothing," Joy started, but grabbed him in a big hug, and, for once, he did not stiffen up.

Dani slammed open the sliding glass door up above. "Hey, Mom says to get in here right now. The dragons are coming a lot faster!"

Chapter 60

The weather was now on every channel, not only locally. It was a strange enough event that meteorologists were on TV everywhere doing their best to explain the unexplainable. Climate scientists were trying to reconcile the phenomena with changing global temperatures and wind patterns; spinning rain bands surrounded the low-pressure zones and had pushed up waves along the Oregon and California coasts. Emergency service personnel were being called in all along the west coast, including those in Crescent City. The seaside town had been hit before; there was the devastating tsunami of 1964 which killed 11 people, and the less destructive one of 2011 in which one person was killed. Of course, those catastrophes were caused by far-away earthquakes, but severe storms could also be destructive. As such, the local hardware store was running out of plywood and sandbags as those with low-lying homes sought to prepare for the worst.

Shou made good time along the Redwood Highway until she entered Crescent City's south side of town. At that point, she found herself competing with locals as they tried to get all of their errands taken care of before the impending storm hit. She thought, hoped perhaps, that many would head inland. Unfortunately, these sturdy folks weren't ready to abandon their homes just because of the possibility of a little rain and wind. That line of thinking could be disastrous if the dragons fought right over their heads—Shou had seen it happen before.

A child clinging to her mother's hand pointed as Shou drove by with her Honda, which was loaded full of forest animals with a doe strapped to the hood of the car. Shou chastised herself for forgetting and quickly darkened the car's windows and made the deer appear as a canoe. It looked a little silly on a compact car, but Shou did not have time to think on it too much. As they made their way through town, Shou left her window open to search for the telltale signs of Berit's mischief.

They were there, along with some faint undertones from her accomplices. However, the much stronger smell of TJ's magic masquerading as bear poop informed her that many crises had been averted.

Shou pulled across the street from Justin's house and started to tell all her dragon critters to wait in the car, but one look at the ragtag group shoved in together and she decided against it. She opened the passenger side door and out jumped the two rabbits, the fox, and the squirrel. The doe freed herself from the hood. They were immediately pelted with wind-driven rain. Shou ushered them across the street and to the front door. It was locked, so she rang the bell. A tall man in his forties appeared, and Shou recognized Dr. Murry, Justin's father.

"Oh, Mrs. Wang, we've been waiting for...is that squirrel blue? Oh, and there's a rabbit, no two, and oh, never mind. What the hell, I've got a bear in my living room. Come on in." He motioned for them to enter and stepped aside. "Would you like me to get some towels?

Before Shou could answer the question, the fox and the doe shook themselves free of excess water. A loud crash from the living room brought them around and TJ bounded into the foyer.

"Shou, my sister, you're here! Give me some love! Whoa, is that Elenore? And Reggie? Wow, Shou you brought the whole crew."

Steve pushed in beside the surfers to see who had arrived at the front door. "Dudes, check it, it's a whole petting zoo!" Ramone announced.

"Oh, it's a bunny," Dani yelled. "Let me pet the bunny!"

For a second, like everyone else, Steve saw all the cute woodland animals. But then, in the occasional microburst of light, he'd catch their true forms. Dragons, all of them, though some seemed smaller than the others. It made him jump back and trip into Justin and Joy. Shou caught the movement and looked right at him. "Can we all come in out of this doorway?" she asked.

Everyone pulled back to let the newcomers into the living room. Dani had to be restrained by her mother from fondling one of the grey rabbits, who was about ten seconds away from zapping the child with a bit of magic. Shou gave the poor dragonette a warning look; she had already told them to avoid using magic around the boy, Steve.

TJ tried to introduce everyone with only minimal success since not everyone spoke bear. Meanwhile, Shou went immediately to Steve. "What is it? What made you jump?"

"I'm sorry. It's just that, every few seconds I saw flashes, like, I can't explain it."

"Go on," Shou prompted.

"Th-Th-They're all d-d-dragons aren't they? I mean, they're like TJ, right?"

Shou nodded, "That's right, of course they are. Like TJ said, this is Elenore and Reggie." She pointed to the bunnies. "And this is Katrina," Shou pointed to the doe who did a dainty curtsey. "Where is...Oh, there's Sam." The fox was holding a can of peanuts and waved. "And that leaves Jack..." Shou stopped in mid-sentence. She looked around. "Has anyone seen a squirrel, a blue squirrel?"

Dr. Murry spoke up, "He was here when you came in."

Shou knew immediately that the newcomer was gone.

"Wh-Wh-What's w-w-wrong, Sh-Sh-Shou?"

"Steve, your stuttering's getting worse again," Joy remarked. "Why all of a sudden? It's like, as soon as you get around..."

Both Justin and Joy said it at the same time, "Dragons!"

"Wha-Wha-What d-d-do you mean?" Steve asked.

"Your stutter, Steve," Joy elaborated. "You almost never stutter anymore unless you get really upset, but since we have all these dragons around, it's like, you're kind of like you were when we were little. You know what I mean?"

"Is this true, Steve?" Shou asked.

Steve shrugged, now self-conscious about his speech. "And you're seeing us as we really are? Without really trying?" Shou asked. "How do you see me now?"

"An old, Ch-Ch-Chinese lady. Sorry," Steve apologized. "I s-s-see, maybe red scales…"

A loud bang interrupted them. A decent-sized branch had broken away from a tree in the backyard and slammed against the sliding glass door. "This storm is getting violent," Roger announced.

"I didn't think to get any lumber to board the house up," Justin's father replied.

"I've got some in the shed back home," Roger replied.

"No, Roger," Jeanie said, "it's too windy now. It would be dangerous to try to get back to the house."

"Not if we—"

TJ stood up and growled, "I got this. Let me do a little magic and we'll have this place zipped up so tight—"

"No," Shou boomed. "No magic around the boy. We don't know what it will do to him, or us for that matter. Is there a better shelter?"

"Wait, wait," Justin's mom, the other Dr. Murry said. "We've got a ton of stuff in the garage. We can even use some of those old boards and that pile of old wetsuits to cover up the windows. We can nail some of those across the windows."

The surfers looked as if someone had spray-painted the Statue of Liberty. "But Mom—"

"Those boards might be the only thing between us and the storm," she said.

Larry nodded bravely, a testament to his evolution into adulthood. Fred and Ramone looked on in shock.

"I need a minute," Ramone said and stepped into the garage.

"I should check on him," Fred announced before following.

"I've got a box of four-inch wood screws in my truck," Roger announced, "and a cordless drill in my toolbox. Come on, Larry, we'll grab the boys to help us."

While Roger ran to his truck, Larry went to the garage where he found Fred and Ramone facing a stack of various board. "What's up, brahs?"

Ramone sniffed and rubbed his sleeve across his nose, "She wants us to use surfboards to block the windows, brah. She wants us to drill into the boards."

Fred turned to Larry, "There's got to be a better way."

Larry grabbed them both and pulled them along, "Come on, brahs, it'll be all right."

Ramone gulped, "Adulting is so bogus."

Another loud noise, this time thunder, shook the house and all the lights blinked momentarily. Dani dropped the bunny she had pinned on the couch and ran to her mother. Granny asked if everyone was okay, and then stopped as something on the television caught her attention. "Oh my," she said, "look, look at the TV, everyone!"

A tornado had hit the town of Brookings, Oregon, and it was   heading   south.

Chapter 61

Berit, Brita, and Halldor loped through the forest outside of town. The punishing rain slid easily off their dragon forms and animals instinctively got out of their way. Berit maneuvered through the trees like a skier through a slalom gate; the other two kept pace. They went north, south, west, and east, increasing the size of the circle with each loop. They were hunting. A short time earlier, Berit had taken her laptop and smashed it against the wall. Her ride through town had assured her that their magic had been neutralized; all their efforts may not have helped their dragon at all. Berit wanted permission to directly attack anyone or anything connected to their enemy; in other words, to attack other dragons. Her masters back in Iceland had refused, and, not only that, they had told her to pack up her team and come home. She was no longer needed in the upcoming battle.

When Brita asked about the prohibition against attacking other magical creatures like themselves, Berit lied. She told Brita that this battle was too important, that this fledgling dragon too powerful to be allowed to carry forth an egg. Brita started to protest, insisting that she wanted to see the instructions from back home, but Berit only smiled and pointed to the wrecked computer. "Not an option, my dear." Brita looked to Halldor for support, who as usual, only shrugged.

Berit could smell both of the great dragons now, one to the north and the other rushing to meet it. This storm, she knew, was the result of her dragon's powerful magic. It would grow in intensity until the two dragons clashed. Berit hoped the battle would be here, right on top of this stupid little village that had given her such grief. To the poor, unwitting humans who were trying to shutter up their homes, it would appear as if heaven itself had opened up to punish them. As delicious as the thought of this entire town being destroyed might be, it did not console her. She had failed. All her plans had been thwarted, and she was angry.

They were out here somewhere, Shou and her dragonettes, her tiny army of bugs and rodents. And they would pay. Suddenly, Halldor stopped and stood to his full height of eight feet, his honey-brown color visible even in the torrential rain. He had caught a scent. Berit and Brita bounded after him, sliding on the wet pine needles and slick mud down into a steep ravine. At the bottom, strung between two moss-covered rocks, an intricate web shook back and forth in the wind. A black dot the size of a nickel clung tightly to the middle. Berit saw past the spider's illusion to the golden-red dragonette that peered back at her with unblinking eyes. Before the thing could move, she struck, launching herself through the air. She didn't even bother with magic, just teeth and claws. Such was the ferocity of the attack that Brita and Halldor could only watch in horror. Berit turned her head at them, her fangs glistening with dark dragon blood. "One down. Now, let's find the others." Berit had killed a dragon.

Chapter 62

"Roger," Granny called into the garage. "Roger, there's a tornado headed this way!" When he didn't answer, she ran past the confused surfers out into the storm and found him unloading some things from his truck.

"Mom, get back inside!"

Granny pulled him close and yelled into his ear about the tornado. "What? Are you sure?" he screamed back. "How close?"

"Brookings."

"Come on," Roger urged, pulling his mother along. Once they were back inside, he grabbed the rope that dangled from the automatic garage door opener and yanked it down manually. It continued to shake as the storm beat against it, but they could hear each other now. "Mom, we've got to get something to cover up these windows; they're all over the house."

"But Son, didn't you hear me? There's a tornado headed this way."

"You said it was in Brookings," Roger interrupted. "That's still a good ways away and we don't know that it will head here. Right now, our biggest concern is keeping everyone from being shredded by glass." His mother nodded as he continued, "Try and keep an eye on the weather, but get everyone into the hallway away from the windows. The boys and I will be in as soon as we can. If the tornado looks like it's getting closer, we'll drop everything and come in."

Roger grabbed what he needed and bolted back into the elements. Granny went back inside, and Jeanie immediately came up to her. "Where are they? Why aren't they back in here?"

Granny relayed Roger's instructions while Justin's parents shooed the kids into the hallway. The adults and woodland creatures continued to hover around the television in the family room.

"Why don't we head for a shelter?" Joy asked.

"Yeah," Justin agreed. "Hey, Mom, can't we go find a shelter?" he yelled.

She came over to answer, "No, dear, with the wind and debris, it's too dangerous to drive anywhere."

Joy's phone rang. It was her parents. She couldn't hear them very well, so she started moving around the house looking for a better signal.

"Hey," Justin said, "you okay?"

Steve shrugged, "Y-Y-Yeah, I guess."

"No, you got something going on in your head, I can tell. What is it?"

"L-L-Look at them, the d-d-dragons," Steve began, "they could use magic to protect us. Or m-m-maybe even the town. But they're not."

"That's because you might...Oh, you think they don't want to do magic around you or it might make you sick again."

"Or t-t-take away their powers," Steve added.

The sound of Roger's drill penetrating the house echoed in the hallway despite the howling wind. "Maybe they won't need to," Justin replied.

Steve didn't answer. He was thinking. Part of him knew that, if he left, Shou and the rest could use magic to protect the house. But he knew that was foolish; no one would let him go, and even if he did sneak out, they'd come looking for him. A crash in one of the bedrooms grabbed his attention, forcing him and Justin to run and see what had happened. Something had blown into it, shattering glass all over the floor. Ramone and Fred suddenly appeared with a surfboard and tried to hold it up to cover the hole. They had just managed to get it into place when a burst of wind ripped the board right out of their hands, sending it flying off down the street. Steve saw the shocked expression on their faces. "Get out and shut the door!" Ramone yelled.

Steve nodded and backed away. With the window blown out, the storm was louder than ever, even in the hall. "It's getting worse," Justin stated.

Apparently, it was. The front door flung open, revealing Roger followed by the surfers. They pushed the door back into place, shivering in the entryway. Justin's mother ran and got them an armful of towels. As everyone clumped up again, Roger explained that they couldn't hang on to anything because the wind had gotten too strong. They had managed only to cover the front of the house.

The lights flickered twice and then went out completely. A couple of cell phones suddenly appeared, and Steve watched them dance around the house until Justin's dad and brother returned with the three cheap plastic flashlights stored under the kitchen sink. Steve sidled past Dani, who asked where he was going. Ignoring her, he found Shou.

Very slowly and carefully, Steve said, "You have to use your magic."

Even in the gloom, Steve could see her shake her head. "We can't risk it. It could hurt you."

"No wait, listen, please," Steve implored. "I-I-I d-d-don't think it works that way." He took a moment to breath and then continued slowly and deliberately. "I t-t-think I can control it. The first time, I w-w-was very upset, and during the fire, I was almost hypnotized by the m-m-magic. I'm calm right now and, even though we're in d-d-danger, I think I can stop myself from stealing your magic."

"My man here might be right," TJ agreed, shaking his big bear head up and down.

"But we can't risk it," Shou answered. "If Berit shows up—"

"And he siphons away our magic, he'll do the same to her," he finished. "I say we chance it."

Another crash, this time sounding like it came from the garage, galvanized Shou into action. "Okay, but not you, TJ. I'll get one of the others to try a little magic first. That way, if Steve does absorb the magic—"

"I can still fight. Word."

One of the tiny rabbits, Reggie, stood in the driveway. To human eyes, he would have been a speck of gray in the pouring rain. The wind should have picked him up and whipped him away, but to Shou and TJ watching from the garage, the creature braving the hurricane appeared in its true form, a substantial, squatty, purple dragon. Despite the hurricane, its voice cut through the howling winds and slowly, items on the garage floor began to shake, and then rise up in the air. A tarp shot out and wrapped itself around TJ, who had to fight to get it off his head. Next came a long board, a relic of less athletic surfing, an ice chest, and a couple of wetsuits. Shou watched as they zoomed out into the storm and attached themselves to different windows around the house.

Steve stood back to let the little rabbit back inside. As Sebastian shook the rain off, Steve caught flashes of purple and wondered if something was wrong with his eyes. Before he could think on it further, Shou appeared by his side. "Well?" she asked anxiously, "Anything?"

Steve shook his head, still a little afraid to open his mouth.

"Thank the Great Dragon," Shou replied.

Chapter 63

TJ brushed by, almost knocking Steve over as he came back into the house, "My bad," he declared before joining Fred at the fridge. The house was in complete gloom now, with the windows covered. "Mom, where are you?" Dani yelled. "I can't see anything."

A beam of light swept across the floor and stopped in front of Steve and Shou. "So, is it safe?" Jeanie asked. "Can you do magic around Steve?"

The lights came back on before Shou answered her question. The old woman smiled, "Yes, Steve was right. We can use magic around him as long as he doesn't get too upset. But safe? No, my dear, I don't know if anyone is safe."

"B-B-But you can use your magic!" Steve insisted. "Can't you—"

"No, we can protect this house, I think. Maybe we can try and help out some of your neighbors, too. That is if…" Shou lapsed into thought.

"What is it, Shou?" Jeanie asked.

Shou was interrupted by the blaring of the television, which someone had reset. Ramone had the remote and was turning the volume up even higher. "Everyone, check it, this is epic. I mean like epically bad."

Everyone gathered to watch the broadcast. Two storms were headed directly toward each other. Already the storm surge was up to eight feet and another tornado had been reported spinning off from the northern hurricane. All residents along northern California and southern Oregon coasts were to take shelter immediately.

"Shou, isn't there anything we can do?" Roger asked. "How much worse is this going to get?"

Joy ran into the room, "I was on the phone with Mom, but we got cut off. I told them I was going to be all right, but I'm worried about them."

"Where are they?" Roger asked.

"They were at Dr. Phyllis's office. It's in the hospital." Joy answered.

"They'll be all right," Roger assured her. "There's a good shelter there."

"What about my mom?" Ramone asked entering the conversation. "We don't have a shelter."

"Mine, neither. I mean, my grandparents don't have a shelter or anything," Fred added.

"Or Anthony, or most of our friends," Roger added.

Shou considered before answering. There were limits to what she could do to help the humans caught in a battle between great dragons. "We can try and help. My friends and I can split up and help who we can."

"My mom?" Ramone asked.

Shou nodded.

"Hey, Shou," TJ yelled from the kitchen. "You smelling this?"

"What is it?" Shou asked, then leaned in towards a window. "Damn, Berit's out there!"

Chapter 64

Trees went down, centuries-old mammoths toppling like dominoes. Electrical lines fell with them and sparked in the rain. The sky thundered, and lightning crisscrossed the black clouds above. The wind was sweeping away anything not tied down: tin storage sheds, old roof tiles, flags, laundry, swing sets, and trashcans. The town had lost power and no one with any sense was outside. An emergency siren sounded, barely audible above the wind.

Three forms slipped easily into town, ignoring the deteriorating conditions. They moved like waves, propelling their long sleek bodies with their powerful legs. They were met with empty streets and abandoned cars. Lanterns, candles, and flashlights moved about in shuttered houses as they passed. Berit ignored these. Letting her nose and her exceptional senses search for others like herself, she had begun to reach the more populated part of town when she saw it, a lone home, lit up by magic. It was like a lighthouse in a sea of darkness. Berit pointed her head in its direction for her friends. "They've left the light on for us," she laughed.

"Stay here!" Shou shouted. Then she led TJ and their woodland friends out the front door. Steve ran to the kitchen and peered out through a small space that a surfboard hadn't covered, but he couldn't see anything. Joy joined him. "What is it? What's going on?"

"Berit is out there," Steve answered.

"Are you sure? What does she want?"

"I-I-I don't know," he answered. "I can't s-s-see anything. C-C-Come on, let's try Justin's room. That's where the window was b-b-broken out."

"Hey, where is Justin?" Joy asked.

But Steve was already on his way down the hall. He reached Justin's door and yanked it open. Joy bumped into Steve. "Why'd you stop? Oh. What are you doing, Justin?"

Justin was on his hands and knees scooping glass into a pile, already having cut himself in several places. Joy squeezed past Steve and dropped down next to Justin. She grabbed his arms and forced him to look at her. "Stop it, Justin. You're hurting yourself."

"Everything's destroyed," he wailed. "Look at my room, all my stuff. All my collections…"

Steve crouched down as well, careful to avoid the remaining glass. "It-It-It will be alright. C-C-Come on get up and we'll help you."

"No, no, no, no. Go away," he screamed. "I'll do it myself! It's my room. I know where everything goes."

Joy looked to Steve for help. "Go get his mom," he mouthed. She ran out of the room while Steve tried to calm his best friend down. Joy returned moments later with his parents, who gently, but firmly, took hold of Justin and led him out while he continued to yell.

"I've never seen him like that before," Joy said.

"I have," Steve admitted. "B-B-But never that b-b-bad before. It's his room. All of his things are messed up."

Joy got a worried look on her face. "Does that mean that he's back to, well, normal? Or, you know what I mean, being himself?"

"I guess," Steve said.

Joy did not say anything.

"Oh, your mom…"

"Doesn't matter right now. Come on, let's see what's happening outside."

The pair stepped around the remaining glass and debris strewn about. They had a better view from there, able to peer out a six-inch gap below the stretched wetsuit covering the window.

"Can you see anything?" Joy asked.

The slashing rain had only gotten worse. "No, not really. It's too dark and the rain—"

A boom of thunder shook the house, followed almost instantaneously by a flash of lightning. In that moment, Steve saw all the minor dragons facing off in the street. And he saw them as they were, scaled, snake-like creatures of different sizes and colors. Then the sky went black again.

"Did you see—"

"All the dragons in the street?" Joy continued. "Yeah, I did."

Steve thought for a second. "If you can see them, I don't th-th-think they're hiding their true identities anymore."

"What does that mean?"

"Probably nothing good."

Jeanie appeared at the open doorway. "What are you two doing? Come on, get away from that window. It's not safe in here. Is that glass all over the floor?"

"Yeah, but—" Steve started to say.

Jeanie pointed, "Come on, out of here. All you kids need to get in the master bathroom; it's the safest place in the house."

Chapter 65

Sitting on the side of the tub, Steve reflected on adult stupidity for the umpteenth time. If it was so unsafe, then why weren't they all huddled in here too? Instead, there was sort of a pecking order of safety with Justin, Joy, Dani, and himself here, Larry and his friends in the hall, and all the old folks watching the storm on TV in the family room. Occasionally, someone would come in and check on them. "This is s-s-stupid," he groused.

Joy was fidgeting with her phone, "Nothing, I can't get anything…"

Justin said nothing, but sat in the corner with his arms around his legs, rocking himself. When Steve's dad looked in on them, Steve asked what was happening.

"Even with the magic, the television signal is starting to fade in and out," Roger explained. "But it looks like the storms are coming together."

"Coming together where, Mr. Batista?" Joy asked.

Before he could answer, all the lights went out. First, there was a crash, and then someone screamed. "Stay put, don't move," Roger said before running out of the room.

"W-W What's happening now?" Steve asked.

More crashes, and the sound of wind and rain. Justin finally roused himself, "The magic's gone. It's not protecting the house anymore." He started to get up.

"Where are you going?" Steve asked.

"I'm going to my room before it gets completely destroyed. All my stuff—"

Joy stepped in front of him, "No, Justin, you can't. There's glass everywhere. If there's no magic protecting the house, then that wind will be blowing everything away."

Justin tried to step around her, "Exactly, all my things will be…they'll all be gone."

Steve joined her, "N-N-No, Justin, you can't. You have t-t-to stay here."

"I do not!" he screamed. "It's my room and if I can save anything—"

Larry came running in. "What's the matter? I heard someone yell."

"He wants to go back to his room and save his things," Joy explained.

"Ah, brah, you can't. All the bedrooms are getting swamped with rain. All the boards and things we used to cover the windows are gone. Rain and wind are coming in everywhere."

Something shook the whole house. It sounded like a jumbo jet was coming in to land and could be heard over the warring winds. "What was that?" Larry asked.

"Look, look out the glass door!" Jeanie screamed from the family room.

That was enough. All the kids broke out of the bathroom to join the adults who were gathered in front of the sliding door despite the danger of something crashing in. Outside, up against the swirling grey and black clouds, was a monster, a shiny black dragon, longer than a football field, and it just flew over the house. "It's enormous!" Granny exclaimed.

"Where's it going?

"Looks like it's going out to sea."

"No, wait, it's—"

"Turning, it's turning around."

"Oh, my God, it's turning around. Get back!"

"It's coming this way."

"No, look everyone," Dani shouted. "Look, there's another one!"

A smaller, bright-green dragon slammed into the first one. Its roar drowned out the storm. The monstrous dragon sprayed an arc of fire after the other one.

"It's our dragon! It's our dragon!" Dani screamed in delight.

The black dragon twisted itself around and whipped its massive tail into Steve's dragon, swatting it and sending it tumbling to the ground. Before Dragau could recover, the monster shot a stream of fire after it. It missed its mark.

"Get back, everyone!" Roger yelled and grabbed Joy and Steve. They weren't fast enough.

The fire hit the back of the house and exploded. What windows remained were blown inward and the walls were engulfed in flames. "Fire!"

Steve was momentarily knocked down by the concussive blast, but unhurt. Fred and Ramone, who were closest to the exterior wall, were thrown completely across the room. Granny was down with her sweater on fire. Joy stumbled forward, fighting the increasing smoke, and smothered the flames with a couch cushion. Justin's mom grabbed the fire extinguisher from under the kitchen sink and started spraying indiscriminately.

The entire rear of the house was on fire. Instinctively, everyone moved toward the front. Larry helped Joy with Granny, who was only semi-conscious. Justin's dad screamed for them to go to the garage, while Roger half-carried, half-dragged the two unconscious surfers away from the flames. Steve grabbed Dani's hand and pulled her along.

"Who are we missing?" Roger asked. "Jeanie, help me, do we have everyone."

"Justin," Jeanie said. "I don't see Justin."

His mom started back to the house, but Roger stopped her. "No, stop. He's here!" She ran over to her son and wrapped him up in her arms.

"We can't stay here. The rest of the house will be consumed soon and smoke's already coming in," Justin's father stated. He went to the rolling garage door that shook with the wind and started to pull it up manually. Larry joined him and the two managed to pull it up to knee height to clear the air.

Roger's EMT training took over and he quickly triaged those who were injured and unconscious. Granny was miraculously okay, and the surfers were coming around. Everyone had cuts and bruises, though. More dark smoke continued to pour in from under the door to the house. Steve found some rags and stuffed them into the gap. It slowed down the toxic fumes, but the air was heavy and foul.

Larry ignored the soaking and attempted to lift the door even higher to clear out more of the bad air. As he got it up past his chest, he stopped. "Oh, no, come see this!"

Dragons were fighting in the street.

Chapter 66

Shou sliced the empty air with her claws. The blue dragon, the one called Brita, ducked and swung her tail into Shou's face. She was fast. But so was Shou. She caught the tail with her powerful fangs and yanked the younger dragon off her hind legs. With a mighty flip of her neck, Shou flung the blue dragon high into the air. Brita crashed to the ground, breaking a patch of sidewalk. The respite gave Shou a chance to think. This was wrong, so wrong; she did not want this fight. The great dragons fought. Period. Though they were on different sides, the minor dragons rarely, if ever, fought each other directly. Shou feared what Berit had started.

Shou saw that the young dragon was starting to rise. This one was tough; they all were. Given a few more centuries, they might even rival Berit and herself. Thinking of Berit made Shou look around for her ancient nemesis. TJ was holding out against her, barely. He, too, was powerful, perhaps the strongest she had ever brought here. But Berit was older, far older, and, with dragons, age often meant power. She winced when Berit used her magic to pluck a metal trashcan out of the air and smash it against TJ's head. Shou had to get to him; only she had a chance against Berit. She looked for the other one, the honey-gold one, and found it fighting against two of her friends. They were fighting valiantly, but had no chance. They simply weren't strong enough.

One of their number, Elenore, was already dead, struck down immediately when Berit had done the unthinkable and attacked without warning. Another was barely holding on. Shou was in an impossible situation: she did not want to kill her own kind, but how could she stop Berit otherwise?

A car door zipped by and Shou realized that she had to keep her attention on one battle at a time. Somehow, she had to end this and help her friend before Berit destroyed him as well.

Shou used some of her own magic and clapped Brita between two abandoned cars. The dragon screamed in fury, but was momentarily pinned. Shou was rushing to TJ's aid when the great green dragon came smashing to the earth. Its impact rocked the ground and knocked them all down. Amazingly, Dragau lifted himself up, listed unsteadily, and shook his giant head. Shou could see where his beautiful luminescent scales were scorched black. For a second, he looked at Shou and something passed between them. Yes, the great dragon had understood her back in the cave. He had to take the fight out to sea. He took off and shot a jet of fire of his own right back at the dark terror that was bearing down on them. But, as Dragau tried to veer off and head to the ocean, the larger dragon cut him off.

Shou gasped as the black dragon snapped the air, just missing the smaller one. Something sizzled and then they heard a pop. Shou turned to see Berit using magic directly against TJ now. Another sizzle, and an explosion threw the bear into the air. TJ hit hard and didn't immediately move. Shou ran to his side and rolled the scorched bear over. "Is all good, baby!" he whispered. "Just got to lay here in timeout for a minute and resuscitate."

Shou felt a staticky feeling in the air again; Berit was summoning more magic. Shou reared up as tall as she could and brought forth her own. It surrounded her in a brilliant blue aura. Before Berit could unleash any more harm on Shou's friends, Shou struck out all at once. She sent the swirling blue fire into all three of their enemies. Halldor and Brita screamed, and Berit was lifted into the air and spun around and around. And the magic kept coming. Shou felt the magic flood into her as if she were some kind of conductor. Something was augmenting her own powerful magic. Shou had never felt so powerful and then, shockingly, she understood.

It was the great dragon. It was giving its own magic to her, trying to save her and her friends, trying to protect the minor dragons that shared its home. Shou pulled the magic back.

Berit dropped immediately. The other two slumped down on the ground, not moving. But they weren't dead, Shou knew. She searched a sky that was filled with black clouds and fire. There, there they were. The mighty black dragon had Dragau's leg in its mouth while its claws raked the smaller dragon's side.

Dragau was trying to free himself. Shou focused all the magic she could and tried to will it back to the green dragon, back to its source. But it was too late, there wasn't enough magic left. In seconds, the battle would be over.

The older dragon opened its terrible mouth to get a better hold, and then, suddenly, Dragau slashed its adversary across the face, enough to momentarily stun it. The great beast swung its head like a battering ram, knocking Dragau senseless. He fell limply all the way down to the rocky cliffs that ringed the beach. The black dragon roared in triumph and sent a stream of fire after its fallen foe.

It would be over soon. Dragau was not moving; he was a helpless target now. The great dragon, ancient and powerful, would destroy him and steal his magic. Shou fell into despair; there was no hope. Maybe, though, she could protect her friends. A shorn limb from a downed tree shot through the air and hit her in the head, sending her reeling. Berit was back up.

Chapter 67

Steve marveled at the way the magic was used between the dragons, almost like seeing a deadly laser light show. He saw Berit attack TJ and watched in amazement as Shou struck back against all three dragons. But then she stopped, and Steve saw the bright blue magic build, only to shoot off to the sky. It took him a minute, but then he understood: Shou was giving it back, giving it back to his dragon. He did not know she could do that. Why would she? What was…and that's when he heard the crash. He knew—knew—that it was his dragon, and that he was in pain.

Steve looked around to see if anyone else could sense it, but everyone was watching the battle. Steve wasn't even sure if they all saw what he saw. Shou stood alone in the middle of the street, and then something hit her, a tree branch the size of his leg. Now the only one standing was Berit. Steve gritted his teeth, his dragon's agony leaking out, and made a decision. He wouldn't stand back and watch those who protected him and his kind die. He just wouldn't. He bolted, ducking out of the garage into the storm, and past the hands of several adults who seemed too stunned to stop him.

Steve put himself in front of the sinewy beast that stalked toward Shou. Her eyes were bright yellow and reminded him of another set that threatened him not long ago. He was scared. He started talking to Shou, begging her to get up. Shou's eyes opened and looked into his own. In an instant, Steve understood all that was happening, and he felt Shou's sorrow. He kept talking to her, telling her not to give up.

Meanwhile, Joy was trying to calm Justin down; Steve running outside had totally freaked him out. "Oh no…" Justin said, forcing her to follow Justin's wide eyes to where Steve stood. The blue dragon loomed over Steve and Shou, menacing and terrible all at once. Joy huffed and looked Justin directly in the eye, "I'm going to get him. Stay here." She sprinted outside, ducking past the adults with a surprising nimbleness.

Berit, seemingly irritated by the constant barrage of human spectators, hissed, and the garage door slammed shut. The sound caused Steve to look up. Suddenly, there it was, that abrupt, sickly feeling in his stomach. Only this time, he welcomed it. He started talking, not caring at all about how little sense it made.

He was aware of Joy kneeling next to him. "How is she?" she asked.

Steve didn't answer. Instead, he kept talking to the prone red dragon. Berit screamed again and Steve could see her magic, like a whirlwind of color. So he took it; he took it all. Holding on to Shou like an anchor, he saw the colors and pulled them into himself. His mind expanded; he saw the magic all around him, zipping through the air like bullet tracers. He caught them as they flew by. There was the golden dragon, unconscious, but not dead. Steve took his magic. And the deep, dark blue dragon, just beginning to rise. Steve took hers as well. He felt the unbelievable power well up inside him. It was too much. His mind was starting to slip. He was going to pass out like before, or worse.

Then Shou was there with him, calming his mind. Joy was there, too, holding his other hand. Steve sensed what Shou wanted him to do. There, on the edge of the cliff overlooking the shore, lay the body of the green dragon, beaten, broken, but not dead. Steve called to his dragon, as he had years before. He answered, and Steve willed all the magic that he had captured into Dragau. The transference was awkward, it almost felt like his soul was being ripped away, but he held on as long as he could until all he had was a trickle of magic left to offer...and then it was gone.

He opened his eyes. Everyone was there, being pelted by the rain. His dad helped him sit up. "W-W-What h-h-happened?"

Most of the adults seemed to wonder that themselves, but Joy leaned in to answer him. "You absorbed all their magic, again," Joy yelled over the squalling wind.

"Which meant we could get out of the garage," his dad continued, nodding in understanding.

Weakly, Steve looked around. Berit was on the ground, not moving. Shou was right next to him. He reached out, and she took his hand in her own claw.

"Oh, thank God. You're alive!" Steve said.

Shou only nodded. Steve stood slowly, leaning into the wind. He looked up and saw his dragon. It was flying again! He almost jumped for joy, but something was wrong. He could see that it was weak. He closed his eyes and realized that he still had a connection to the dragon. It was too badly beaten to defeat the greater dragon. The magic Steve had given it was barely enough to get it moving again. All it could hope to do now was to try and lure the other dragon out to sea in order to save the town.

"No," Steve said aloud. "N-N-No, n-n-no, n-n-no."

The black dragon flew past Steve's dragon and clipped it with one of its enormous wings. The green dragon spun for a second and then regained its control, still trying for the open ocean. Steve watched the black dragon with a deep hatred. He started talking again, not blinking as he fixed his sight on the monster.

"No!" a voice screamed in his head.

Shou reached out, "No, Steve, you can't. It's a great dragon. It will destroy you."

Justin's dad said something about finding shelter which Steve ignored. "B-B-But I-I-I have to do something. C-C-Can't we d-d-do something?"

The battle raged overhead, a mixture of lightning and fire and twisting clouds. Jeanie pointed, "We have to go now! Those clouds look wrong, somehow."

As if to accentuate the point, there was a flash and then a boom followed by the explosion of a power pole. A sparking transformer fell; TJ scooped up Dani right before it landed on her.

"Everyone, move now!" Roger screamed. "Follow me next door!"

Roger led them to the neighbor's house, which was boarded up properly for a storm. He beat on the plywood that covered the front door, aware that even if there was anyone home, they probably wouldn't hear him. TJ handed Dani over to her mom and gently pushed Roger out of the way. "I got this," he said and ripped the wood away from the siding.

Everyone squeezed by the propped-up sheet of wood and into a darkened hallway. Justin's mom yelled for their neighbors by name, but there was no reply. "They must have evacuated," Jeanie observed. Shou was the last to enter, and she surprised everyone by being in her human form.

"Hang on, everybody," came a call from the kitchen. "I think Eloise keeps her flashlight under the kitchen sink."

"How'd she know that?" Justin asked.

Steve turned to his friend, "What?"

"How'd my mom know where Eloise leaves her flashlight?"

"Who cares, Justin?" Joy butted in. "Hey, you doing okay?"

"Yeah, I'm fine, but I can't understand why my mom would—"

"God, would you shut up about the stupid flashlight?" Joy said. "Maybe she was here during a storm or a power outage or something."

A beam of light swept past the teens. "Is everyone okay?"

"Yeah, we're fine, Mom," Justin replied. "But how come you knew there was a flashlight under the sink?"

"Oh my God," Joy swore.

"We've got t-t-to d-d-do something," Steve cried. "Can't anyone think of anything? Our dragon is going to get killed."

Shou moved next to her young friend, easily stepping around the soaked and freezing humans in the dark. "We tried everything we could, young man. There's nothing left for us, but to wait this out and try to help any way we can."

"Are you sure, Shou?" Justin asked.

"Sure about what, child?" she asked.

"I've been thinking about—"

"Oh here we go again—" Joy began.

"No, w-w-wait, Joy," Steve said. "Let h-h-him talk."

Justin continued, "Okay, so Shou, you've been bringing dragons here for years, right? How come?"

"Originally? Because it was so isolated. There were practically no humans here except for a few scattered Indian tribes and some trappers."

"Yeah, but there was something else you said…about this place being special, a magical source you said," Justin continued.

"I did," Shou agreed. "You know, I think that's what first brought me here, actually. It's a place where the earth's magic is still very strong. Often that's the case where few humans have settled. Except this place seems to maintain its energy, despite your presence."

Joy suddenly perked up, "Wait a minute, Justin, are you thinking—"

"Yeah, I am," he finished.

"W-W-What are you two talking about?" Steve asked.

Dani started to jump up and down. "Don't you get it? Take the earth's magic!"

"Is it possible…?" Shou pondered aloud.

TJ clapped his paws together, "Booyahh, it is, it is. You could help him, Shou. We could all help him!"

"C-C-Could I, Shou? Could I h-h-help the dragon that way?'

"I don't know. Tapping into natural magic is different than what you have been able to do so far. You may not be able to. Even if you do, I don't know what the side effects might be."

"W-W-We have to t-t-try. And h-h-hurry. He's going to die," Steve insisted.

"Steve—" Jeanie began, but Steve was already shaking his head, his eyes determined.

"H-H-He's willing t-t-to die. F-F-For any one of us, he w-w-would. I c-c-can't let him w-w-without trying."

Roger placed his hand on his wife's shoulder, who grasped it and turned away. He glanced over at Shou, "What do we do?"

Chapter 68

Steve sat in a circle formed by woodland creatures and one old Chinese lady in the middle of the living room floor. All the furniture was pushed back to give them room, and the other humans were waiting in another part of the house. Shou wasn't sure how regular human senses would react to what they were going to try, even though some of those humans were not, strictly speaking, regular. Shou was going to attempt something that in all her long years she had never attempted—leaching magic directly from the earth herself. And, to make matters worse, she was using a human as a conductor.

A memory suddenly flashed in her head, one of a boy grasping a great dragon's magic and the mark it had left on him. Shou had warned him not to touch the egg, that no human ever should. But still she had sent the magic off, the magic that would one day be Dragau, with Steve's ancestors, hundreds of years before their dragon was born. Had they heeded her, or had others handled the magic? Was this why Steve could do the things he could? They were questions she needed answers to, but there was no time, now. If they were going to save Dragau, Steve was their only hope.

The room pulsed with magic as the small group began communicating as dragons do, with feelings, sights, smells, and, lastly, their dissonant speech. Behind his closed eyes, Steve knew the room must be glowing. He could follow the dragons as Shou led them through the forest, everything so clear, like seeing the world through a microscope and yet, at the same time, managing not to miss a single thing; he could smell—could sense—the rich ground, and the pine trees, and the animals. Everywhere he looked, everything was alive— every bush and pebble and ant and stream. And everything emitted an aura, its own tiny field of magic.

There was a difference between this connection and what Steve had experienced with his own dragon. Then, he had seen not only what Dragau saw, but what other creatures did, too. That was still happening, though to a lesser degree, but Shou's sense of magic, which she detected through smell, was extraordinary, even beyond his own dragon's. It was this sense that she used to scour the forest for the deepest, strongest magic. As best he could describe it, Shou perceived magic as a kind of odor, or better yet, a whole spice rack of odors. Steve didn't have the words for all the distinct smells that filled his brain. TJ smelled like leather and coffee, another dragon like cinnamon, another maybe like pumpkin pie, or whatever the spices in the pie were, maybe cloves? There were other smells, fantastic combinations he could never hope to identify or describe.

Steve followed Shou's nose through mountains. There was a moment of hesitation. The mighty dragons. Their magic was awesome, overpowering. Again, he had no words. His human brain, which was not designed to process dragon magic on that scale, formed visual representations in his mind to cope. His dragon was like the forest in spring, tree bark, wild ferns, and wet earth. The other was immense and oppressive, like ash and smoke, like a volcano. Steve began to lose himself in those smells, and Shou had to snatch him back.

"That's not what we're looking for," she said.

There were other smells, distant, human smells—the smell of towns and cities, repugnant according to their scale. Shou had to separate those, as well. It was taking time, longer than Steve thought it should. He started to worry that they wouldn't find the magic in time.

"Patience," Shou advised, and then, finally, there it was, like a drink of the sweetest water on a hot summer day, and it wasn't just one place, one magical well; it was all over. It seeped up through the earth and flowed freely throughout in the spots humans had left alone—a spring of untapped, untainted magic.

"Here," Shou whispered, and Steve began to speak. Steve felt himself floating, carried away on a magical, never-ending stream. It was so beautiful, as if the world was made of crystal, or encased in crystal. It seemed perfect, and all Steve wanted to do was walk around in it. He knew there was something he should be doing, something extremely important, but he couldn't remember what it was. He felt whole and at peace. Except…was that someone calling his name? His name…what was his name? It didn't matter. Nothing mattered.

"Something is wrong," Shou said aloud. The connection to Steve was dwindling; he was slipping away, getting lost in the magic. She called to him—nothing. TJ and the other dragons tried as well.

"We have to get him back now!" Shou said.

"Try his family," TJ suggested.

"Right." Shou called out in her human voice. Roger rushed in, followed immediately by Jeanie and then the others. He threw up his arm to block the blinding light. "Uh, I can't see a thing. What is it, Shou? What's wrong?

"The light won't hurt you, any of you," Shou exclaimed. "Come in closer." Shou waited for them to creep in. "I'm losing him to the magic," she explained. "He won't answer me. You have to help me bring him back."

Jeanie squinted, trying to see Shou. "How?"

Shou took a moment to answer, "You and his father and grandmother, get Dani and Justin and Joy. Squeeze in here and we'll all try to get him back."

Moments later, everyone joined the circle and grasped hands. "Now, I want you all to say his name over and over until I tell you to stop. And think of him, as much about him as you can. He's lost, and we have to bring him back."

Something, something was trying to get his attention, like a slip of memory ducking back into the attic of his mind. There it was again. What was it saying? For a moment, Steve waivered. Voices, they were calling. What were they saying? It didn't matter. Here was all that mattered. He was part of here.

"No," a new voice, a stronger voice, interjected. "You do not belong here. This is not a place for mortals."

"Who are you?" Steve asked.

"A friend, a friend to you and to your dragons. This is my home, and you cannot stay."

A crushing pain squeezed at Steve's heart. "I have to stay. This is where I belong."

"You came here for a reason. Can you remember it?"

"A reason? What reason…Oh, wait." A flood of memories came to him, and a purpose. "I know who I am."

"And what you must do. Go back to your friends, your family. Help your dragon if you can."

"Who are you?"

"A friend. We'll see each other again."

The crystalline world receded, and Steve heard Shou and then Joy and then everyone else, chanting his name. Steve couldn't remember what he'd been doing, but he felt surprisingly well-rested and relaxed. He looked around at his friends and family and felt a rush of contentment. Joy saw him looking at her first.

"Steve!" she cried.

"Hey, Joy," Steve said, grinning. "What's up?"

Joy socked him in the arm.

"Hey!" Steve rubbed at the sore spot, "What was that for?"

"For scaring us half—"

"Joy," Shou interrupted, "there's no time. Steve, you have to pay attention," Shou said, "The magic is flowing through you now. You've done it! I can sense it flowing through you. Don't try to control it. Just let it fill you up. Do you see it?"

Steve held up a hand to his face and smiled blissfully as he turned it, marveling. "Yes, I see it."

"Good. Wrap yourself up in it like a warm blanket. Let it fill you up, but continue to listen to my voice, and the voices of your loved ones. Now," Shou continued, "can you find your dragon?"

Steve nodded, still smiling. He shut his eyes and reached out, but then recoiled, his expression pained. "He's hurt so badly. He's trying to escape, but he can't," Steve cried.

"Call to him. Call him with me."

"He can't hear me. He's in too much pain. He's going to die."

"No, Steve, listen. Try harder. With your voice, in your mind, reach out for him."

Steve refocused all his thoughts on touching his dragon. He muttered over and over, "Dragau, here. I'm here. You are not alone."

Flashes of pain, of terror, filled his head. His dragon was fighting for his life. Steve almost pulled away, but his dragon needed him. Steve felt for the connection he and Dragau had once shared. His dragon resisted, not wanting Steve to experience the horror of the battle. *I'm here to help you,* Steve thought. *We're all here to help you.* Steve willed the torrent of magic directly to his dragon. Steve felt Dragau's shock.

"Ah, thank you, my friends!" Steve heard in his head.

Chapter 69

The storm over Crescent City had intensified; the eye was incredibly small, erratic, and unstable. Winds continued to tightly rotate at over a hundred miles an hour, ripping off older roofs and siding, sweeping unsecured decks, toppling sickly trees. Gusts, substantially stronger, collapsed some rickety structures, including some neglected homes. A storm surge all up and down the northern coast was causing all kinds of havoc. Many of the docks in Crescent City's curved harbor were wiped out and the boats were stacked together like misshapen Legos. Lake Earl, the large lagoon north of Steve's house, was flooding, threatening homes and livestock; even sections of the Smith River were rising to dangerous levels.

Because of previous tsunamis, Crescent City had a robust plan to evacuate the population to higher ground. Most of the inhabitants had driven inland—apart from the inmates locked up in Pelican Bay Prison, emergency workers, and a scattering of those stubborn individuals who refused to leave their homes no matter what the dangers. Of those that remained, no one was outside to witness the epic battle overhead. No one except Steve. He was now linked to his dragon, much like he had been during their battle with the demon Mammon. Still, no matter how many times he linked minds with Dragau, Steve never stopped marveling at the experience.

Steve saw the ground below, impossibly far below, zip by. He could feel the air stream around the giant wings. He was flying. But the thrill was short-lived; ahead he could see the massive black dragon coming out of the equally black clouds. It opened its terrible maw and an explosion of fire shot straight for them. Dragau flew a tight spiral around the flame, never changing direction. Steve could feel the heat and hear the air sizzle as the dragon cork-screwed about the flame, heading directly to the monster ahead. Then, Steve realized what his dragon was doing—the flame reversed itself! His dragon used the magic to twist the flame backward and now he flung it right back into the face of the beast who sent it.

Steve did not understand much about dragon physics or anatomy. Dragons lived in fire, breathed it, and spit it out, but apparently, could be injured by it—even if it was their own flames. He suspected dragon magic had its own peculiar rules. Regardless, the black dragon screamed as its own fire flashed all over its head. Steve knew they had hurt it.

Steve's dragon seized the moment and raked the larger dragon's back with its own magical flame. The beast arched its shoulders and shot its wings out to keep from falling and that's when Dragau attacked. It shot back and forth across the injured dragon, mobbing it like a sparrow attacking a hawk. The size difference, which had once tipped the scales in the ancient dragon's favor, was quickly becoming a hindrance; by the time the ancient dragon turned to fend off the Dragau, he was already gone, only to shoot back again to tear another chunk out of his enemy.

The immensely powerful dragon would not give up, however. It snapped its head and neck back and forth at the dive-bombing dragon. It scorched the sky with streams of fire. It screamed in anger and frustration. But it was useless. Dragau attacked again and again, and, almost imperceptibly, the great black wings began to beat slower and slower, until, eventually, they could not keep the larger creature aloft. As it fell, Steve's dragon landed on its back and tore into it—scales and flesh flew and rained down below. Dragau was doing more than killing; he was searching, digging for something.

The dragons hit the beach together, but Steve's dragon was unhurt. He stayed atop the larger animal, ripping into its flesh and then found what he'd been looking for. Next to the beating heart, a white, glowing orb pulsed. Steve saw a green claw reach in and take it. Then he and his dragon lifted, cradling the magical ball like priceless china. Steve looked down, as did his dragon, and saw the great dark shape below. Steve knew it was dead, and he felt for a moment his friend's sadness and regret.

His dragon arched around and bathed the carcass in flames, giving it the only burial appropriate for a great dragon. "Leave me," Steve heard clearly in his own head. The last impression he had was of his dragon flying up, and up, like he may never come back down.

Chapter 70

Without dragon magic to fuel the storm, it simply died, adding another mysterious element to a freakish weather anomaly that meteorologists would never be able to figure out or explain. Once the hurricane-force winds stopped, silence stepped in. "You hear that?" Joy asked. "What is that?"

"Why are you yelling? I don't hear anything," Justin replied.

"Huh, oh, sorry. That's what I mean," Joy continued. "The wind's gone. Come on, let's see what's up." She grabbed him by the hand and hauled him past the adults who were huddled together, speculating about what the quiet meant.

"Hey," Jeanie called. "Wait!"

Dani squeezed past them all to be the first to ask, "So, what happened? Is it over? Did we win? How's our dragon? Where'd it—"

Joy caught her and cupped her mouth. "Give' em a chance, Dani."

She pulled Joy's hand off and glared at her. "Fine. Well?" she asked.

Steve looked at Shou and then wrapped his arms around her. Shou hugged him back. TJ laughed and encircled them along with the rest of the woodland creatures. "Give me some love! Ding Dong, the witch is dead!"

"What's he talking about?" Dani asked.

Justin answered, "Wizard of Oz. When Dorothy kills the witch."

"What?" Joy asked.

"You know, the movie, The Wizard of Oz. It's the scene when—"

"Never mind," Dani said. "We won!"

The surfers were the first out the door. Fred ran immediately around the house for a view of the ocean. Ramone was right behind, "Waves, come on, let there be waves!" But when they reached the fence and looked over, all they saw was a calm grey ocean far below. "No, no, no!" Ramone yelled. "There has to be waves after a storm like this! Aw, man, nothing but some chop..."

Fred nodded in sympathy, "Just a bunch of white wash, brah...it's..."

"Tragic," Ramone added.

"Yeah," Fred agreed. "Oooh, looky. Fattest barbeque in the whole world!" He pointed to the burning remains of the massive dragon below.

"Brahs," Larry said after catching up. "Look at this mess, man." He pointed back out to the street, which was covered with tree limbs, leaves, trash, clothes, water, and several injured automobiles. A couple of electrical poles were down. A dog started barking down the street.

Shou led everyone else out. Steve was talking excitedly to his friends, trying to answer their questions about what had happened. Dani ran to where the surfers watched the burning dragon. "Eww, it stinks," she announced. "Hey, hey, everybody, come see this!" she screamed.

"Where's our dragon, Steve?" Dani asked.

Steve started to mentally search for it, but then shook his head. He didn't know if he could contact it right now, or if he should even try. He left everyone staring at the quickly disappearing remains of the deceased dragon while he looked for Shou.

Shou stood apart from her fellow dragons. She had her nose up and was sniffing the air. "What is it, Shou?" Steve asked.

TJ waddled over on all fours and then stood up next to them. "She's gone."

Shou nodded.

"Who?" Steve asked. "Oh, you mean Berit. Where is she? Are they all gone?"

Shou looked at TJ before answering. "They're all gone. I can still smell them, barely. They must be moving fast."

"Should we go after them?" TJ asked.

"Best not," Shou answered. "After all, they lost." Quietly under her breath, she said, "Ah, Berit, what have you done this time?"

"What do you mean, Shou? Is she going to be back?" Steve asked.

Like any kindly aunt, Shou took his hand in a very human-like gesture. "Not today, my excellent guardian. You were stupendous, did I tell you that?"

Steve reddened.

To be on the safe side, Shou sent the surviving three minor dragons away to keep an eye out for Berit and her friends. She also wanted them to spread the word to any other magical creatures that the immediate crisis was over. TJ yawned. Shou's smile added more wrinkles to her face. "You getting tired, my old friend?"

"Naw, I'm up for whatever you need. What'cha wanna do next?"

"Well, if you have it in you, I thought we might go spread a little magic around and see what we can save in this town."

"Okey dokey with me," TJ answered, "but we got to magic me up some grub." He pulled some excess skin off his slightly diminished belly. "I gotsta do some serious carb loading before winter."

"We'll get you fed."

"Shou, what should we do now?" Steve interrupted. "I mean about Dragau?"

"Your dragon won't forget you, Steve. For now, let me go find TJ something to eat." She kissed him on the forehead and walked away, followed by a lumbering black bear.

Chapter 71

Everyone had to deplane in London. That was fine with Berit; sitting this close to humans for so long had made her skin itch. Fortunately, she and her companions had first-class seats and did not have sit shoulder to shoulder with the rest of the passengers. Berit had even dealt with that annoying attendant who felt compelled to interrupt her one too many times; he was locked in the lavatory nursing his upset stomach.

The trio was the first off the plane—a beautiful, Nordic, nuclear family returning home from a holiday. Halldor immediately went searching for a smoking area. He had developed some kind of twisted psychological addiction to human cigarettes—ludicrous, but Berit did not stop him.

Brita lagged behind, a pronounced limp slowing her down. Shou had nearly crushed her leg, so even disguised as a gorgeous human female, she had a crippled limb. One airport worker asked if she needed assistance, to which she replied, "Piss off." That was about the only thing she had said since reaching the airport back in California, which was fine with Berit.

Berit sat near a coffee bar, where the odors—cinnamon, nutmeg, cloves, allspice, and, of course, fresh-ground coffee—successfully masked that wretched human stench. Brita stood nearby, leaning on her good leg. "Hm," Berit snorted, "Shou has made an enemy for life in that one. Good, maybe she won't dispute my side of this when we get back."

Berit was seething. Her failure burned her like poison. She wanted to explode, again. It wouldn't help. In fact, it would only make things worse. Right now, she needed a cool head. She had failed, and not only that, she had changed the rules of the game. It wasn't only anger gnawing at her, it was also fear. How would her masters react when she got home?

How had they lost? She replayed the battle and everything leading up to it a thousand times. Could she have done anything differently? She didn't think so. Would her masters condemn her for failing, for intensifying the war? It was coming anyway, she told herself, whether they liked it or not. If they didn't crush these humans soon, the chattering monkeys would be unstoppable. No, she might have crossed some lines, but those lines had to be crossed. And the great ones needed her. No one was better at destabilizing human beings than she was. She was still fretting over her meeting with her clan's leaders when Halldor returned.

He looked slightly dejected as he approached and sat next to Berit. He sat, shifted restlessly, obviously wanting to talk about something. Berit tried to ignore him. Sometimes he acted all too human. He sighed.

"What? What is it?" Berit finally asked.

"I can't smoke in the terminal. I'd have to leave security and go outside."

Berit's eyes narrowed and she emphasized each syllable of each word like a staccato, "You-are-a-dra-gon. Go smoke wherever you want!"

"Yeah, but—"

"Did you hear what I said?"

The ambient air temperature had suddenly gone up several degrees. A woman sitting a few feet away took off her sweater, while an older gentleman dropped his coffee on the floor when it suddenly started boiling in its cup. Halldor stood up, "You know, I think I'll go get some gum."

Chapter 72

Justin's house was a wreck. A crew was there replacing windows. Another company would come and fix the damaged roof. The garage door wouldn't shut, and part of the deck had collapsed—all future projects once the rest of the insurance money arrived. Justin's parents had been forced to send him to Steve's house because he'd been losing his mind over his destroyed room. Steve lay on his bed, half listening to his best friend go on and on about all the things he lost, including his trashed computer.

Occasionally, Steve would flip his soccer ball up with a backspin to see how close he could get to the ceiling without hitting it. He could hear Dani banging around in her room, probably rearranging it again. School was out and would be until next week at a minimum—too much water damage mostly, plus the electricity was still out in many places.

"I should be home, helping out, finding my things," Justin insisted.

"Yup," Steve agreed.

"I bet my computer is completely gone, all my bookmarks, photos…"

"Probably."

Jeanie poked her head in and Steve perked up. "What's up, Mom? Can we go out yet?"

She sighed, "No, sorry, babe. It's too dangerous. Power lines are down, and there's debris all over the place. The city's only beginning to get clean-up crews out."

"But Dad's gone out."

"Because they need him at the hospital," Jeanie said. "A lot of folks were injured or can't get into town, so he's helping out the regular EMTs."

"Can't we walk around the neighborhood? Or ride our bikes?"

"Steve," his mom started, "it's only been two days. Can't you play a game or something?"

"We have, Mom. We've played *Clue*, and *Risk*, and *Life*, plus a hundred games of *Yahtzee*. I'm gamed out."

"Okay, I get it," Jeanie began. "You stay right in the yard, nowhere else. You don't even cross the street. You understand?"

Steve dropped the ball and jumped off the bed. He grabbed Justin by the arm and pulled his reluctant friend out of the bedroom. Before he could get outside, his mother added. "If Dani finds out, I'm sending her out with you."

Steve suddenly got very quiet and tiptoed out the front door. Once outside, he felt better, less like a rat in a cage. He walked around the yard, picking up pieces of junk, bits of wood, or clothing. Some of his neighbors were out, too, dragging branches away to the street. A group of people had gathered at Mrs. Wilson's house and looked like they were trying to clear away the whole front porch; her house got socked hard. He recognized one or two of the good Samaritans and figured the rest must be from her church. A loud green military truck rolled down the next street and, despite his mother's warning, he ran after it. "Look," Steve pointed, "it's the National Guard. How cool!"

"Steve! Get back in the yard, or you can come inside," a familiar voice screamed from his house.

"Man, we can't do anything," Steve complained

Before he could protest any more, there was a rumble in the sky. "Great, more rain. Just what we need."

The sudden downpour forced everyone to take cover. Steve and Justin started to run for the house, but immediately stopped. They weren't wet. The deluge was so thick, it was like looking through beveled glass: everything was grey and wavy. Steve looked at his friend, who was equally stunned. Then there was an enormous thud and Steve felt the ground shake. Steve turned to the sound and there before him was his dragon.

For the first time in days, Justin was animated, "Steve, Steve, it's Dragau, it's Dragau."

"I know. I can see, too," Steve agreed.

The bright green dragon, shimmering with water, bent its front legs and lowered its large face down to the stunned boys. It didn't say anything, but Steve thought it was smiling at him, at both of them. The eyes were friendly, so friendly. Steve reached out and touched the dragon's forehead, like petting a massive horse.

The second he touched it, though, he was transported somewhere else. A cave. *Man,* he thought, *we must have a ton of caves around here.* He looked for Justin, but did not see him. "Justin?"

"He's fine," a voice said. "Do you know where you are?"

"Well, I was in my front yard, but now..." A picture entered Steve's head and he knew exactly where the dragon had selected his next lair. "This is close," Steve stated. "Aren't you worried about people?"

Instead of a reply, Steve felt a rush of feelings and pictures. Many of them were of him. Steve understood. "You're offering me a choice, aren't you? But don't you need us? Who will feed you while you're sleeping? Who will, ah, now I get it. That's why you're so close to the shore. You could go hunt yourself. But I thought if you were awake, you know, you would go berserk, or something."

"Not now," the dragon answered. "Once we destroyed the great dragon, I became a little stronger. I won't need to eat as often, and I can hunt in the open ocean without endangering humans."

"People could still see you," Steve insisted.

"Possible, but not likely."

"Wouldn't you get lonely? There'd be no one to sing to you like my dad does."

"No, I wouldn't be lonely. I am connected through the earth's magic to many lives. I also believe Shou and her friends will seek me out now." The dragon hesitated, "I would miss your father's songs, and someday, perhaps, yours."

Steve thought about all the ramifications of what the dragon was suggesting. "Would, would the magic be gone? Would I stop being able to do the things, you know?"

"You have magic all your own, Steve. You are special even among dragon tenders, but if you choose it, you can have a normal human life."

Steve hesitated, "What about Shou? And TJ? And Justin and Joy. They were involved in all this, too."

"I owe your friends a great deal; I'll be talking to them. As for Shou and TJ, they have each other and me. Magic or not, I think they will always value your friendship."

Steve realized that, in many ways, his dragon was offering what he'd wanted ever since he'd hopped into the back of his dad's truck one fateful morning: to be free of all this supernatural craziness. No more whispering about him in school. No more accidental explosions or accidents with animals. No more demons. No more stutter?

"Gone," Dragau said.

"But...I don't know what to do," Steve admitted. "I mean, it's been what I've wanted for two years, and then Berit shows up and everything gets out of control, and...wait a minute. This isn't over, is it? Berit and her side will be back, won't they? Shou said there's a battle going on."

"None of that would be your problem. In fact, without the magic, your friends and family would be a lot safer. At least at first..." Dragau trailed off, as if he hadn't meant to mention that last part.

"What do you mean, 'at first'?"

"Nothing. You must understand that the struggle between the great dragons has been going on for centuries. This latest skirmish might be it for a long time."

"Or it might not, that's what you're saying. It might only be the start of something, right?"

The dragon didn't answer right away. "Steve, you cannot right the world. This is your chance to change your life. The world will go on no matter what you do, and the world of dragons will go on without you. You must decide what is right for you."

"I can't right now. I can't decide. I don't know what to do."

"You will, and when you do, I'll know."

Steve opened his eyes. He was standing in the middle of the street. The rain had stopped, and his mother was calling him back to the house. Justin was next to him. They were dry.

Steve turned to his buddy, "Did he say anything to you?"

Justin shrugged. "Nope. Was he supposed to?"

Steve looked away, hoping Justin wasn't too disappointed that Dragau had only spoken to Steve. "I guess not."

Chapter 73

Cell service throughout most of the northern coast was spotty or non-existent during the storm and had not been entirely restored even two days later. Joy tried one more time to call her friends with the same frustrating result. Her house had survived mostly intact, but some of their neighbors had enough damage for her and her parents to have plenty to do. The roads were clogged up, which meant her dad was not going back to work for a while and had time on his hands.

Joy had just taken a break after dragging a big tree limb off a neighbor's fence when she saw her dad helping another neighbor ease what was left of a broken window out of a kitchen. She didn't see her mom until she walked right up behind her. "Hey, sweetheart, you okay?"

Joy smiled at her, "Hi, Mom. I'm fine. Where were you?"

"The wind smashed in the glass patio door across the street, so I'm helping Trudy clean up. I was going to get the Shop-Vac your father has in the garage."

"I can get it for you," Joy offered.

"That's fine, baby, but why don't you take a little break first. We've got a bunch of big glass pieces to clean up first, so take your time. Get a peanut butter sandwich."

"You mean a peanut butter and jelly sandwich."

"No, don't open up the fridge to get the jelly. I'm hoping if they get power back on maybe we won't have to throw everything out."

"It's been two days, Mom," Joy pointed out.

"I know, but it's been cool weather, so maybe we'll get lucky. Go on and take five." She reached over and gave Joy a kiss on the cheek.

Joy trudged back to her house, only now realizing how tired she was. She entered the gloom of the kitchen and opened the pantry door. With a little squinting, she could make out the bread and Jiffy. She started to reach for them, only to decide that she didn't have the energy to eat. Instead, she went to the large sectional in the media room and kicked off her shoes. She curled up in the elbow of the big couch and immediately dropped off.

The first thing Joy noticed was the sound of breaking surf and the intermittent crash of waves against the rocks. It was calming, peaceful. "Hello, Joy," a voice said.

Joy was not startled in the least. Somehow, she knew it was Steve's dragon. "Hello," she replied.

More gentle lapping of the waves. "I wanted to thank you."

Joy felt warm all over. "You're welcome."

"You have a question. But to answer, I must hear it asked."

"My mom, they promised she would be cured," Joy started. "Yes."

"Did they lie to me? Could they have cured her permanently? I mean, would they have?"

"They could have, yes," the dragon began. "Would they cure her indefinitely? Who can say? Maybe they would have held up their end of the bargain, and maybe they would have come back wanting something else at a later date. Did you ever consider why your mother became ill in the first place?"

"She's always had…Oh, you mean why did she stop taking her medication? You think they…"

The dragon stayed silent and let Joy think. *So,* Joy thought, *they might have caused it. How could I trust them if they were the ones who made her sick to begin with?*

"I don't know for sure that they did, just as I don't know if they would have kept their word."

"But you can cure her, can't you?" Joy asked.

"Yes. I could, and I would if you asked. You deserve to be rewarded for all you've done," the dragon agreed. "However, to cure her, I must change her."

"What do you mean?"

"Has your mom been ill her whole life?"

"I don't know. At least as long as I can remember," Joy answered.

"Then her illness is part of who she is. If I take away part of who she is, then I forever change her whole."

"But not in a bad way. She just wouldn't be bipolar anymore," Joy explained. "Isn't that what her medication does anyway?"

"I can't answer that. I believe even taking her medicine, or not taking it, is part of who she is. Being human is just that, I think—choosing. Now it is your turn, Joy, because it doesn't matter what I think. It's up to you."

Joy thought very carefully. Her mom had gone back to her doctor; she was back on her medication, but would it last? "She's fine right now. Is that magic?"

"No, she is not enchanted."

"So, her medication is still working," Joy thought aloud. "There's no way we can know if it will always work, or if she'll always take it."

"No, there is no way to know," the dragon agreed.

What should she do? Was it the right thing to wish her mom's illness away? What was wrong with that? She would be cured. But would it be real? Would it make her a different person? Did Joy even have the right to make that decision?

"Joy?"

"Cure her," Joy said. "If you can, cure her."

"It is done. She won't carry that burden any longer," the dragon assured her. "Ah, but there's something else, isn't there?"

Joy did not answer. She felt too ashamed to say it aloud. She worried about her mother all the time, but there was another fear lurking at the back of her mind, always—a shadow that followed her everywhere. What if she had the same disorder lying dormant inside her? What if, one day, she, too, would end up having to take medication, to cling to her sense of self every day and hope it would be enough? This was not a fear she'd shared with anyone—not with Steve or Justin, not even with her parents. Nevertheless, the fear of mental illness had been a dark and constant companion.

"Your mother's burden is not yours, Joy."

Joy started to cry.

Chapter 74

Shou returned to her car with a plastic bag full of Hostess cupcakes and Twinkies. She opened the door and tossed the bag at TJ. "That's it. That's all the store had left," she said testily. This was the third time TJ had made her stop at a convenience store and buy up all the junk food inside.

TJ ripped open a clear plastic wrapper and started to shove a pair of cream-filled yellow desserts into his mouth. When he saw the look Shou was giving him he stopped, his paws and face covered in white fluff and yellow crumbs. "I have to fatten up. Winter is coming."

"Aren't you supposed to eat nuts and berries?" Shou asked.

"Don't judge me!"

Shou climbed back into the driver's seat and pointed the car south. TJ reached in the bag and pulled out a box of Nutty Bars. "Hey, look, these have peanut butter. See, right here."

"Oh, forget it," Shou said. "Any place look good yet for me to drop you off?"

Chew, chew, "Naw, keep driving."

Shou looked in the rearview mirror. "I don't see why you didn't want to stay around Crescent City. I thought you liked those kids."

"Oh, them babies was great, no doubt. But come on, Shou, that backwater town? Naw, boo, I gotsta be where the action is."

"You're going to hibernate."

"Yeah, yeah, I know. But afterwards, it's all black and silver—Oakland, boo. What about you? What'cha gonna do?"

"First, I need to reassure my human family that I'm all right," Shou explained. "Then, I will probably do a little traveling and meet up with a few old friends." Shou grew grim, "Berit changed the rules of engagement. I hope she did it all on her own, but if not, then…we might be in for some dangerous times ahead."

"Speaking of Berit, where do you think she went?"

"No clue. I lost her scent, so I assume she's long gone."

"And the kids? What about those kids? They gonna be okay?"

"For now, I think they'll be fine. Dragau will look after them until I get back. Hopefully nothing bad happens before then."

Chapter 75

The way down to the beach was always dicey, and when it was wet it was downright treacherous. All the recent rain made it even more so. Justin inched his way down, taking one baby step at a time. More than once he started to fall and used the surfboard to keep his balance. His brother would have killed him if he saw him banging the board on the ground. Of course, his brother would have surely killed him if he caught him sneaking down to the beach by himself.

When Justin finally made it to the bottom of the cliff, he looked up, searching for anyone who might tell on him. It was early yet, cold and misty. The fog moved in with the air off the ocean in large grey clouds. The sun looked like it was going to take the morning off, which was fine with Justin.

He attached the leash to his ankle like he'd been taught and realized that he hadn't zipped up his wetsuit. He reached back for the dangling zipper, which hung like a tail, and managed to coax it halfway up, but then spent the next five minutes trying to get it to close completely, grasping behind his back with each hand to try and snatch the cord. Thank goodness no one was around to watch his struggles; there was no way they would let him in the water if he couldn't even zip up his suit.

When he was all ready to go, he faced the grey ocean. His pulse was racing, and he asked himself for the twentieth time if this was a good idea. After all, how could he expect to remain his same old self and still be able to surf? But that was what he asked for, and, even if he didn't exactly trust himself, he trusted the dragon. A seagull mocked him from above and spurred him into action. "Okay, you stupid bird, I'm going."

Justin tried to dance into the water, holding the board over his head like he'd seen his brother do. After smacking his own noggin more than once, he decided to drag the board behind him. He got about waist high in the churning water and tried lying on the board. He kept tipping over. Finally, after several tries, he got himself situated and started paddling in the prone position. The first little wave that came along crashed into the front of the board and knocked him into the water. He had only gone about three feet. "Ah, this is stupid," he said aloud. "Why did I think this was a good idea?"

The cry from the seagull hovering right above his head made Justin look up. "What? What is it, you?" He stopped. Something about the bird and the way it was looking at him, almost like it wanted to tell him something, made him pause. That was dumb; it was Steve who talked to animals. Justin was just about to ignore it when a big wave hit him, ripping the board away and yanking him off his feet. Justin stood up, spitting salt water and started to turn around. This time the bird flew right in front of him, cutting him off. "Ah, come on!" he yelled at it. When the bird swooped in again, he said, "Fine, I'll try it one more time. I can't believe I let some crazy dream make me come down here."

Justin pulled the cord to his board back and slowly pointed it out into the open ocean. This time, however, something felt different. He was excited, but felt more relaxed. He pulled himself up and lay his head on the board. He could hear the ocean growl all around him. He paddled first with his left arm and then his right, back and forth. A wave came, and he pushed the nose of the board down, leaving a gap between the board and his body that the water could pass right through. His confidence grew, and he paddled harder. He made his way farther and farther from shore and stopped at the place where the water flattened and the waves began their run to the beach. He sat up and straddled the board with perfect balance. Somewhere out there a swell was forming that would hit the up-rise of the shore and turn into a righteously rideable wave.

Three hours later, Justin trudged up the cliff, slipping and sliding all the way to the top. All the exhilarating rides were beginning to meld into one memory of joy and freedom and speed on the water. It was a shame his brother wasn't there to watch. His only spectator had been that persistent seagull. That didn't matter, though; Justin was not doing this to show off. In fact, he didn't want anyone to know about this. For a few magical hours, this clumsy, autistic kid could disappear and be spectacular. That had been the dragon's gift, a gift that Justin had kept secret from his best friend. He felt a little bad about that, but, after losing everything in his room, it felt good to have something of his own again that nobody would touch.

Luckily, no one watching him struggle to drag the surfboard up the steep hill would ever accuse him of being the surf ninja who shredded waves like a pro barely moments ago. When Justin reached the peak, he turned around, looked back over the ocean—down to where the water hurled itself against the rocks, a battle that had been going on forever—and smiled.

Chapter 76

Spring in Crescent City meant rain, but so did winter, fall, and summer. However, today was a bright, clear sunny exception. Steve thought that should mean riding his bike all over town. What it actually meant, according to his father, was that it was a perfect day to mow the lawn. Steve dumped the cuttings into a lawn bag and rolled the mower onto the patio to hose it off. Steve thought it was dumb to worry about cleaning it after each use, but that was how his dad wanted it done. When he'd finished, he plopped himself down on one of the Adirondack chairs and took a big swig of the iced tea his mother had put out for him.

The sun felt marvelous now that he was done working and sweating. He leaned back and enjoyed the golden glow through his closed lids. His thoughts drifted over the last couple of months. School was fine and spring soccer was starting up. The town was still cleaning up after the storm. There were no recent surprises, no magic, no explosions, no villains, and no stutter. Normal. Joy was in an especially good mood; her mom was still doing okay. Justin was back to his weird self, though he must have been spending a lot of time outside because he was getting really tan. Everything was back to normal. Well, maybe not back—things were not exactly normal before—but things were good, which is the only normal Steve cared about.

Sadly, normal also meant no visits from Shou, no TJ, though he should still be hibernating. Steve hadn't dreamt of dragons since Dragau's visit. Steve sighed and opened his eyes. Immediately, he saw the purple spots as his eyes adjusted. When they quit watering, he saw a blip in the air. It was a butterfly; Steve could tell by its fluttering wings and schizoid flight pattern. He didn't know what kind.

Steve watched it zigzag, not landing on anything. He tried to tell what color its wings were, like Justin had taught him to do to determine its type. As it got closer, Steve saw that the wings were black and yellow with specks of blue—pretty, but not a species he recognized. Species...wow, he had spent too much time with his bug-collecting buddy. It was beautiful, though, so beautiful. He mumbled softly, a whisper, something maybe only a butterfly could hear, or perhaps a dragon. The tri-colored butterfly landed on his outstretched index finger, and Steve smiled.

THE END

Steve and his friends will return in the final installment of the Modern Dragon Chronicles, *You Can't Teach an Old Dragon New Tricks*. To take an exclusive look at the opening chapter, simply read on!

Did you enjoy this book? The next step...

Reviews tell us many things: the good, the bad, the traffic we'll have to deal with to get there...but for an author, nothing is more important than hearing from fans. While this novel has been crafted with love and attention, this is only part of what it takes to make sure as many people have access to it as possible. That is why you, **dedicated and forthright reader**, have been tasked with this mission, should you choose to accept it:

Review this book.

Be kind, be gentle, but, above all, be honest.

Oh, and thank you! Without you, none of this would be possible or, let's be honest, nearly as fun.

Get your FREE Book!

Long before Steve met his dragon, a Portuguese village under the protection of a powerful talisman came face to face with an infamous plague that ravaged all of Europe…but was it a plague, or an infestation? And what role did Steve's ancestors play in stopping it? To get answers to these questions and more, check out the extraordinary prequel to The Modern Dragon Chronicles, *It's a Dragon's Life*, by going to Ty Burson's website **www.tyburson.com,** clicking the link, and letting him know where to send your free copy!

YOU CAN'T TEACH
AN OLD DRAGON
NEW TRICKS

TY BURSON
THE MODERN DRAGON CHRONICLES

Chapter 1

Senior year, one of the biggest wastes of time for anyone not on the fast track to college. At least, that's what Steve was thinking as he ate his Egg McMuffin in the school's parking lot. He dug into the pocket of his jeans and pulled out his phone. It was 8:37 and he had already missed first period. Pre-calculus. *Are you kidding me, geometry at 7:45 in the morning?* he thought. What twisted administrator thought that up? Pre-Calc at 3 o'clock was ugly enough, but at 7:30? It was child abuse, state-sanctioned torture. Moreover, it was a make-up class he needed to pass to graduate. And, to top it off, most of the other kids in the class were freshmen and sophomores, eager little mathematicians climbing the ladder to calculus while Steve doodled through the pre-dawn brain vice. Steve had avoided taking math as long as he could, but his time had run out. Plus, his mom had insisted on it— otherwise he'd be taking remedial math in college for no credit. If he went to college.

Steve reached into the glove box and pulled out the knob to manually roll down the window. Very little on the old family truck worked like it was originally supposed to, but when his dad had given it to him for his senior year, Steve had been grateful. Besides, all the old beater's rusted quirks gave it a certain endearingly cranky personality.

A cool morning chill stole away some of the sun-trapped heat from the truck's cab. Steve checked his phone again, 8:49. He sighed. Maybe one of his friends would want to skip. He thought about all the things they could do. They could go on up into the mountains and roam among the giant redwoods, or catch a few steelheads in the Smith River, or feed the seagulls out at the marina. They could take the old dirt bike out to the dunes, or grab a coffee at Denny's, or hang out with crazy Dave who carved driftwood animals north of town. They could do all those things and more, but what Steve could not do was shove himself into a plastic desk under a lifeless florescent sky.

But despite daydreaming about all the adventures he could have in his own backyard—his own Northern California paradise—he knew that his two best friends would never join him. Justin had found a second home at school and was completely wrapped up in the robotic program. Plus, he had a girlfriend, sort of—a concept that Steve was still getting used to. And then there was Joy, who wouldn't skip anyway, but was presently weighing the best offers from a number of colleges—all of them interested in the star volleyball player with a 4.3 GPA. Both were already focusing on life after high school, so there was no way Steve was going to get either to play hooky. That left a minor league group of friends, people he knew from soccer or some of his classes, a questionable sub-set of anti-schoolers including burn-outs, surfers, and out-of-season athletes. But since he didn't smoke, rarely surfed, and had practice today, he was left without a truancy support group.

Of course, he could strike out on his own and drive down the coast to visit the dragon. Dragau had made its lair well to the south, just off the Coastal Highway, and was magically hidden away from human intruders. Dragau was the dragon his father and his father's father had had served, the same dragon that destroyed Mammon the demon along with Steve and his friends, and perhaps the only remaining Great Dragon still trying to protect Steve and the rest of the human race. Unfortunately, Dragau was fighting his own kind, and he was losing.

Steve warmed to the idea of dropping by to see his dragon, maybe even get a little advice...but Steve's problems seemed so insignificant, and he didn't want to bother his friend. Plus, the trip to the lair would take most of the morning and land him in serious hot water with his parents. One class skipped would probably mean a few extra chores and a promise to do better; half a day and he'd be handing over the keys to the truck. He looked at his phone—8:55. He stepped out of the truck, taking a final bite of the cold breakfast sandwich, which now had about as much flavor as the day ahead.

Giving the empty parking a final, wistful look, Steve moved to beat the next bell. The office buzzed open the front door, and he was forced to sign himself in. Somewhere an evil program was starting a chain reaction that would result in a truancy letter home. His signature and a camera would back up the letter's veracity should he deny it. He was living on borrowed time.

The bell sounded, and Steve joined a churning river of teenage bodies flowing to their next class. His tributary led to the English hallway, where he found his class and settling himself at his desk, in the row next to the windows. *So close and yet so far,* he thought as he slunk down, assuming the senior position, the one that displayed total apathy toward the subject and school in general. Fortunately, this class was slightly less painful than the pre-dawn mathematics torment because it wasn't packed with underclassmen; juniors or seniors only in British and World Literature.

They were studying Chaucer's Canterbury Tales, which, once you figured out the weird language, were kind of entertaining, especially since his crazy lit teacher liked to have everyone act out specific parts. After the obligatory groans and gripes, most of the kids had begun to look forward to this break in their monotonous schedules.

A familiar voice roused him from his torpor. "Did you watch the PBS program like she asked?"

"Huh?" Steve turned around to talk to the girl who sat behind him.

"This, dummy," she said pointing to a handout with five questions referring to the program they were supposed to watch over the weekend. Hers was completely filled out.

"Crap, I forgot. Here let me see it."

"Forget it, champ," she said. "If I had to sit through a two-hour documentary on Chaucer, then so do you if you want credit. What's up with you lately, anyway? I bet you have a straight "F" for homework."

Steve only shrugged and turned back around. *What's wrong with me?* he asked himself. He had never been a stellar student, but he hadn't hated school. Right now, everything about it caused his soul to itch. But before he could self-evaluate any further, the teacher swirled in. She was obviously a new teacher; she still swirled. The last of the kids bolted through the door like they were sliding into home plate just as the tardy bell sounded, practically right on her heels.

The teacher pointed to the book shelves housing the five-pound literature books while she typed in her attendance. The automatons in the front seats retrieved enough copies for everyone in their rows. The teacher announced the page number, which was of course followed quickly by a dozen students asking for the page number a second time. As Steve absently flopped over a couple of hundred pages at a time, he imagined the teacher announcing, "Open up to page 45, 011." He actually stopped at 432, part-way through The Miller's Tale, the 14th century equivalent to an "R" rated comedy. For a happy minute, Steve thought the teacher would forget to ask for the homework. "Oh, and put your assignments in the tray. I'll give you completion grades, and we'll discuss the answers tomorrow."

Darn it. Well, maybe he could find the program on YouTube and still watch it for tomorrow's class. But Steve knew he wouldn't bother.

They were right in the middle of a funny part of the story, Nicholas farting in Absalan's face, when a tapping at the window caught Steve's attention. He turned away from the bawdy tale to see a squirrel peering back at him through the second-story window. With its tiny hands cupped around its face, it appeared to be looking for someone. Steve had a sinking feeling it might be him. Then, the critter started motioning like it wanted in. Instead of acknowledging it, Steve secretly glanced around to see who else might be watching. Thus far, everyone was following the story.

Steve's experience with squirrels was extensive. A pair of desperadoes lived in the walnut tree next to his house and took twisted pleasure in raining shelled nuts down on his patio. When he'd tried to shoo them away, they'd mocked him and flicked their half-eaten nuts at him. Therefore, Steve knew a squirrel banging on his school's window was not too farfetched. However, when it suddenly started changing colors—red, then black, and finally to blue—Steve knew he wasn't dealing with an ordinary critter. However, when Steve refused to acknowledge it, the squirrel became even more insistent and began rapping on the glass. Finally, obviously frustrated, it reached back and gave the window one last deliberate thump before impatiently folding its arms.

One thing battling demons and dragons had taught Steve was not to doubt his sanity. So, when the weird and the strange came knocking—or, in this case, a blue squirrel—it merited his attention. Still, he had no idea how he was supposed to get up in the middle of class and open the window for what had to be a minor dragon, disguised like the ones who fought along his side a few years ago. They weren't as powerful as his friends Shou or TJ, and nothing like the great dragons, but they were still magical.

But, before he could figure out a way to see what this one wanted, the squirrel suddenly looked up like it was frightened. It spared Steve one dirty look before it jumped off the ledge. Forgetting about the class, Steve jumped to the window, in time to catch a reddish-brown blur flash past the glass. A second later, a wicked-looking hawk rose up, flapping its wings while the blue squirrel dangled precariously from one even wickeder-looking claw. The squirrel was twisting and squirming and biting to break free. It was so fierce that the bird had to let go and the squirrel tumbled to the ground. Fortunately, it landed unhurt and scurried away to the cover of some trees before the hawk could dive again.

When Steve turned around, the entire class had stopped—even Ellie, who had been reading her part with complete abandon, was staring at him. The silence that hung in the air was deafening.

"Everything all right?" the teacher asked.

"Sorry, I, uh, t-t-thought a bird was going to h-h-hit the window." As he slid back into his seat, he realized that he had stuttered, something he seldom did anymore. For a moment, he was afraid everyone would start laughing at him, like back in elementary school, but no one said a word; instead, they looked at him like as if he were an alien bug. He wasn't sure that was an improvement. He lifted the textbook, the gargantuan size of which he suddenly appreciated, and waited for Ellie to resume her inspired rendition of the awaking of the carpenter.

Acknowledgments

To my children, the most interesting characters I know; to Susan and Kathy, for their excellent questions and feedback; and for Kerri, my partner and supporter in all things.

About the Author

TY BURSON was born in Riverside, California. His mother and her family emigrated from Canada, while most of his father's people hailed from Oklahoma. After completing an Associate's Degree in general education, Ty joined the Air Force. Ty signed on to be a Russian Crypto-logic Linguist, went off to basic training, and eventually ended up in Monterey, California. It was there that Ty met his future wife, Kerri.

Ty finished his Bachelor's degree before leaving the Air Force. Eventually, four kids and a couple of career changes later, Ty went back to school, got his teaching certification, joined the Air National Guard, and began teaching middle school in Florissant, Missouri.

It was at a conference for middle school teachers that Ty got the idea for a lucky dragon that protected a fishing village. A protagonist with a stutter and a demon came along much later. While the novel got shelved when Ty decided that he had to have a Doctorate in Education, it never entirely left his mind—as few wonderful ideas ever do.

Currently, Ty and his family live in Maryland, where he continues to teach after completing his Doctorate and retiring from the Air National Guard in 2011. Ty is known for entertaining his students with funny poems and stories, and for wearing bizarre, entertaining ties.

Made in the USA
Middletown, DE
21 July 2023